# BRITISH GIRL FOUND DEAD

ROWLAND STONE

First published in 2021 by Bloodhound Books.

www.bloodhoundbooks.com

Print ISBN 978-1-914614-05-7

*For Dad.*

# PROLOGUE

She stumbled out of the nightclub, his arm around her waist for support, both of them wasted, gabbling, unsteady on their feet.

She tried to remember his name.

Did it matter? Not in Magaluf.

*Magaluf.*

*Shagaluf.*

They moved on, down a side street, further away from the lights and chaos of the main drag, Punta Ballena, and into the hazy darkness.

She knew where they were going. It was kind of inevitable.

They crossed over the boardwalk until she felt her shoes crunch onto the soft, warm sand of the beach.

They walked on twenty, maybe thirty metres, until they were out of sight of the street lights, with just what reflected off that night's half-moon for help.

After a few more steps, he stopped, satisfied they had the requisite privacy, and leant in to kiss her.

Then the hand, running over her skirt, under the hem,

making its way up her legs, stroking, briefly, before it found its way inside her knickers and started pulling at the material.

She put her hand inside the waist of his trousers and slipped it inside his pants, running it over his buttocks and then moving it, inelegantly, round to the front. She felt his body jolt and he inhaled sharply as she squeezed him.

'Condom?' she asked.

'Really?'

She gave him another squeeze.

'Okay,' he said.

He reached a hand into his pocket, pulled out his wallet and started leafing through it.

She dropped to the sand and started to rearrange her underwear. God, it was such a cliché, such a dirty, drunken, hopelessly Magaluf way of going about things.

But what the hell. It was her holiday.

He knelt down in front of her, moving in towards her, kissing and fumbling until her body shivered with the excitement of it. She closed her eyes and disappeared off somewhere else as he started to build up a rhythm. She held him close as he started to quicken. Faster and faster.

'Gentle, gentle,' she whispered in his ear, but he didn't seem to hear her, just kept on with his thrusting. She gave up, clung on tight to his T-shirt, breathed in his musky deodorant, and focused on the sounds behind him, the gentle wash of the sea, the faraway bass of the clubs and the soft tread of feet on the sand.

Footsteps. A little faster, getting louder as they got nearer.

'Hey,' she said, but he was too busy.

'Someone's...'

The man was walking fast, just a few feet away, some kind of hood on his head, a glint of metal in his right hand. The footsteps closer, near enough now to see that horrible, coarse sacking over his head with the two clumsily cut holes where his eyes should be.

She felt her stomach contract as the muscles the length of her body stiffened. She tried to scream but her mouth and throat were dry.

'You all right?' her lover said, just before the sickening thud of the length of metal impacted on his skull and he went down in a heap on top of her. She screamed and tried to push him off, but he was heavy. Very heavy.

She thrashed manically, pushing with her arms and kicking with her heels, but the man with the coarse hood knelt on top of both of them, pinning them down with his knees, a knife in his right hand stabbing repeatedly into the back and side of her man, in and out, six, seven, eight times, until she lost count, feeling her clothes becoming wet with his blood.

She screamed, sounds coming out freely now, loud and clear.

'Shut the fuck up,' the man growled in her ear, an accent, a bit like her own: British, vaguely southern.

She screamed again and he slapped her across the face, gripping her wrist, hard.

He rolled the deadweight of her lover off her, then twisted her arm into a vicious half-nelson and manoeuvred her around until she was lying on her front.

'Not a fucking word,' he growled, grabbing a handful of her hair in his fist and pulling hard enough that any movement of her neck came with excruciating pain.

He positioned himself behind her, and pushed her face down into the sand and he started to force himself upon her.

She tried her best to cut herself off, tried to separate her mind from her body, to regulate her breathing, to think of what she would do when she got home and back to the UK.

But she couldn't blank out the sound of the man's voice and its hateful mantra.

'Slut, slut, slut,' he said, his hot, heavy breath in her ear. 'You're a dirty slut, slut, slut.'

# 1

## FOUR YEARS LATER

'Elaine, you've got to help me,' Karim says.

There's dark bruising around his right eye, and an ugly, green, half-moon of blood underneath his left. His right cheekbone has red striations across it, like it's been dragged over sandpaper. His nose is swollen with a single, thin line of dried blood across it that suggests it's broken. His upper lip is fat and split.

'I need to claim asylum,' he adds.

We're sitting in a cordoned-off meeting room, separated from the rest of the British consulate by glass dividers. Outside, in the reception area, a dozen sunburnt British holidaymakers are seated, waiting to be called to the serving counter, where my colleagues will deal with their problems from the other side of a bombproof glass screen. A little boy in a monster truck T-shirt is pushing a toy car along the floor underneath the portrait of the Queen. He looks over and holds his car up for me to see. A flicker of a smile from me, then it's back to Karim.

'You're a British citizen, Karim. This is the British consulate. You can't claim asylum in Britain if you're a British citizen.'

'Not asylum then,' Karim says.

His breath reeks of cigarettes, clothes stink of stale sweat, like a down and out. 'Where the law can't get you.'

'Refuge?' I ask.

'Refuge, yeah. I want to claim it.'

There's a nagging itch at my elbow and I rub the eczema through my cardigan.

'Listen, Karim, refuge is something that's given to someone that's in imminent danger from the authorities in the country they're in, usually for political reasons. Are you in imminent danger?'

'Yes, that's my point.'

'From whom?'

'The cops.'

I sag into my seat, looking out across the office for a momentary distraction.

'I know the police here, Karim. You're not going to convince any UK official that the Spanish police pose a threat to your life.'

The colour drains from his face and his fidgeting increases in intensity. He's picking at the skin below his already scrappy-looking nails. He starts looking around again, staring at the waiting room, as if he expects someone to come in at any moment.

'I didn't kill her,' he says, and my shoulders stiffen slightly. 'Never touched, never so much as harmed a hair on the girl's head, I swear it, swear it on my life,' he says, babbling a thousand words a minute, as if he's on the clock and has to get everything out before his hour is up.

It starts to dawn on me that he's on something.

I'm no expert on these things, fifty-four and never even smoked a joint, but even I can recognise the signs: the jitteriness, pink skin, layer of sweat on his forehead, manic countenance and inability to concentrate.

'You know me, Elaine,' he continues. 'Know me as well as

anyone probably knows me. You know that I wouldn't do that, couldn't do that. That's just not me, Elaine, just not who I am. I wouldn't kill anyone.'

He taps his foot fast on the ground like he's keeping rhythm in a band, while his right hand fingers a *See Majorca* drinks mat.

'Karim,' I say, holding my hand up to interrupt his flow. 'You need to calm down, and take me back to the start. Who is this girl? What exactly is it you've been accused of?'

He leans in.

'Fucking police is accusing me. Or they will be, if they get hold of me,' he says, his Leeds brogue hitting the swear words with northern gusto.

'Accusing you of what, Karim?'

'The girl what's washed up dead this morning. They're saying I've done it, and I've never even touched her.'

'What dead girl? We've not heard anything here about a dead girl.'

'You will,' he says.

'A British girl?' I ask.

'Guess so.'

The vein on the right side of my forehead is pulsing now and the nerves start to inch their way towards my tummy.

He turns to look out at the office, nervous, checking who's there. Then he whips his head back round to me, his eyes wide and wild.

'It's like I say, there I am with this girl, in Kiss club, of course, because that's just where you go, isn't it? I mean, there's nothing odd about that, it's where everyone ends up and, you know, I'm part of that scene. So, I'm there with this girl and we're together and that, nothing sinister, like, it's just the way we are. Didn't do nothing bad or anything, just, you know, a kiss and a cuddle. But they're not going to have that, are they? They've decided I did it and don't care about the truth. They reckon I've killed her, don't they? Because I was dancing with her and that, and they don't like me anyway, because of my record and because I don't just sit there, handing them money and doffing my cap like a good boy. You got to help me, Elaine. Please, you know I can't go back to prison. I'd rather top myself. Please, Elaine, help me.'

He's staring at me, his eyes pleading for me to believe him, his face fidgety, eyes blinking rapidly.

'Who is this girl and how do you know she's dead?'

He sits back.

'Don't know her name. She went off at some point. And then later, after the club, I'm round my mate's and my flatmate's texting me and saying there's police round our place asking for me cos the girl's been found murdered, on the beach, and they want me, don't they?'

My stomach tightens.

'You're sure that's why they're looking for you?'

He nods.

'Police crawling round Magaluf, up and down the strip, the beach, you name it. But I know what they'll do second they find me: fit me up for it. And with my record, what chance have I got? It's why I've come here, because I didn't do it, Elaine. You've got to believe me. I didn't touch her and I can't go back to prison.'

He might look tired and his face drained, but his eyes are alert, imploring me to take his side.

And I'm inclined to. I'm no expert, but I've been dealing with people like Karim for seven years now, since I got the job as the British Vice-Consul, and I'm pretty good at telling when someone's lying and someone's telling the truth. I can spot the tells, the shifty glances, attempts to avoid eye contact, physical distractions, playing with fingernails, fiddling with their hair, etc. And I know Karim. Know him too well. Over six years now: five as an inmate at the Centro Penitenciario, the island's main prison. It was my job to give him consular assistance, as I have to any Brit who's unlucky, or stupid enough, to wind up in a Majorcan jail cell. In Karim's case, he had been convicted of drug dealing. Nothing particularly serious, just cannabis and a bit of cocaine, but it wasn't his first offence and the courts lost patience with him and decided to give him something stiffer.

Which is how he and I became friends. For five years I visited him once a month to check he was okay. His dad, a Pakistani taxi driver in Bradford, walked out on him and his two sisters when he was six, and hasn't been in touch since. His white, British mum still lives in West Yorkshire, an alcoholic with an occasional cleaning job and barely a penny to her name. Which meant I was the only friendly face he ever saw. And it's because I know him so well, know, deep down, what a placid soul he is, that my instinct is that he's telling the truth.

His hand is lying on the table, the fingers still tapping away slowly along the top. I reach over and add my hand to his. He looks up at me.

'I believe you, Karim,' I say, and I see the muscles in his face begin to relax.

'Thank you,' he says, his eyes open and honest again.

'But there's only so much I can do.'

He lets out an audible stream of air.

'Can't you get me back to Britain somehow? You must know people that can do that. You're the embassy aren't you?'

'We're the consulate. I can't just get you back to the UK.'

Hand goes into his pocket, pulls out a mangled pack of chewing gum and starts ripping a couple of pieces out with his teeth.

'What can I do then?'

'You need to do this properly,' I say. 'You can't run away from the police indefinitely. You're better off fronting this up. I know the police in Calvià. I can talk to them, arrange for you to go to them, politely, sensibly, help you find a lawyer, let you put your side of the story, properly, on the record, and make sure it's investigated properly. That way, we can be sure the evidence will show you're innocent. Do you understand?'

He stands up, scraping his chair on the ground as he does so, starts walking over to the window, then to the wall, mumbling 'Fuck's sake' under his breath, again and again.

'I can't go to the police, Elaine. They hate my guts.'

'Karim, it's not a choice. They're going to pick you up one way or the other. If you work with me, we can show them you've got nothing to hide and they'll treat you reasonably.'

He's fidgety still, walking from one side of the room to another. Taking out a packet of cigarettes, then thinking better of it and putting it back in his pocket.

'Will you let me sort things out with the police for you?' I ask, but he ignores me.

'Karim,' I say, louder, with more authority. 'This will all be all right, but you have to work with me.'

He looks over at me, trying to read my face, checking whether to believe me.

'Well?' I ask.

He nods, almost imperceptibly, and sits down at the table.

There's a dull tap on the window. Soraya, one of our junior officers, is waving at me. She shapes her hand to look like a telephone and holds it to her ear. 'Can't it wait?' I mouth, but she shakes her head. I apologise to Karim and tell him I'll be back in a moment.

Over at my desk, the telephone handset is lying on the desk, off its cradle.

'It's Miguel,' Soraya says.

The deputy chief of the Policia Local in Calvià, which is why it couldn't wait.

I thank her and pick up the phone.

'Miguel, what can I do for you?' I say in Spanish, with forced breeziness.

Normally, Miguel's full of pleasantries. But, today, there's none of it – he's straight to the point, gruff and formal.

'Your friend, Karim Ansari, have you seen him recently?'

I swallow.

'Why?'

'Girl washed up on the beach in Magaluf this morning. One of yours. British. Had her throat slashed so deep, it nearly severed her head. Been raped as well.'

'I see,' I say, trying to betray as little emotion as I can, but the acid is tingling through my arms and neck. Soraya has noticed. She looks at me, narrows her eyes, mouths, 'You okay?'

A nod and a smile from me, a little too quickly to be reassuring.

A young girl, raped and murdered. Body discovered this morning, Monday sixteenth of June. It's grim enough on its own without the additional train of thought it sets off, the things of which it reminds me. The last time something like this happened. Four years ago. Same town, same beach. A girl raped, stabbed and left for dead.

The 'Crude Hood'.

That was what the papers dubbed him.

*The victim described the man as middle-aged, heavily built and wearing a crudely fashioned hood.*

A bit of sacking tied around the neck with some string. Two holes cut out for the eyes.

She was with someone. Sex on the beach.

Then the Crude Hood arrives.

The man left bleeding out on the sand, fighting for his life. Stabbed nine times – somehow, he survived.

Her, tied up and raped. Her throat slashed once, non-fatally – she turned her head at the last moment.

He got disturbed.

Ran off.

And it wasn't just the attack. There was the shambles of a police investigation that followed. Cops immediately putting all their effort into pinning it on a single suspect, Glen Mills, a young British bar-worker with a history of mental health problems and a long rap sheet of petty crime. He spent four weeks at the Penitenciario pleading his innocence and threatening to commit suicide if no one would listen to him. At the end of the fifth week no one had, and he succeeded. It was left to me to ring his mum and tell her. Case closed, as far the Guardia Civil was concerned – they had their man. Until CCTV evidence turned up of Glen Mills breaking into a convenience store in Portals Nous at the same time he was supposed to have been carrying out the attack on the beach. The police had to reopen the investigation but, four years on, still no arrests have been made.

In the interview room, Karim's standing at the window, staring at me. I pray Miguel isn't making the same mistake again.

'Karim's the last person seen with her, so we need to talk to him,' Miguel says.

I'm not saying or doing anything but Karim's face twitches as he looks at me. A microscopic shake of his head, then he's moving, towards the door, then out of the room, fumbling for the button to release the dividing door.

I put my hand over the mouthpiece and call out to him.

'Karim, wait.'

But the glass between us is soundproof and all he can probably see is my mouth moving up and down.

He squeezes his way through the groups of people in reception and then he's out of the consulate altogether, heading down the stairs and into the city beyond.

The muscles in my neck stiffen again. Miguel's voice hums through the earpiece.

'He's with you?' Miguel asks.

'Was,' I say. 'He's just gone.'

'Where?' he asks.

'I don't know. He saw me talking to you and just went.'

No reply from Miguel. Instead, he's barking instructions in rapid Spanish to whoever else is in his office.

Then he's back on to me:

'What's he told you?'

'Not a lot, and anything he has said is in confidence.'

There's a pause and then some more Spanish in the background. Then Miguel's back on the line.

'Wait where you are,' he says. 'I'm sending a car.'

'For me?'

'Yes.'

'Miguel, I can't come to Magaluf. I've got a waiting room full of people, work to do, a consulate to run.'

'You'll wait where you are – one of my men will be with you shortly and he'll bring you over.'

'For God's sake, Miguel, you can't just haul me over there like I'm a suspect.'

'You're the last person to have seen our chief suspect, so I think you'll find, I can.'

## 2

We pull up outside the front entrance to Calvià Police Station, a brand-new monstrosity the district council somehow found the money to build just before the financial crash. It's all marbled walls and cantilevered glass atriums and serves both the Policia Local, the small municipal force who do most of the day-to-day policing here, and the Guardia Civil, the paramilitary police who take on the big crimes.

The officer assigned to drive me here from Palma signs me in at the front desk and I'm given a 'Visitante' pass to wear around my neck. He shows me to a lift that takes us to the fourth floor and directs me into an institutional interview room. There's a table in the centre with audio recording equipment on top of it, currently turned off. One thin, horizontal window, high up in the wall, lends us some daylight. I'm pointed to one of two chairs and left. I take out my phone and flick through my messages. There's one from Louise in the office, detailing the afternoon's roster of new casework: an old girl's had a heart attack in Andratx and died, aged ninety-one; a twenty-six-year-old British lad is in Son Espases hospital after being hit by a car in the early hours of the morning, and it's currently unclear if he'll be able to walk again; a guy has rung up, furious that we haven't sorted a telegram from the Queen for his mum's 100th birthday party; and a six-year-old boy's experienced severe lacerations to his face after his dad let him go out, unattended, on a jet-ski.

I'm just emailing Louise back when the door opens and a short, grubby-looking man in suit trousers and an open-necked shirt comes in. His skin is swarthy and pockmarked, and the stale smell of strong cigarettes, recently smoked, trails in with him.

He introduces himself as Inspector David Nabarro from the Guardia Civil.

'You are Elaine Martin, the British Vice-Consul?' he asks in Spanish.

'That's right,' I reply, recrossing my legs.

'I'm leading the investigation into the death of the British girl who was found this morning. I understand you recently met with Karim Ansari?'

'He came to the consulate wanting to speak with me. It's open to the public.'

'About what time was this?' he asks.

'About 4pm,' I say.

He doesn't take notes.

'Did he say what he wanted?'

He looks longingly at the recording equipment on the desk. I know he'd like to switch it on, interview me under caution, but things aren't at that stage just yet.

I lean back in my seat.

'I'm sure you can understand that any conversations I have with British citizens in the consulate are, by their very nature, confidential,' I say.

He scowls at me.

'What could he have said that you would want to keep confidential?' he asks.

Exhalation of breath. Already getting tired of this now. Start thinking of home. Where Nick is. My husband. What's he up to now? Bottle of Scotch, bottle of tequila? Probably.

'If I told you that, it clearly wouldn't be confidential, would it, Inspector Nabarro?'

'A British girl was raped and murdered last night,' he says, making a point of looking me in the eye as he hits the two verbs. 'You don't want to help us find the killer?'

'I would love to. And perhaps you can tell me what Karim has to do with this?'

'At this stage, that's confidential,' he says.

'What is there about it that you would want to keep confidential?'

Smirk on his face now. Turning into a grin.

A bastard's grin.

He changes tack.

'Do you know where Karim is now?'

'No.'

'Can you think where he might be?'

'No.'

'Where does he usually go? What does he like to do? Where does he spend his free time?'

'I don't know.'

'You're not being very co-operative, Miss Martin.'

'It's Mrs Martin.'

He's pissed off now. Pulls up a chair directly opposite me and sits in it. Sizing me up, looking me up and down. Trying to unnerve me. Hand goes to the holster on his belt. Pulls his phone out. Flicks through, finds something, then turns it to face me. It's an image of a girl. Can't tell much about her face. Covered in blood; giant pool of it around the head and body. Skirt pulled up over her waist, legs splayed, pubic hair matted with blood. Then there's the neck. Jesus. It's at the sort of unholy angle that instantly makes me feel nauseous.

Blood seeping into the sand like spilt paint.

Just like four years ago.

The Crude Hood.

I turn away, swallowing down the bile.

'Michelle Fraser,' he says. 'British. Twenty-two years old. She'll never see twenty-three. Has a three-year-old son. Had,' he corrects himself, looking at me, as if I was somehow involved. 'What did Karim Ansari tell you and where was he on his way to?'

I think. Think hard. What harm could it do? Karim told me hardly anything. Nothing that could have a bearing on this.

I look Nabarro in the eye.

'Anything Karim said to me is confidential.'

He turns his hands into fists and slams them on the desk. I jump from my seat, shocked. He curses in Spanish. Ugly words about sluts, mothers, whores. The door opens with force. It's Miguel: immaculate navy-blue uniform, walnut skin, crow's feet around his eyes. His gaze narrows as he sees me standing defensively, a look of shock on my face.

'What's this?' he asks Nabarro.

Nabarro looks at him, half angry, half embarrassed.

'I was asking Miss Martin about Karim Ansari,' he says.

'*Mrs* Martin,' Miguel says. 'She's our guest, not our witness.'

Miguel turns to me, face softening.

'Are you okay?'

'Fine,' I say. I force a smile in Nabarro's direction.

'Come to my office,' Miguel says to me. I take small steps towards him.

He turns to Nabarro, scowling.

~

Miguel's office is not far off the size of a tennis court. That's how it works with public servants out here: the head of Palma's binmen has an office twice the size of the British Ambassador's in Madrid. As the deputy chief of the Policia Local, Miguel's is, of course, bigger than the head of the binmen's.

Miguel takes a seat behind his large oak partners' desk, and points me to the cushioned, burgundy leather chair opposite.

'I'm sorry,' he says, digging through one of his desk drawers and producing a bottle of sherry and two glasses. 'Fucking Guardia Civil.'

'They're involved already?' I ask.

Miguel shrugs.

'Standard practice to hand over murders, but we normally get a few days first. We're in the transition phase.'

'What does that mean?'

'We do the donkey work until they're ready to take over properly. Bunch of pumped-up adrenaline junkies. They'd frame their own grandmothers if it closed a case. You seen the picture of her yet?'

The photo on the phone. The blood, the face, that neck.

I nod.

'Look,' he says, pouring out two sherries, a big one and a little one, 'Nabarro jumped ahead of himself. He agreed to let me talk to you first. I'm still being allowed a foothold in this investigation at least, liaison and all that. He wasn't meant to speak to you unless we're forced to arrest you.'

He passes the little sherry to me. I don't thank him.

'And when's that going to be?' I ask, feeling his eyes on me again, light dancing around them.

'If you obstruct our investigation,' he says.

That smile.

'I'm sorry,' he says. 'You were meant to be brought straight to me. It appears Inspector Nabarro was keen for the first word.

He's stressed. Everyone is. This girl has thrown everything in the air.'

*That face. That neck.*

I push my sherry glass back towards Miguel.

'Not on work hours,' I say. He looks vaguely surprised, adds mine to his, then takes a sip.

'Can you tell me what's happened?' I ask.

'They found the body about 7am this morning,' he says. 'A jogger on the beach. They alerted police. Victim's a British holidaymaker, here for a week with friends. She's from Colchester,' he says, his accent butchering the name of the town.

He taps something into his computer and turns the monitor round to face me. There's a passport photo of a young woman, early twenties, pretty, brown hair in a neat bob with traces of a blonde dye job still growing out at the ends. She looks serious, like she's applying for a job interview, a tiredness to the edges of her pale white skin.

'Michelle Fraser,' he says. 'We're waiting for the autopsy for confirmation, but there is bruising and abrasion around the vagina too. We think she was raped, then murdered.'

*Blood. Face. Neck.*

The bile again. I swallow.

'And why are you saying Karim's involved?'

'At the moment, that information's part of an ongoing police investigation, so must remain confidential.'

'I see.'

Miguel leans in. Sherry and aftershave, almost certainly designer.

'Off the record,' he says in a voice just above a whisper, 'about midnight last night, Michelle's boyfriend, Ben, got into a fight with someone in Kiss nightclub. It spilled out into the street until one of my patrols interrupted. It was Karim that Ben was fighting with.'

I frown.

'Fighting about what?'

'Apparently, Ben had had an argument with Michelle. She had gone to Kiss without him. She had met Karim there and one thing had led to another. Ben had arrived and not been too happy about seeing them together. It was Paint Night, after all.'

Kiss's infamous Paint Night.

Ten paint guns spraying fluorescent substances over several hundred revellers to a soundtrack of the latest in euphoric house music. Clubbers encouraged to wear as little as possible, supposedly so as not to ruin their clothes. In reality, something approaching a 500-person orgy. The cause, two years ago, of Kiss losing its licence. It got it back a few weeks later. No one's quite sure how or why.

'Doesn't being in a fight make Ben the main suspect?'

'No. He was with us.'

I nod to indicate I understand. A night in one of the cells here. A wipe-clean foam mattress and a long-life pastry for breakfast.

'That doesn't mean *Karim* did anything,' I say.

'He wasn't arrested and went back into the club. He was the last person seen with her alive.'

'Any forensics?' I ask.

'Might be. There was a white, shiny substance on her upper thigh. Might be semen. It's with the lab now. And they found GHB in her system. It's a regular out here. Party drug. Common in date-rape cases. Makes someone tired and groggy. They lose control. Often lose their memory of the last few hours. Hard to detect. We found half a litre of it in Karim's apartment. So you see, we're quite keen to find Karim. And you're the last person that's seen him.'

'So you tell me.'

I shift in my chair, not liking the way it sounds; like I'm a suspect.

'Do you know where he is?' Miguel asks.

'Haven't a clue.'

'But he's in Palma?'

'Well, the consulate is, and he came to see me there.'

'Why did he come to see you?'

'Wanted to talk.'

Miguel leans back and looks out of his window. The view is of corrugated iron roofs, warehouse units and sparsely used car parks.

'What did he tell you?'

'As you well know, Miguel, anything I'm told in the privacy of the British consulate is in strict confidence between me and the visitor.'

He shrugs and sips his sherry again.

*That face. That neck.*

I lean in to him.

'Off the record,' I say. Miguel's head flicks round to face me. 'He didn't tell me very much. He was agitated and flustered and looked, and smelt, like he hadn't slept. He said nothing about where he'd come from or where he was going to go, and very little about last night's events. The only thing I will tell you is that he was absolutely adamant he had nothing to do with anything that happened to the girl. And, for the record, I believe him.'

Miguel laughs, blowing acrid air through his teeth in the process.

'Don't believe it, Elaine,' he says. 'He's a well-known liar.'

I try to hold his gaze, but he won't look me in the eyes. Instead, he turns back to his sherry glass and drains it.

'He's a lot of things,' I say, 'but he's not a murderer, and I should know, I've met enough of them out here.'

'You and me both.'

'Haven't you got CCTV from the club?' I ask. 'Can't you see who she left with? Where she went?'

He shakes his head.

'Only up to a point. She didn't leave through any of the main entrances, so we don't know who she went with or how. We think she might have gone out of the east door, which is a service entrance, one not covered by cameras. So it must have been someone who knew the place well. Someone like Karim. There's no CCTV of Karim leaving the club either. Which is another reason we think they left together.'

'You don't know that.'

Miguel shrugs his shoulders and takes another sip of his sherry.

And now I'm worried. Now I can see what Karim was saying. Miguel's not just making enquiries here. He already seems to think he's got his man. And that means they'll waste several days trying to prove it was him, while whoever did do it, could be busy getting ready for their flight home. And, when they find Karim, he'll be slapped back into the Penitenciario, and I'll have another suicidal prisoner on my hands; another potential Glen Mills.

'Doesn't it remind you of anything?' I ask.

He looks at me quizzically, narrows his eyes.

'Four years ago,' I say, 'on the beach at Magaluf. The couple stabbed by the guy in the hood.'

He shrugs his shoulders, says he doesn't see the link.

'Same beach, similar MOs,' I say, but Miguel's not having it.

'That was a long time ago,' he says. 'Different case.'

'But there are definite similarities. And we know Karim was already inside then, on drugs charges.'

'There are similarities with lots of bad things that you Brits do to each other in Magaluf,' he says. 'Just ask Karim.'

Whatever I say, he's not going to be interested. Already made his mind up. It's Karim he wants, just as four years ago it was Glen Mills.

'So, what happens now?' I ask.

'I've got teams in Palma looking for him,' Miguel says. 'The Policia Nacional and Policia Local there are helping too. We'll find him, and then Spanish justice will take its course.'

'And what's that supposed to mean?'

The shrug again.

'I'll need to speak to her family,' I say.

'I know.'

'Do they know their daughter's dead?'

'They've been informed,' he says. 'You should get in touch with them. They're arriving to view the body tomorrow.'

'Tomorrow?'

I almost get up from my seat. It's usually the consulate that oversees visits to mortuaries and undertakers. It's one of the most difficult jobs we do.

Miguel reads the panic on my face and smiles – the sort of thing that amuses him.

His mobile rings. He checks the number.

'Excuse me,' he says, answering the phone and walking out of the office.

Another young life wasted. Another pair of grieving parents to liaise with. The meeting, the trip to the mortuary to view the body, the arrangements to get it back to the UK, the press descending on Palma, getting up our noses. More tales of debauched youths and binge-drinking. Mum and Dad beside themselves, wanting to get the body back, the paperwork, the money, the sheer goddamn tragedy of it all.

*That face. That neck.*

Miguel walks back in, angry.

'Lab came back on the substance on Michelle Fraser's thigh,' he says.

'The semen?'

Miguel shakes his head.

'Spermicidal fluid. From a condom.'

I close my eyes for a second to take it in – nothing to implicate Karim.

'So, no DNA, which means Karim's in the clear then.'

I sit back, trying to stifle a smile.

Miguel just shrugs.

'Karim must have been careful,' he says, looking at me, a smile creeping round the edges of his mouth.

I don't react.

'Nasty piece of work, Karim,' he says. 'Now, if you don't mind, I've got to try and find the bastard.'

He turns to his computer.

'You can find your own way back,' he adds, without looking up.

# 3

The evening is wearing on and I'm stood outside the police station in the tiny corner of shade thrown by the glass portico that sits over the main doors. It's over thirty degrees and there's still no sign of the taxi that was meant to be here forty minutes ago. My headache is pounding and my throat is dry and I haven't brought any water. I could go back inside but I don't want to give the surly woman on reception the pleasure. Instead, I turn to my phone and dial the cab company again. They promise my car will be with me in the next five minutes.

I slump to my haunches and sit. It's undignified and uncomfortable, but I'm uncomfortable anyway. This case. This suspect. It's not the murder that's bothering me. It's the rape.

They're not unusual out here. Far too common: more rapes happen here than anywhere else in the whole of Spain. In high season, we probably have a girl a week who's reporting some form of non-consensual sexual activity. For every one reported, I expect there are ten more where the woman says nothing: can't remember enough about it, doesn't want the hassle, blames herself, got too wasted, thinks it will never stand up in court.

*Magaluf.*

*Shagaluf.*

It's the perfect place for creeps to take advantage of girls, too often drunk and vulnerable.

But this is different.

Women get raped here. Men get stabbed or murdered. But, even in Magaluf, the two rarely mix. Not had a girl stabbed here for years, not in an anonymous attack. Not since the 'Crude Hood'.

The memories of that summer four years ago flood back. Dealing with the two stunned families of the victims. Trying to help Glen Mills, then having to deal with his family after, first, his suicide, and then him getting cleared. Watching a police force, and decent police officers, worm their way deeper and deeper into a rabbit hole, convinced they had their man, pouring manpower into finding evidence to confirm it, then having to rip up their entire case as it becomes obvious they've not only got it wrong, but that their mistakes have cost another young life and that the sick bastard who's actually done it, is out there walking free.

And four years on, he's still out there having never been caught.

But surely it can't be him again? The Crude Hood.

There are similarities: the knife; the time and location, on the beach, in the hours of darkness.

The club: Kiss.

But four years ago, there was no GHB. And this time there's no stabbed sexual partner.

The taxi arrives. I give him instructions to where my car's parked, in Palma, in the car park underneath the consulate. I'm itching to go back to the office, to look at the case files. To remind myself of the details of what happened, who said what, when and where. To try and get clear in my own mind whether this new atrocity could possibly be linked, or whether I'm just putting two and two together and making five. But I'm hot and tired and it's getting late, and I know I can't put off facing Nick for ever, so I decide to leave the files till the morning.

I check my emails on my phone as we drive. Louise has been in touch with the hospital about the lad from the car crash. He still doesn't know if he'll be able to walk, and he's lost his passport. She's set up for me to go and see him there the day after tomorrow. She's also been in touch with Michelle Fraser's parents. They are indeed arriving tomorrow, and I've been booked to take them to the undertaker in the afternoon, to view their daughter's body. My stomach muscles tighten as I read it. I try to put the next two days out of my mind, but my thoughts keep turning to Karim.

I desperately, desperately don't want it to be him, and not just because he's a friend, albeit an odd one. Not just because I've invested so much time in trying to help him get his life back together.

Nothing to do with that.

Because I see so much of Jonathan in him. The son I lost eight years ago, who took his own life in such awful circumstances. And I don't want to see another young life ruined.

The cabbie drops me outside the consulate. As it's gone five, it won't be open anymore, so I go straight down to the car park, get into my car and drive home.

I live in Santa Luisa, a medieval town up in the hills north of Palma. It's beautiful and largely untouched by modern developments or tourists. A place to hide away from the rest of the world, if that were possible.

I park my car on the street in front of the house, unlock the front door and step inside. My house is old, seventeenth century, built of stone that keeps it dark and cool when the sun's out, and warm when it's not. I check my watch: it's not far off midnight.

I drop my bag and cardie on the chair by the chest of drawers, take off my shoes and pad my way to the living room.

There's a light on.

Ominous.

I walk through and the stench hits me before the sight. Nick is spread out on the sofa, the telly still flickering away, a repeat of *Under the Hammer* and the best part of a dozen bottles of beer and a couple of bottles of whisky lying on the floor, empty, his chin and shirt and part of my sofa coated in vomit.

I screw my eyes up and try not to cry.

The smell is foul, like a soil pipe blocked with rotten eggs.

I go closer to him, make a point of breathing through my mouth and kiss his head. His hair smells of apple shampoo and sweat. I call his name, softly at first and then louder, until I'm practically screaming in his ear.

Nothing.

Twenty-six years of marriage.

I shake him by the arm, then by both arms.

Still nothing.

One of his "blow-outs" then, as he calls them. He's had them from time to time since Jonathan died, but since he lost his job at the car showroom two years ago, they've been happening with increasing regularity. This is his second this week.

I go into the kitchen and get a bowl of water, a cloth and some paper towels. I do a rough cleaning-up job, wiping the sick off him, picking up the bigger bits with the paper towelling, doing my best not to gag.

Egg and soil pipe.

When I'm done, the stench is still terrible, but it's better. A bit better. I dispose of the cloths, towels and what's in the bowl, wash my hands and go upstairs.

I should really have a shower, wash the worst of the day away, but I'm too tired. Instead, I change into my nightie, put my phone on to charge, and get into bed.

I'm woken by my mobile ringing. It's one of those nice polyphonic ringtones that, when you first set it, sounds like it could never be unpleasant to the ear, a sort of jaunty little polka. Right now, as I rub my face and try to come to terms with being awake, it sounds like the devil's own cacophony.

My eyes are adjusting to the light when it finally stops ringing. I blink until I'm able to focus and check the call history. It's Louise. Four missed calls, a voicemail and some texts. I open the first one:

Little girl's gone missing in Magaluf.

Christ.

I try not to panic. Deep breaths, in and out. Doesn't mean she's properly missing. Probably just got lost, or staying with a friend or hiding in a basement or got lost trying to find a toy. Doesn't mean anything bad's happened to her. Doesn't mean she's not coming back. Doesn't mean the British tabloid press will descend on us for weeks on end.

Like the last time.

I check the time: 10am.

Jesus. She must be wondering what the hell's happened to me. Two missing people. Meant to message her last night to say I'd be late in. Meant to. Forgot.

I text her to say I was at the Policia Local until very late but will be in as soon as I can. I get out of my nightie and start hunting for a towel. Then I remember Nick. I can't hear anything. Haven't heard anything. Shower first, then deal with him.

I'm about to enter the bathroom when I hear my phone going again.

I pause, weigh up ignoring it for a second, then answer it.

'Elaine?'

'Yes, Louise, it's me.'

'So sorry to bother you, I know you had a late one, but I just wanted to let you know that the parents...'

'Parents?'

'Of the little girl. The one that's gone missing. Well, they're here. In one of the meeting rooms. I'm doing my best but they really want to see someone senior. I just thought you should know. They're beside themselves. And get this, turns out their girl went missing just down the road from where that other girl got murdered, and on the same night!'

I swallow hard.

'I'll be there in thirty minutes,' I say, throwing the towel onto the bed and reaching for my clothes.

# 4

My little SEAT's going as fast as the bashed-up piece of tin can manage. It's fifteen years old and only passed this year's *Inspección técnica de vehículos*, the Spanish MOT, after I came to an 'agreement' with the local garage – they gave the car the benefit of the doubt when it came to some of the paperwork and I gave them €200. It was still cheaper than having to buy a new one. That will have to wait until Nick gets a job.

Nick.

*Beer bottles. Whisky bottles. Vomit.*

He never wanted to come back to Spain. It was me that made him. Despite having Spanish parents, he grew up in England. They were refugees who emigrated after getting fed up with Franco.

Nick loved England. He was happy there. He had me, and a good job and a good house. He didn't want to move.

I made him.

It was after Jonathan died. Eight years ago. I couldn't bear to stay in England any longer, in that little market town, in the

Midlands, in the house where Jonathan had grown up, all the memories, all the moments, all the ghosts.

The room where I found him that Sunday afternoon.

I begged Nick for a fresh start. Got on my knees and begged him. Cried my eyes out until he agreed. We sold the house and our timeshare on Majorca to buy this place. I got the job at the consulate. Nick couldn't get the job he wanted, so ended up taking a sales position at a VW dealership in Palma, until it closed and he was made redundant. And that's the way it's been ever since. Because that's the problem with Spain: there are no jobs in Spain, no jobs if you're young and definitely no jobs if you're re-entering the jobs market at the age of fifty-six.

So now Nick's got no job, no friends and nothing to do with his day. The only thing he's got left is me, and, these days, it looks very much like that might not be enough.

I discuss this every other week with Miriam, the counsellor, at her little consultation room on the outskirts of Palma. Nick thinks it's to discuss grief, to chat about Jonathan, get it all out. He doesn't know that, these days, most of our discussion is about him.

He was still lying on the sofa when I went to leave the house. I roused him briefly and he did, at least, stir. He wasn't in a good way. He looked, smelt and sounded like a vagrant. Said his head hurt, and a few other things besides.

I tried, and failed, to help him stand up. Instead, he propped himself up on the sofa. I put some coffee on for him, gave him a glass of water and told him we'd talk later. But what is there to talk about? Our marriage? What's left of it. Is it still functioning? Can you breathe life back into a corpse?

It's nearly midday by the time I get to the city. I work my way through Palma's back roads, thinking about Karim. Where he might be. What he might be doing. How he might be feeling.

On my mind, too, what happened four years ago. My memory is vague about it. I know it was a couple, on the beach, and it was brutal. I know a knife was involved and it was another horrible rape. But I can't remember any faces, any details, any names, except one: the Crude Hood. But there will be records. We'll have kept on file everything we did to help the family and help the police. I'll look it out when I get in, when I've dealt with the missing girl that is – wherever she is. I feel tense again just thinking about it; a young girl, on her own, somewhere in Magaluf, amongst the drunks and the drugs and God knows what else. I don't know how long she's been missing. Hopefully just a few hours. The shorter the period, the more chance we'll find her safe and well. Hope it's a simple story of little girl lost, little girl found; that it's not linked to anything that went on two nights ago, on that beach. I bite my lip and mutter something between a wish and a prayer, and then I drive down the ramp into the underground car park of the anonymous office block that contains the British consulate, just off the Plaça d'Espanya.

By the time I walk through the main door, the reception area is already full of people. Mainly they look tired and hungover. Most have grim looks on their faces which is understandable when you want to be on the beach but, instead, you've got to trek to the middle of a big city to try and sort out some miserable bit of paperwork or other.

About half the workload is sorting out replacement passports for people who've been careless and either lost, damaged or destroyed theirs. The rest is a mixture of advising on how to report crimes, helping out with accidents, or aiding the repatriation of bodies. Sometimes we get something nice: helping to register an early birth or a marriage, the arrival of a

Royal Navy warship into harbour, or there's a British VIP in town, but those occasions are rare. Most of the time, the only reason anyone needs to see us is because something bad has happened to them in the one week a year they're meant to be having fun.

I push my way past a man with a sizeable cotton-wool pad micro-taped to his face, press the code for the connecting door, and walk into the main, open-plan office. Today, at least, there's a full team. The junior officials, Duncan and Soraya, only here for the busy summer months, are working the front desk, dealing with the public's queries. My fellow Vice-Consul, Rodrigo, is sat, as ever, doing something on his computer – almost certainly answering his emails, which is about the limit of his contributions these days. If things went on merit, he'd have been sacked years ago. Unfortunately, having worked in the consulate for over twenty-eight years, he's now unsackable as, with that time served, Spanish employment law would mean he'd be due a payout approaching €175,000. So instead, he turns up to the office, puts his feet up and does almost nothing while the rest of us shoulder his workload.

There's a yelp from behind me.

It's Louise, emerging from one of the interview rooms, her walnut-brown brow breaking into worry lines.

'Elaine, thank God,' she says.

I nod to acknowledge her, then head towards my desk and dump my bag on top.

'Are you okay?'

She comes right up to me, starts whispering.

'They're in there, in the Family Room. I put them in there because, you know, it's bigger and a bit nicer.'

The Family Room, also known as Interview Room 3, is where people get taken for the difficult conversations. It has sofas instead of chairs and prints of Majorca on the walls instead of

Foreign Office information posters. It's designed to put people at ease when we need to tell them that their loved one is injured or paralysed or, more often than not, dead.

'They're very... jumpy,' she continues in that perennially upbeat way of hers, which feels particularly inappropriate right now.

'I'm not surprised,' I say. 'What are their names?'

'Mr and Mrs Walsh,' she says.

'Are there any more details?'

'Daughter, Kayleigh, twelve years old, was last seen the day before yesterday, but they didn't realise she was missing until late yesterday afternoon.'

I frown.

'Twelve? Jesus. How did they not realise?' I ask.

'I'll let them fill you in,' Louise says, relief on her face, only too pleased to hand this one over.

The Family Room has a large window that looks out across our office area. On the other side of it, I can see two people sat, fidgeting on the sofas. The man looks to be in his late forties, head shaven to the skin. He's rocking back and forth on his seat, staring at the wall and, from time to time, nibbling at his fingernail. The woman's concentrating on her phone. Her hair is a shock, short and spiked like a 1980s model. She looks a similar age to her partner, but small where he's broad.

'Is Miguel onto this?' I ask.

Louise nods.

'They've had teams out searching all morning,' she says.

I nod and make my way over to the Family Room. The door's ajar but I knock anyway and step into the room.

I introduce myself and take a seat on the opposite sofa from the couple. They tell me their names are Mike and Helen, that they live near Worcester and that Kayleigh is the youngest of their two daughters. They're out here for two weeks and were due to fly back this evening.

Up close, you can see the strain immediately. Mike's skin might be beach brown, but there are dark rings under his eyes and his eyelids are tinged with red. Helen looks a state. Her eyelids are low and her face drained from lack of sleep. What make-up she's applied has been wiped away where the tears have rolled. She gazes at me but her mind looks like it's elsewhere. The corner of a packet of sleeping pills sticks out of the top of her handbag.

'I understand you've already spoken to the police,' I say.

They both nod.

'First thing we did,' Mike adds, 'when we realised.'

'Good,' I say. Praise and reward. Make them feel more positive. 'The most important thing is that the police are working on it. I know several of the officers in Calvià; they're good people. They'll be doing everything they can. Now, I don't want to distress you but I'd be very grateful if you could talk me through what happened, from your point of view. That will get me up to speed and then I can talk you through what we can do here.'

They look at each other, trying to work out who'll lead.

Mike takes charge, asserting himself.

'We'd had a good day on the beach,' he says, in a strong Midlands burr, 'and we'd put the girls down for the night. We left Kayleigh with her sister, Stacey, cos she's sixteen, like, and was meant to look after her while we went out. We're here with friends, you see. Ollie and Jean. They're also staying in Palma Nova, at the Mercurial. Got kids a similar age. They're who's looking after Stace right now.'

'Which hotel are *you* at?' I ask.

'The Excelsior,' Mike says.

'Do you mind if I take notes?' I ask, reaching for my pad.

Mike gestures that that's not a problem, and I write down the name of the hotel.

'So, we leave about eight o'clock and go out to Luigi's with Ollie and Jean and have a nice meal and then go on for a few drinks. Nothing crazy, like, just in Palma Nova. We do a spot of karaoke, few beers and shots, then we go home.'

'We had our phones on us all the time,' Helen chips in quickly. 'Stacey was under strict instructions – anything happens, to call us straight away.'

'Of course,' I say, and look down at my notebook so I don't feel forced to nod. 'So what time did you get back?'

They share a glance, furtive, both look down at their shoes.

'Don't know exactly,' Mike says. 'Helen thinks it was about five. I think it was more like four.'

'In the morning?' I ask instinctively. They both look a bit hurt.

'We don't know exactly what time it was,' Helen says, on the defensive again. 'But everything seemed normal enough when we went to bed.'

She's prickly now, and jumpy. I want to ask if she checked on the girls when they got back, but I don't want to get her back up again. I just assume they didn't.

'So, when did you realise that Kayleigh was missing?' I continue.

'Second we got up,' Mike says.

'Which was when?'

They share a glance. An unspoken debate, *Do you want to do it, or me?*

Helen takes it.

'About two,' she says, no AM or PM specified. 'We assumed everything was fine, so we just slept it off.'

'And that's when you called the police?'

Another shared glance.

Helen again.

'Neither Kayleigh nor Stacey were in the room when we got up, but we expected that. Stacey had planned to go straight to the beach and we assumed she'd taken Kayleigh with her. It was only when she got back, about five, wanting her tea and that, that we found out Kayleigh wasn't there.'

I look at Helen, trying to make sense of her story. They seem like nice people; normal, decent. But, two daughters, left on their own while they go out till five in the morning, then sleep it off till gone two the next afternoon. Helen fixes me with a stare as if to say, *Don't go there, not now, not today.*

'Was there a reason Stacey hadn't raised the alarm earlier?' I ask.

Mike leans forward.

'So,' he says, feeling more confident on this one, 'she fell asleep not long after we'd left for our night out and didn't wake till ten-ish the next day. When Kayleigh wasn't there, she just assumed she'd already gone to meet friends down the beach. They've made friends with quite a few other youngsters, you see. That's one of the nice things about Palma Nova – it's a very family-friendly place.'

'And when she hadn't turned up by the afternoon?'

'She assumed Kayleigh was back with us,' Mike says.

'It was only when we all got back together,' Helen chips in, 'that we realised none of us had seen her.'

'Which is when you raised the alarm?'

'That's right,' Mike says, and sinks back into the sofa.

I make a little note of the times on my notepad. When I look up, Helen's crying. I lean in, put a hand on her knee.

'It's okay,' I say, sympathetic, professional, official. 'These things happen all the time. She's probably just–'

'You must think we're the worst parents in the world,' she cuts in. 'And we are. We fucking are.'

'Come on, love, that's not fair,' Mike says.

'Oh, shut up, Mike, of course we are. Leaving two teenage girls on their own while we go off and get trashed. I said we shouldn't but you were full of it, weren't you, wanted to do your fucking karaoke, didn't you? "They'll be fine. This is a nice, friendly place. You only live once". Well, well done, Mike, cos now we've lost our little girl and we don't know what's fucking happened to her.'

She's standing now, leering into his face, cheeks red and glowing, tears and spittle flying.

She turns to me and I think she's going to attack me.

'Where are the toilets,' she says, a command, not a question.

I tell her and she storms off.

Silence in the room. Mike bewildered. He coughs, trying to regain composure.

'She's very upset about it all,' he says.

Statement of the obvious.

'Very emotional right now,' he continues. 'They mean everything to her.'

'Is there CCTV at the hotel?' I ask. 'Have the police checked it? Is there any sign of Kayleigh leaving the building?'

'First thing we did after ringing the police,' he says. 'I went straight down to reception and I demanded they show us the CCTV. They wanted to wait till the police got there but I said, "Listen here, amigo, my daughter's missing, now you show me that CCTV before you go missing as well, capisce" and they bloody well did what I said.'

'And?' I say.

He looks at me, furrowing his brow, confused.

'Did it show what time she left the building?' I ask.

'Course not.'

It's Helen, coming back into the room. She's splashed water

on her face but her cheeks are still red and her eyes surrounded by black rings.

'Nothing of her leaving any of the entrances or exits,' she continues. 'But our apartment's on the ground floor. She probably climbed out the window and walked. No cameras there, so no idea. They'll have to check every CCTV camera in the area to find her and that could take days.'

I nod, make another note, then offer them a cup of tea. They decline, but I desperately need a coffee so make my excuses and head to the kitchen. While the coffee machine's chugging its gruel into a cup, I take out my mobile and call Miguel. He answers.

'The girl, Kayleigh Walsh,' I say. 'What's the latest?'

'Wait a moment,' he says. I hear a door open and Miguel shouting at his subordinates for an update. There's some Spanish in the background that I can't make out, then he's back on the line.

'She's not turned up yet,' he says. 'We're checking CCTV and patrols are out looking. Soon as we hear anything, we'll call.'

'What's your hunch?' I ask.

He laughs.

'She'll turn up,' he says. 'Just young girls getting up to something. Are the parents with you?' he asks.

I tell him they are.

'Can you ask them for a photo?' he asks. 'We'll give it a few more hours, then we'll need to put out something to the media. Picture always helps.'

A press release.

'You know what will happen when the British press hear there's a little girl missing in Magaluf?' I say, butterflies in my stomach.

He doesn't say anything, just gives out a dismissive breath.

'If you could scan it directly to me,' he says, and the line goes dead.

Back in the Family Room, Mike and Helen are now sat on opposite sides of the sofa, a couple of feet of empty beige cushion between them.

I explain to them that, while Kayleigh's unaccounted for, we'll do everything we can to help them but emphasise that our powers are limited. I say we can liaise with the police on their behalf, can put out unofficial feelers around the British community on the island, and that we're happy to put up posters in the consulate itself. But we can't go looking for Kayleigh ourselves, that's the job of the police and they're much better placed to do it. They sort of nod, but don't seem too interested.

'I've spoken to the police in Calvià,' I say, 'and they've assured me they've got their full resources on the job, looking for Kayleigh. They're being very sensible about things and are sure she will turn up soon. They deal with these kinds of incidents quite often. One thing they did say was that if Kayleigh hasn't turned up in a few hours, the next step would be to alert the media, which will help get people looking for her. Please don't be alarmed, it's absolutely standard procedure and will only help in the search.'

Helen looks at Mike, tears forming at the corner of her eyes. He reaches over, puts a hand on her knee, gives it a clumsy pat, then removes it.

'They have asked whether you'd be able to provide a photo of Kayleigh they could give to the media. Would that be possible?'

Helen reaches for her phone and starts thumbing through her photos until she's found one she likes. She gives me the handset.

The girl I'm looking at could pass for anything from fifteen to twenty. She's tall, like her dad, dressed for a night out in a cocktail dress, with make-up and salon-styled hair.

'Her end-of-year prom,' Helen says. 'They do them each year at her school.'

'She's very... grown-up,' I say.

'She'll be thirteen in a couple of months,' Mike chips in. 'I don't know where the time goes.'

I leave Helen and Mike in the Family Room. They seem at a bit of a loss as to what to do and aren't in any rush to leave the consulate, so I leave them to their own devices.

I head back into the main office. On the other side of the glass, the reception area is now crammed with people. Duncan and Soraya are both busy dealing with visitors at the front desk. Duncan's running through the procedure for replacing a lost passport with a harried-looking blonde woman who's trying to take in what he's saying while also dealing with her six-year-old daughter, who's crying her eyes out. Soraya's listening intently to a big, red-faced man whose sunburnt chest sticks out through the open neck of his sweaty fawn-coloured shirt. He looks flustered about something, his eyes flickering left and right as he speaks, refusing to settle.

I head over to my desk to send the photo of Kayleigh on to Miguel. The latest issue of the *Majorca Daily Bulletin* is lying on top of my computer keyboard. There's a banner headline reading: 'British Girl Found Dead', and, underneath, the same photo of Michelle Fraser that Miguel showed me in his office: the pretty eyes, the brown bob, the growing out blonde hair.

*The blood. The face. The neck.*

Raped and murdered.

Magaluf beach.

Kiss.

I decide to postpone emailing Miguel for a minute and, instead, open up our Aristotle database – they're all named after Greek philosophers. Aristotle is where we keep all our casework stretching back for the last ten years plus. Once it's open, I bring up a search box and type in: '*Crude Hood*'.

Nothing.

I put in '*crudely fashioned hood*' and there's a hit. Four years ago. Magaluf. Same beach. Same time of day.

The victims: Matthew Houghton and Laura Neil. Met at Kiss that night. Walked to the beach. Interrupted by a man in a 'crudely fashioned hood'.

*String round the neck. Two holes cut out for the eyes.*

Matthew stabbed nine times. Survived, just. Rushed to Son Espases. Intensive Care. Laura held down and violently raped. Neck slashed, but not fatally. Also recovering in Son Espases.

There are details of the consular assistance offered. My predecessor, Imogen, now retired, visited both in hospital. Assisted relatives coming over. Matthew had travel insurance. Helped him get a medical transfer back to a UK hospital.

There are contact numbers.

It's been four years.

There are similarities in the cases: same town, same beach, same hours of darkness. Rape with a knife. Slash to the neck.

Could it be?

I pick up my deskphone, dial 0044 and then Laura's contact number – a mobile. It rings once, twice, three times. Answerphone. I leave a message. Explain I'm calling from the British consulate in Palma, Majorca, say that I'd like to talk to her about what happened to her four years ago. I add that, although I know it might not be something she wants to relive, we've had another attack that has similarities and that it might be useful to hear her side.

I finish the message and put the phone down. Then I turn to my mobile, scan through it for the photo from the Walsh family and forward it to my work email account. I then attach it to a blank email and start composing a message to Miguel.

```
Photo as requested. Family understandably very
concerned. Going to head to Magaluf later to
ask around British businesses, talk to Freddie
etc… see if they've seen or heard anything.
Let me know if I can be any help. Regds,
Elaine.
```

Things are getting more vocal at the front desk now. I look up. The sunburnt man in the fawn-coloured shirt is riled about something. I can hear snatches of his voice through the intercom: '…got to be fucking joking.' 'Fucking shambles.' 'Pay my taxes.' 'Fucking disgrace.'

Soraya looks over at me, hand trembling, eyes pleading. I click send on the email, stand up and head over to her.

I lean into the microphone and press the 'talk' button.

'What seems to be the problem, sir?' I ask.

'Problem is this prissy little shit for brains doesn't know her arse from her elbow,' he says in a nasal, Estuary whine. 'I'm giving very simple instructions and she can't seem to cope. Can barely speak English. Understand? Comprende?'

I turn the microphone off and tell Soraya to take five. She walks away and I turn the microphone back on and lean into it.

'Perhaps you can explain to me what the problem is,' I say.

'And who the fuck are you then?' the man says, his weak chin jumping to and fro.

I can feel my hands shaking a little. It takes a lot for a man in his sixties to make me nervous, but even with the glass between us, his aggression is palpable.

'I'm the British Vice-Consul here in Majorca,' I say, 'and I must ask you to refrain from using such language, sir, or I'll have no choice but to ask you to leave.'

I cast a glance over to my left and the door of the reception, where Javier sits, our armed security guard. He's looking at us nervously, but the pistol on his waist seems to have the desired effect.

The weak-chinned man rolls his eyes and gathers himself.

'I'm sorry,' he says. 'I just get so angry when people can't do their jobs properly–'

'Soraya's an experienced member of my team who does an excellent job,' I break in. 'I'm sure speaking to her in this way didn't help matters. Now perhaps you could tell me what's wrong, Mr...'

'McLellan,' he says, 'Aiden McLellan. It's my mother. Blanche. That name mean anything to you?'

I stare blankly, turning her name over. Nothing. McLellan pre-empts me.

'Not a clue, have you? Bloody should seeing as you caused all this.'

I think hard. Blanche McLellan. Still nothing. I start to speak, hesitantly, but he interrupts before I've formed a word.

'She lives here. British, mind, but lives here now. It's her hundredth birthday a week on Saturday. Registering anything now?'

The name – still nothing, but the birthday starts to ring a bell. To try and keep in touch with our residents out here, we have an unofficial register of UK citizens living permanently in Majorca, pieced together from those that have told us they're here, and those that have registered with the local council. It's not complete or official and is undoubtedly full of holes, but it was felt to be worth doing. And we have a new scheme now. Brainchild of Vanessa, the Consul General, in Barcelona. Any time any of our residents is about to reach their hundredth, we contact them to congratulate them, and see if they want a telegram from the Queen. Vanessa calls it 'outreach'; 'good PR'. We call it a pain in the neck.

'Is this about a telegram from the palace?' I ask.

He nods, giving me a sarcastic smile.

'Nice one, Sherlock,' he says, giving me a slow handclap. 'You should know seeing as you put the idea in her head. All she can talk about. Had to bring forward my holiday so's I'm here for the big day. Then, when I get here and ask for it at the home, they say they know nothing about it. Nothing's arrived. I turn up here, having made all that journey, and that...' he gestures with his head to where Soraya was standing, 'well, she says she doesn't know anything about it either. Says she's all very busy and she'll ask around and someone will get back to me. Well, that's just not fucking good enough.'

'Sir,' I say. A glance towards Javier and McLellan puts his hands up.

'I'm sorry,' he says. 'I just get wound up.'

'I understand,' I say. 'I'm sure one of the team has been looking into it.'

'Of course,' he says, calming down. 'And she's been told one of you would come and present it to her. As a representative of the Queen. That better still be happening and all.'

My heart sinks. I don't know who promised it, but it's not going to be me.

'Who was it you spoke to?' I ask.

'A man,' he says.

Probably Rodrigo.

'In that case, we'll make sure someone's there. Now, if you'll take a seat, I will ask around and get back to you as soon as I can.'

'Well, that's just it,' he says, cheeks going red again, eyes flickering once more. 'I'm fed up of waiting around. That's all I ever get from you lot. "I'll get back to you", "take a seat", "someone will be with you shortly". Well, I've had it up to here.'

'Mr McLellan, we are extremely busy right now as we've had a British tourist killed in very unfortunate circumstances and we have a little girl currently missing, so, as I'm sure you can appreciate, our resources are somewhat stretched at the moment. Now, I do not know at this moment in time where your telegram is. To find out, I need to go and ask my colleagues. So, while I appreciate your frustration at not getting immediate answers to your questions, I'm sure *you* will appreciate I will need time to find out what's happened.'

He nods, puts his hands up again as a way of apology and takes a step back.

'Thank you,' I say to McLellan and watch as he takes a seat. The next woman in line steps up to the window, scrawny, sun-damaged skin, pinched face. I ask her if she'll kindly wait while I get my colleague. Soraya's back now, sitting at her desk, fresh make-up applied where she's been crying. She gets up and takes over from me.

I walk over to Rodrigo.

'This 100th birthday telegram,' I say. He gives me a blank look. 'What's the latest?'

He shrugs.

'I asked you to look into it,' I say. 'I emailed you yesterday.'

Another shrug.

'It's on my to-do list,' he says, his deep Spanish accent mangling the words. Twenty-eight years working in the British consulate and he still speaks English like a tourist.

'The birthday's in ten days,' I say. 'We've made this lady a promise.'

The shrug again.

I lean in, just a few inches from his face. Breath smells of cigarettes and chewing gum.

'That guy over there,' I say, pointing where McLellan's sat, 'wants an update. So, whenever you're ready, I want you to give him one. If you don't, I'll have no choice but to ring Vanessa and say that you're disobeying a strict instruction. Do you understand?'

'We're both Vice-Consuls,' he says, eyes narrowing. Gum and fags. 'You cannot instruct me.'

'I can't, but Vanessa can, and will,' I say.

Vanessa has been trying to find a way to sack Rodrigo for the last two years.

Rodrigo shrugs again, but the confidence has drained away.

I hold his gaze for a couple of lingering seconds, then turn away.

There's a buzz on my phone. Miguel. Text message.

Guess who we've picked up? You might want to come and provide some consular assistance.

Karim.

I check the time. I'm meant to be meeting Michelle Fraser's parents in fifteen minutes.

I text back.

I'll be over late afternoon.

I grab my handbag and cardie and walk towards the connecting door between the office and reception.

Code in. Clunk, click.

I open it and stick my head through.

'Mr McLellan,' I say, and he looks over at me. 'My colleague Rodrigo's looking into your telegram. He'll be with you in just a second.'

He nods, a hint of gratitude, and I head for the exit.

# 5

Two pm and I'm in the lobby of the Paramour Hotel, waiting on another set of grieving parents.

Ray and Cathy Fraser.

Michelle's mum and dad.

After five minutes, a middle-aged, pale-faced couple emerge from the lift looking a bit lost, eyes wandering round reception.

The Frasers, I assume.

They're dressed smartly, as if they're going to a function of some sort, Ray in a plain-blue, button-down shirt and tan chinos, Cathy in a grey blouse and navy-blue, knee-length skirt.

I introduce myself. We have a brief conversation about their journey over here, then I suggest driving them to the funeral home, as it will be easier than them trying to follow me in their hire car.

They don't take much convincing.

Cathy sits in the passenger seat of my car, Ray in the middle seat behind us.

They're silent and nervous, not wanting to make conversation, heads moving left and right, up and down, unable to focus on anything for more than a few seconds.

I tell them how sorry I am about 'everything' and ask them how they are.

Cathy looks at Ray and he shrugs.

'You know. Each day at a time,' he says.

We drive on in silence as I negotiate the inner ring road, crawl through traffic in Amanecer, until we finally reach the motorway.

Half an hour later, we're sitting in the waiting room at the Pinoso Funeral Home, which is situated on a hill overlooking the outskirts of Palma.

Ray and Cathy are sitting on the sofa opposite me, faces drained and grey, holding hands so tightly that their knuckles have turned white. Ray stares ahead, eyes trained on the wall, his face a blank sheet of emotion. Cathy is visibly shaking, foot tapping and left hand alternately scratching at her knee, her thigh, her right wrist, her left cheek.

A woman emerges, white blouse, charcoal-grey pencil skirt.

'Mr and Mrs Fraser?' she asks in strongly accented English.

They nod.

She switches to Spanish.

'The room is ready for you if you would like to come this way,' she says. The Frasers stare at her blankly.

I lean forward.

'Thank you,' I say in Spanish. 'I can take them from here.'

'You're sure?' she says, then looks at the Frasers, who are staring at her in trepidation.

She turns back to me.

'You've done it enough times, I guess,' she says, before turning and walking away.

I stand up.

'The room's ready,' I say. 'I'll walk you down.'

They nod, momentarily relieved, then stand up and follow me.

We go through a fire door, down a short, plain corridor, at the end of which is a grander wood-effect door.

I push the handle and gesture them in.

The Viewing Room.

Infamous, in consular circles.

In contrast to the waiting room, the walls are painted in warm colours, with a handful of tasteful paintings of Majorca hung around them. Flowers in subdued shades of red and yellow stand in vases on a shelf along one wall.

In the centre of the room is a simple pine table on which the shape of a body is completely covered by a clean, white sheet.

Ray and Cathy arrange themselves on one side of it. Cathy is shaking now, still gripping Ray's hand as if it was welded to hers.

'I'll leave you alone now,' I say, edging towards the door.

'Would you mind staying?' Cathy asks.

I look at her, raising my brow.

'It's just, just in case,' she says.

*In case of what?* I think.

'Of course,' I say, shuffling towards the back of the room.

This is the last thing I want.

Ray leans forward and grips the top of the sheet, then gently rolls it down to reveal Michelle's face.

The staff at Pinoso have done an exceptional job, even by their own high standards. There's no sign of any abrasions on her face, just a slight yellowing to the skin. They've dressed her in a high-collared blouse, so wherever her throat was slashed is no longer visible.

She's much prettier than in the passport photo – youthful, tight skin, dimpled cheeks and delicate eyes, nose and mouth.

She looks immaculate and peaceful. Her eyes are closed but

she looks as though she might at any moment open them and say hello.

But she doesn't.

Instead, she lies there, brown hair spread on the pillow that's been carefully placed under her head, the rest of her face peaceful, as though deep in thought.

And that's when it comes: the wail. The purest, most unadulterated sound of human pain I've ever heard – long, low and clear. Cathy almost falls against her daughter as she screams, and Ray does his best to gather her in his arms and keep her upright. Then Cathy reaches out towards Michelle's face, lays her hands on her cheeks, lays her head next to hers and cries quietly to herself. Ray, too, is in tears now, his body convulsing with hard, silent sobs.

I stand there, looking from the floor to Michelle's face and back to the floor as respectfully as I can. The wailing continues – intermittent, anguished howls as Cathy's body convulses.

The image of Jonathan's face pops into my head: his bedroom that Sunday, the rope, the look on his face. I feel a familiar lurch in my stomach. I do my best to bury it back down, deep where it's come from.

I stay with them in that godawful room for a further quarter of an hour, until they're ready to go. I wait until the last tears are shed, the last touch has been administered to their daughter's face and then, quietly and calmly, I show them out.

It's gone 4pm by the time we're heading back and I still feel sick. The sun has burnt through the earlier cloud cover so that the drive back to Palma is in the haze of the summer Majorcan afternoon. The in-car thermometer says it's touching thirty-two degrees outside, and with three people to keep cool, the SEAT's air conditioning is having to fight harder than ever.

Cathy and Ray are staring out of the side windows.

No one says anything until we come off the motorway and reach the first set of traffic lights.

'I always thought she might not make thirty,' Cathy says, looking across at me, then behind to Ray.

I briefly look at her, then turn back to the road. Not sure if I should reply, or not, so I say nothing.

'She lived her life so fast,' Cathy continues, smiling, not crying. 'She moved out from home the second she could, partied so hard, tried a job, quit, moved on, tried another. Same with her boyfriends: tried one, moved on, tried another. Then she had Dylan, and things calmed down a lot and I really thought she was settling down.'

There are tears on her face, but she's not sobbing. There's a tenderness there.

She's quiet for a moment.

'What's going to happen to Dylan?' I ask.

'He'll stay with us,' she says without hesitation. 'We'll start again with him. Bring him up well. Make sure he's told all about his mummy and that he never forgets her. Make sure he makes the right choices in life.'

She looks over at Ray in the back seat, but he's not listening. Instead, he's staring out of the window, tears trailing down his cheeks in steady lines.

I drop the Frasers back at their hotel and promise to keep in touch. Then I get back on the motorway and head in the opposite direction, to Calvià Police Station.

Forty minutes later, I'm sitting opposite Karim in a small

interview room in a secure area of the building, hemmed in by key-coded doors and windowless corridors. He's slumped on the table, half-asleep, but isn't in handcuffs. Once again, there's dormant recording equipment on the table, and not a lot else in the room beyond some laminated fire safety instructions pinned to one wall.

Karim has new abrasions to his left temple to match the ones he had on his right when he came to see me at the consulate.

'What happened there?' I ask, gesturing to my own temple.

He reaches a hand up and strokes the scratches.

'When they arrested me – bastards,' he says.

'That's not good,' I say. 'Have you seen a doctor?'

He frowns and shakes his head dismissively.

'Just a scratch.'

'If they went over the top, I can put in a complaint. It might be Spain but there are still laws about undue force.'

He laughs and leans back in his chair.

'That's a good one. They're all about undue force. Half of them are only in it for the scraps. Reckon they get a kick out of it. Bunch of warped fascists.'

I put my bag down, cross my legs and fix my gaze on him.

'Miguel hasn't told me much. What's the latest?'

He breaks eye contact and looks away.

'Went in front of the judge this morning,' he says. 'Cops gave their side, load of lies and bullshit. Judge looks at me and realises he sent me down five years ago. Asks me a few pointless questions, barely listens to my answers, then orders the investigation and for me to be held. Fucking stitch-up, course it was. Exactly like I told you. They're going to do me for it. They're going to fucking pin this one on me. They've been wanting to get me for so long, and now they've seen their chance. Twenty years in a Spanish jail. Fuck's sake.'

He turns his head to face me again.

'You know what age I'll be when I get out? Fifty. That's half my life.'

Tears now, all down his face, landing in splats on his grubby T-shirt. And I remember Glen Mills, four years ago, same prison, different interview room, different tears – the last time I saw him, before he took his life.

I lean forward and put my hand on his.

'Come on, Karim. Don't get ahead of yourself.'

He looks up at me.

'I'm not guilty. I didn't do fucking anything. But that's not going to change much around here.'

Now it's me that leans back.

'Look, you know I'm not with them and anything you say to me is in confidence. You understand that, right?'

A shrug. Nothing more.

'Karim, look at me. How long have you known me?'

Another shrug. I can smell his breath now, stale and acrid, like he hasn't been near a toothbrush for several days.

'Have I ever been on their side?'

No shrug this time. No response at all.

'You know me. You know you can trust me.'

He looks up slowly, nearly manages a nod.

'Do you want to tell me what happened? Your side of things? Talk me through Sunday night, the morning of Monday the sixteenth of June, from your point of view.'

He sniffs hard, sucking up a mixture of mucus and tears.

'Well?'

He clears his throat.

'So, I'm at Kiss, right, as usual. Just doing my thing, partying, bit of dancing and that.'

'You're there a lot?'

'All the time. Everyone is. Whole of Magaluf revolves around that club.'

'Were you there on your own?'

He cocks his head slightly, looks away.

'You know, there with a few people. Not friends but, you know, acquaintances sort of thing. You know how it is: everyone knows everyone on the strip and most people usually end up at Kiss. I'm there with a few buddies and friends of friends.'

'I understand,' I say, not entirely sure I do.

'And we're having a nice time, chatting, few drinks, bit of dancing, usual sort of thing. It's Paint Night, so you always get a good turnout, especially at this time of year. And I get chatting to this girl, right, the girl what's... you know, been done.'

Unfortunate turn of phrase, but I nod as encouragingly as I can.

'She's a sweetheart and we're just talking and having a bit of a dance and that, and it's all nice and then this guy comes up and just starts on me, out of nowhere.'

'Starts?'

'Gets right up in my face and just starts shouting at me, calling me a c-u-n-t this and a c-u-n-t that.' Karim spells it out to protect my sensitivity. 'And I'm like, "steady on here".'

I can't quite believe he's ever used the phrase 'steady on', but I let it go.

'This guy is Michelle's boyfriend, Ben?'

Karim shrugs.

'It's her boyfriend, don't know his name. He's tall, muscular, got ink all down his right arm. And he starts pushing me a bit, trying to start something. He's bigger than me and got a few kilos on me, too, so I don't fancy my chances much, so I'm like, hey, easy and all that, and then he's just grabbing at the girl. He's got her wrist and he's shaking her really hard by her arm and he's calling her a slut and a bitch and all the names under the sun. And then he just cracks her one, right across the face and, you know, you shouldn't hit a girl and all that, so I lose it and I'm like, get your hands off her, and then he just goes for me, throwing his fists, trying to punch me in the face. Elbows and arms flying at me, and, you know me, Elaine, I'm a lover not a fighter, don't know where to start with my fists, so I'm sort of getting him into a bear hug to stop him because if he lands one on me, it's not going to be nice.'

He demonstrates with his arms, acting out more of a headlock than a bear hug.

'But he's just thrashing about like a wild animal. I've never seen anything like it. Pretty soon we're on the floor and it's like fucking UFC or something, ground and pound: I'm trying to get him in an armlock and he's trying to just batter me, batter my head. By now, floor's cleared around us. There's a few people trying to break it up, few more shouting encouragement, usual Magaluf stuff. And he's stronger than me, so he's finally got my arms pinned so I can't protect my face and he's about to just land one on me, probably break my nose at the very least and I'm waiting for it, waiting to taste the blood, cos it won't be the first time, and then the bouncers have got us, thank fuck, and these guys are mean bastards. I know a few of them, and one of them, this fucking massive fucking Serbian bastard or something, is just rabbit-punching me in the kidneys and, fuck me, this guy really could give me a battering, know what I mean?

'I'm shouting that I didn't start anything, this guy just started on me, but they don't care. They've got me round the head and this other guy, too, and he's trying to kick it off with them, but these guys know what they're doing and they're just frog-marching us, fucking dragging us, off the dance floor, and they get us to the front door and just throw us out, onto the street. You know the main entrance with all the stairs? They pretty much chuck us down them. And we're both at the bottom, trying to pick ourselves up and there's a load of people milling about, waiting to get in, having a smoke and that, and this guy, same guy with the ink on his arm, he looks up and just launches himself at me again. He just flies at me, all fists and "I'm going to fucking kill you" and I'm just trying to stop him battering me.

'We're outside now so the bouncers aren't going to do nothing cos we're not on their patch anymore, and this guy's losing it at me and I'm doing my best to get into a little ball before he does some real damage, and then the cops are there and they separate us, put the restraint ties on, and drag us away from each other. They've got me by the wall of the club and they're asking us what's going on. I explain what's happened, cos I know a few of them and all cos they patrol the strip, and they're having a word with the bouncers who tell them as well and we're all having a chat and this other guy's still struggling and shouting he's going to kill me. I don't know what his problem is, the guy's fucking unhinged. Anyway, I explain and at this point they're reasonable to me and let me go. Then I have a chat with Simon, one of the sane bouncers I know a bit, and explain what happened and he's prepared to let me back in cos he knows I didn't do nothing. The Serbian psycho, mind, he's not too happy about it, but Simon, he knows the deal, so they let me back in and that's the last I hear of the nutter.'

'The boyfriend?'

'Yeah, him.'

'You don't know what happened to him after that?'

He shakes his head.

'Miguel says he got arrested.'

'Serves him bloody right, Elaine. Guy must have been off his head on something to behave like that. Probably had way too much coke. It makes you angry like that if you overdo it.'

'I wouldn't know, Karim.'

He smiles, first time since I've been there. The bridgework I helped get funded.

'Course you wouldn't,' he says. 'Nor would I.'

He winks but I don't smile back. Don't know if I believe him. Sounds a very varnished tale. In my experience, attacks in Magaluf are rarely 'unprovoked'. I'm surprised he didn't get arrested, and amazed he got back into the club. But that's Karim. Say what you like, he's got a certain charm, can wrap all sorts round his little finger.

'So what happened then?' I ask.

'Nothing, really. Went back to how it was before. Bit of dancing, bit of drinking, you know, having fun, the whole Kiss vibe. It was a really nice night for a bit after that.'

'You stayed there all night?'

'Nah, I crashed out about 3 or 4am? Not sure exactly. Went home, got some sleep.'

'And where is home these days?'

He's leaning back now on two of the chair legs, pushing himself backwards and forwards from the table, just how you're warned not to at school.

'Mate of mine's got a place on Torrenova, above a minimart. Let's me crash there.'

'And you didn't see any more of the girl, Michelle?'

'Not really,' he says, slamming the front legs of his chair back onto the ground with a crash. He scratches the side of his head and stares at the fire safety instructions.

'I mean, I talked to her a bit more at the club, but that was it.'

'Talked to her?'

'You know, we had a talk and a bit of a dance and that. Nothing funny though.'

'You didn't leave with her?'

He shakes his head.

'No, nothing like that. Police tell you I had?'

I shake my head.

'Not in so many words. Just said you were one of the last to see her alive. They think she left by a service entrance not covered by any cameras. One only regulars might know about. The inference was pretty clear – that you probably left with her, showed her the way to go.'

'That's what I mean, they make this shit up, just to frame me. They want me to have done this thing just cos they don't like me.'

Now it's me that's scowling.

'Why wouldn't they "like you", Karim?'

'They hate me in this place cos they've got their favourites and I'm not one of them.'

That's the problem with Karim. For all his charm, he's always up to something, swept up in life's underclass.

He rocks his chair back and forth again, glaring at the wall.

'Favourites?'

He shrugs.

'There's a fair few of us regulars, right. You know, ones that live here all year round, that aren't here on holiday. You get to know people, the barmen, club promoters, bouncers, dancers, cops, robbers, you name it. Especially when, like me, you do a bit of work for some of the bars here and there. Some of us, the cops don't mind, let us do our thing. Others, they've earmarked as troublemakers, give us grief whenever they can. That's me, right, just cos they know I've got a record. Makes me a target. It's why I have to make extra sure I don't do nothing wrong, you get me?'

It's my turn to shrug.

'So you had another chat with this girl, had a dance, then didn't see her again?'

'Look,' he says, chair legs slamming down again, leaning in, rancid breath in my face. 'I'll be honest with you, Elaine, cos it's you and we're friends. Once I'm back inside, I get chatting to the girl again–'

'Her name's Michelle.'

'Michelle, right. And we have another chat and a bit of a dance and I think we're getting on famously, right, and so, right, I might misread the signals a bit, cos she's dancing with me all sexy, right, and when a girl dances with me sexy then, you know, I assume they're, you know...'

He waits for me, nudging for me to nod, say I understand, sweating slightly, mouth smiling, eyes urging.

'No, Karim, I don't know. What do you assume?'

'That they're, you know, up for a bit of a kiss and a cuddle and that. I mean, it's Magaluf. Shagaluf, right? Girls want a bit of a holiday romance. Fuck's sake, it's Paint Night at Kiss. I mean, why else would anyone go to Paint Night if they're not up for a bit of a kiss and a cuddle?'

He's looking awkward now, avoiding eye contact, shifting from side to side, rocking back and forth.

'A kiss and a cuddle?'

'You know,' he says. 'Start with a kiss and then see where it goes. So we go to the quiet bar off the dance floor, where it's darker and the music's a bit less school disco, right? And we find a corner to have a bit of a kiss and it's nice and that, and we're having a bit of a cuddle, nothing dirty, but I, like, I must have misread the signs or something cos she just stops and says she likes me and that, but not in that way and that she's going to go off and find her friends or something. So I'm like, that's cool, whatever. I'm not forcing you into nothing or anything, that's not me, no way, gentleman like. And she's off to the toilets or something and I'm like, I've been in a fight, had a bit of a kiss, then been dropped like that, what the fuck's going on tonight? So I just go off at that point, back to the main room, get myself a drink at the bar, gather my thoughts, and I'm there probably another half hour, an hour, and then that's enough for me for one night, so I go home. Next thing I know, I'm being woken up by my phone and my mate's on the line telling me there's cop cars all over the beach cos that girl I met's had her throat slashed or something and I'm thinking, fuck, the cops hate me anyway, they're going to be after me in a shot. They pick me up, I'm fucked. So that's when I go and see you. Because I didn't do it, Elaine. You've got to believe me. You do believe me, right? I never touched that girl. Not in that way. The second I tried, she didn't want to know.'

I believe some of it. Maybe thirty, forty per cent. Is he telling me the truth on the main point? Did he kill her? Do I believe him?

I say nothing.

His face falls.

'Fuck, Elaine, you know me, you've known me years. I know what I am. I know I'm a bit of a scally and that. I mean, Jesus, I'm no angel, but I don't hurt people. I don't cut people. I wouldn't ever, ever hurt a woman, on my mother's life. You've got to believe me.'

He stares at me now, looking for hope, mouth open, all teeth and bridgework.

'If *you* don't believe me,' he says, 'I've got no one.'

'I want to believe you,' I say. 'But my job's not about believing or not believing people. I'm not a detective. I don't investigate. I'm not allowed to. We don't give that sort of support.'

He looks away in disgust, hand rubbing his face.

'If, as you say, you didn't have anything to do with this death, and I've no reason to believe you did, then the evidence will bear that out.'

He laughs, then shakes his head at me, like I'm stupid.

'This is Calvià police we're talking about,' he says. 'They don't do evidence. Last time they sent me down I only had personal use on me and they bulked it out so they could get a bigger sentence. If they don't have evidence, they'll find it.'

'Get a good lawyer, Karim, and they'll make sure that doesn't happen.'

'How?'

'They'll make sure it's investigated properly. That if there's evidence that proves you didn't do it, it's found.'

'Like what?'

'Like CCTV. If you say you left the club and went home, without Michelle, then there'll be CCTV to prove it.'

The laugh. The shaking of the head.

'If that CCTV exists, it'll never see the light of day. I've seen it happen before.'

'What do you mean?'

More head shaking. More looking at me like I'm stupid.

The tears are streaming down his face now. He brushes them away angrily. Stands up, walks over to the wall. Leans on it, starts to rub his head against it.

'It's not about whether I believe you or not,' I say.

Tap, tap, tap, his head against the wall.

'My job is to help you whatever you may or may not have done.'

Tap, tap, tap. Head, wall.

'Have you got legal advice?'

His shoulders are shaking. Sobbing. Gentle sobs.

'I can't go back inside again. Can't.'

Sobs. Tears. Tap, tap, tap.

'I'd rather die. Rather slash my wrists than do a year inside.'

'I know, Karim, and if you're telling me the truth, you won't have to go back inside. The justice system's there to help you, Karim.'

Sobs. Tears. Tap, tap, tap.

Bang.

He hits his head against the wall.

I stand up, walk over to him.

'I'm not going to do it.'

Tap, tap, bang. An ugly red welt on his forehead.

'They're going to do me for it, I know they will.'

Tap, tap, bang.

Bang.

Bang.

Bang, bang, bang.

Blood on the wall. On his forehead.

'Karim, please.'

I put my hands on his arms, try to pull him away. He's too strong.

Bang, bang, bang.

Blood running down his face, mingling with the tears.

'You've got to believe me, I didn't do it. I didn't touch her.'

Bang, bang, bang.

Blood splattering onto my blouse. Images of Glen Mills again – having to make that call to his parents.

'I'd never hurt anyone.'

Bang.

I run for the door, open it, shout for help.

Bang, bang, bang.

There's a nasty gash now on his forehead, running across one temple.

I shout again, put my arms around his waist and beg him to stop.

Feet running. Voices raised. The door opens, shouting, two men and a woman burst in, get the wrong end of the stick, assume he's assaulting me, yank me away, wrestle Karim to the floor. He lands badly, his arm twists unnaturally underneath him, he screams with pain.

I shout in Spanish, try to explain.

'He was self-harming. He didn't touch me.'

One of them holds him tight to the ground. One tries to

cable-tie his hands together, his wrist now hanging limp, broken. One alternates between kidney punches and kicks. Karim screaming.

I can feel my stomach tightening, mind wrestling as to how to make it stop.

'Please, leave him, he's hurt,' I say, but it falls on deaf ears.

'You've got to help me, Elaine. I didn't do it. I didn't do it.'

Two officers now, one on each of Karim's arms, dragging him out.

'Please, Elaine, you've got to help me. Please, please, please!'

# 6

Karim's taken off to the hospital to get his head stitched up and I'm left filling in forms about what happened. Miguel takes me aside for a 'quiet chat'. Apologises on behalf of the officers. Says they thought I was being attacked. They hadn't meant to be quite so 'vigorous' with Karim.

I shrug and say I understand.

But I'm less worried about his officers than the other things Karim's told me.

*You've got to help me, Elaine.*

He says he didn't do it.

*If that CCTV exists, it'll never see the light of day.*

Says he doesn't trust the Calvià police.

*They don't do evidence.*

Says I'm the only one who can help him.

Except we don't investigate crimes at the consulate. Not our job. We're not police.

*If that CCTV exists, it'll never see the light of day.*

Miguel coughs, and I realise he's talking to me. Says he's got other people that might need consular assistance and starts moving off down the corridor. I don't bother to push him for more information, just follow. I've known him long enough to understand he loves to talk in riddles, to provoke my curiosity and then refuse to say any more. He's the kid at primary school who collects insects to torture them, like it's all part of some big joke.

I follow him. On one side of the corridor are doors to small offices. On the other are desks where officers with lanyards sit, tapping at computers and occasionally looking up to study their whiteboards.

Two salute as Miguel walks past.

At the end we reach a fire door, which Miguel holds open for me.

He ushers me down two flights of stairs, through another fire door and then shows me through a door off a small, institutional kitchen. Inside is a large room where four tired-looking teenagers are lounging about on beige banquette seats. None looks older than nineteen or twenty. Two boys, two girls: all four in vests and shorts, mix and match, his and hers. They've divvied up beach footwear: two in flip-flops, two in sandals. All four are white, and three are suffering from different stages of sunburn. Only the blonde girl's not burnt, instead, managing an attractive honeyed gold. The dark-haired girl's goth-white skin has turned an angry pink on her shoulders and neck. The mousey-brown boy's face and shoulders are pink and peeling, and he's got cuts and bruising on his forehead. The big ginger kid's just a mess of skin welts and sores.

Miguel clears his throat and all four stare at me like I'm a supply teacher.

'This is Mrs Martin,' Miguel says. 'She's the British Vice-Consul from Palma. She can help you.'

He turns to me and switches to Spanish.

'The girl's friends. No manners – must have been brought up

by wolves. Got a lot to say about their human rights. I told them you'd be keen to know more.'

He winks, then walks out before I can reply, flashing me a sarcastic smile as he closes the door behind him.

Bastard.

'Who're you?'

It's the dark-haired girl.

'My name's Elaine Martin. I'm the British Vice-Consul here on Majorca.'

'You sound English,' the blonde girl says.

'I am English. I'm married to a Spaniard, hence the name.'

'You're like an ambassador?' the ginger boy asks.

'Not quite,' I say. I'm sure I sound patronising. They don't look like they care. 'I'm employed by the British Foreign Office to help British citizens here.'

'How can you help us?' The dark-haired one again. 'You going to bring Michelle back to life?'

Her face begins to crack up and she starts to sob softly. Her tired eyes are already surrounded by red circles.

I sit down next to her, close but not in her personal space.

'I can help you to liaise with the police. If you want legal advice, I can recommend English-speaking lawyers. I can contact your family back in England and pass on messages if you'd like me to.'

The ginger kid stares at me like a dumb angel, transfixed.

'We want to go home,' the blonde one says.

'What's your name?' I ask, sure I sound patronising.

'Kerry,' she says.

'Do you have a flight booked, Kerry?'

She nods.

'This Saturday?' I ask.

She nods again.

'That's four days away,' I say. 'Has Miguel suggested that might be a problem?'

They stare at me, all four of them, eight eyes in unison. At least two brows ruffle. I realise the name Miguel means nothing to them.

'Miguel is the police officer who was just here. Has he, or any of the other police officers, suggested they might need you to stay beyond Saturday, so you'd miss your flight?'

Kerry strikes up again. Her vest has 'Sex on the Beach' printed across it in garish pink letters.

'They don't know,' she answers. 'Says it depends how things go. I said we got a last-minute, super-saver deal, which only covers up to Saturday. We haven't got money past then for a room or flights or anything. I need to get back for work. If they need us after that, who's paying? You?'

She sits back and crosses her arms, covering up enough of her vest that it just reads, 'Sex'.

'Unfortunately, we can't cover costs on behalf of British citizens,' I say.

'Knew it,' she says. Spits it out, shaking her head, like she's just caught someone in the act of stealing.

'We're here purely in an advisory capacity,' I continue.

'We don't need advice,' says the ginger boy. 'We need cash.'

I lean forward and nod attentively, trying to make myself as open and amenable as possible.

'Look, we don't know yet if you'll have to stay past Saturday,' I say. 'It might very well be that you can go home on the flight you've got booked. Now I know that's a concern for you, so I can ask Mig... the officers in charge where things stand and if they think that might be needed.'

Nothing from three of them. The very slightest of perceptible nods from the blonde girl.

'Have they said what they want you for?' I ask.

Ginger looks at Kerry and they share a look. Mousey-brown tries to catch Kerry's eye. She puts her face in her hands.

Eventually, Kerry pipes up:

'They want statements,' she says.

'Okay. What about?'

Dark-haired shrugs. Blonde leans in.

'About last night. What happened. And the night before. They want us to remember every moment of every day for the last week, basically.'

'And from back home as well,' Kerry adds.

I nod encouragingly.

'That makes sense,' I say. 'That is standard practice. Obviously with... everything that's happened, they want to try and find out what's gone on.'

'Which sick fucker killed Michelle, you mean,' blonde says, eyes red from rubbing.

'They'll be trying to piece together as much as they can about the last few nights,' I say. 'It's really important you help them as much as you can.'

A couple of them share stares again. Then it's back to empty gazes.

'You can have legal advice if you want it,' I continue. 'None of you is under any official caution or suspicion at this stage, as far as I'm aware,' I say, as I realise I don't have a clue whether any of them is under suspicion or not. 'In situations like this, it's entirely normal for some people to want to have a lawyer present when they talk to the police so that–'

'They don't twist your words, try and make you confess when you don't mean it?' the ginger one interrupts.

I shake my head vigorously.

'No, nothing like that. They're not like that here. They're no different from the police back in the UK. They just want to find out what happened.'

'Yeah, right,' Mousey-brown says.

Two of them give out knowing harrumphs.

I ignore them.

'Do any of you want lawyers. At this stage?'

Blank stares. A few shared glances. More blank stares.

'Well, look,' I say, reaching into my bag and pulling out my purse. 'This is my business card.' I pull a few out, hand them to Kerry and indicate she should take one, then pass them on. 'If you decide you want any more help or advice, like you want an English-speaking lawyer or want to know how the system works out here, call me on the number there, day or night. I can't promise I can help, but I can see what we can do.'

Three of them study the card, the coat of arms finally seeming to have some effect on them.

'Is there anything I can do to help in the meantime? Do you want me to contact your hotel, say you're going to be late?'

Two shrugs, two shakes of the head.

I reach into my bag and pull out my notebook and a pen. I turn to a new page.

'Now, it's totally up to you, but if you're happy, I'd like you each to write down your name, address and contact number here so I know where to get hold of you if *I* need to contact *you*. Is that okay?'

Three shrugs, Ginger just gives an empty stare.

I pass the book around and hope to hell they can all write.

I look at the two boys: Mousey-brown and then Ginger.

'Is either of you Michelle's boyfriend?' I ask.

They look at each other, then Mousey-brown pipes up.

'I was. Am.' Thinks about it. 'I mean was,' he says, looking at me.

The bruising and cuts on his forehead start to make sense.

Kerry snorts, sends him an icy stare before handing me back

the paper and pen. I look at it briefly. Ginger is Kai, Mousey-brown is boyfriend Ben, and the dark-haired one is Steph.

I look at Ben. He's staring down at his flip-flops, scratching his groin from the outside of his shorts, avoiding me.

'Are you okay, Ben?' I ask.

He doesn't look up, just grunts.

'I'm guessing this must be particularly hard on you?'

He looks up and shrugs.

I feel a vibration in my pocket and pull out my phone.

It's Miguel.

Media release 8am tomorrow morning. Don't say you haven't been warned.

Kayleigh Walsh.

They've not found her.

Shit.

Within five minutes of the release making its way to the UK news desks, the calls will start. I need to warn Vanessa what's happened and make sure the team's ready for the onslaught, make sure everyone knows what they'll be doing, and then I need to get to Magaluf and start getting word out to the right people.

The whole place is about to go nuts.

I look at my watch. It's late afternoon now and I've not had any lunch.

I nod, put my notebook into my bag and stand up.

'I'm sorry, but I've got to sort something out,' I say. I walk to the door and for some reason, Jonathan pops into my head again, and that last, awful week. How he appeared: his normal, happy self. How he must have felt that he had no one he could talk to, no one who would understand him. How I wish I could have that week again, and what I might say or do differently this time.

I turn back and face the four of them one more time. 'I meant to add,' I say, 'that, obviously, I'm not a police officer or anything like that, so anything you say to me is in absolute confidence. If you feel like you need to speak to someone, even just for a chat, someone that isn't the police or a lawyer, please give me a call.'

None of them says anything. Kai stares at the floor, studying his flip-flops, Ben scratches his groin.

# 7

Seven thirty a.m. at the consulate: five of us are sitting around the big meeting table in the boardroom. Duncan's fiddling with the video screen, checking it's working so Vanessa can call through from Barcelona.

Soraya is sitting alert, pen in hand and notebook ready. Rodrigo is slouched in his chair, tie clip bunching around his 1980s yuppie pin-striped shirt. His hair is shiny and greased back as usual, signet ring tapping up and down on the table like an ageing Spanish Del Boy. Louise makes small talk. Something about the weather and the town hall looking to close part of the MA1 for resurfacing works.

I'm running through the day in my head. I'm set up to go and see the boy from the car crash early afternoon, but Miguel's press release is going out any minute and I've got to make sure we've got enough manpower to handle the inevitable flood of inquiries.

Everybody's nervous. They don't know why we're sitting here, why I've asked for an emergency conference call with all staff and the Consul General. They know job losses are coming. In this day and age, with the Foreign Office's priorities changing, they don't think it's possible to justify five permanent staff for Majorca alone. No one knows where or when the axe will fall.

It should be Rodrigo.

It won't be Rodrigo.

Vanessa crackles through from a meeting room in Barcelona, her chunky coloured-glass necklace the only thing that stops her looking like a headmistress.

'Morning all,' she says.

'Good morning, Vanessa,' I say, taking over. 'Thanks for coming through to us at such short notice. I wouldn't normally call a meeting like this but I think it's important we're all aware about a couple of things.'

Everybody's listening now, even Rodrigo's leant in.

'No problem,' Vanessa says. 'Please go ahead.'

'As some of you probably know by now, a British girl has gone missing in Palma Nova. Kayleigh Walsh is twelve years old and staying at the Excelsior hotel with her parents. On Sunday night they went out, leaving Kayleigh in her bedroom in the care of her sixteen-year-old sister. The sister fell asleep and when she woke up the next morning, there was no sign of Kayleigh. She assumed she'd gone out to meet friends and didn't think too much of it. The parents had had a big night out and were still sleeping things off. When they all finally realise that none of them know where Kayleigh is, it's yesterday evening. That's when they let the police know.'

Louise's nodding gently, the others listening closely. I watch Soraya swallow. Vanessa looks at me, her eyes narrowed.

'I've spoken to Deputy Chief Miguel Fuentes in Calvià. They've got full resources looking for Kayleigh, but he let me know last night that they're putting out a press release shortly. It'll hit the UK news rooms in the next... fifteen to twenty minutes. We know how excited, hysterical even, they can get about missing girls on holiday. I think we need to plan our resources for when that happens. Vanessa, I wanted you to be aware of the situation and to see what you think.'

She takes her time before speaking, getting her thoughts together.

'Do they have any idea where the girl went?' she says after a pause. 'Who she might have been with?'

I shake my head.

'They're trawling through CCTV at the moment, but right now they don't have a lot to go on. That's why they want to go to the media – get her face circulating, see if it brings any leads. That's also why I'm anticipating a lot of interest coming our way.'

'Where are the parents?' Vanessa asks.

'They're staying in Palma Nova. I've had a thorough debrief with them. As you can imagine, they're really worried.'

'I bet they are,' Vanessa says. 'How busy are you at the moment?'

There's a murmur around the room, rueful humphs from Duncan and Louise, a knowing look from Soraya, a grin from Rodrigo.

'Yeah, we're pretty busy, what with high season and the Michelle Fraser murder.'

'The girl in Magaluf?' Vanessa asks.

'That's right,' I say.

'Any news on that?'

'Not at the moment. They've got one suspect. He's being investigated but swears he's innocent.'

'They all say that,' Vanessa says, and there's a snigger behind me.

Rodrigo.

I say nothing.

'Look, I know you're all busy,' Vanessa says, 'but is there

someone you can put on press liaison? Someone who can take the calls and just basically deal with the papers, etc.?'

I look around the room. People avoid making eye contact.

Instinctively I want to say Rodrigo. He has the lightest workload so would seem the obvious candidate. But I know how this situation could blow up and I dread to think what sort of mess he'd make of it.

'Louise,' I say. 'I know you've got a lot on, but if we shifted some of your front-desk duties, is it something you could do?'

'Um,' she says, trying to concoct an excuse.

'Yes, Louise would be an excellent candidate,' Vanessa says, staring her down from the screen.

'I suppose if someone took over some of the other stuff...' murmurs Louise.

No one wants to deal with the British press. They're awful. The rudest, most ungrateful, presumptuous, foul-mouthed, ill-tempered people I've ever dealt with. A few years ago a woman went missing up in the Tramuntana mountains. She went for a walk in the woods and never came back. For two months we had the press camped here, ringing us up, asking us to suggest hotels, translate for them, get them contact numbers for the family, the fire service, mountain rescue and so on. If we refused, or said it was outside our remit, we were told we were useless, a waste of money, jobs-for-lifers sponging off the state, that they'd write stories about what the hell was the point of the British consulate, what were they paying their taxes for. Except we're not funded by taxes. But they didn't care.

'Thank you, Louise,' I say.

She turns pale and stares down at her lap.

Poor woman.

'I'll speak to the consulate in Ibiza,' Vanessa says. 'They're busy but they've not got anything on like you have. I'll see if we can get them to send someone over on secondment for a few weeks. Just until things calm down a bit.'

'That would make a massive difference,' I say.

I can feel the relief in the room.

'What are you planning to do to help?' Vanessa asks.

'Once the press release is out, we'll start circulating some photos of Kayleigh to people we know in the Magaluf area, make sure all the key players put one up, just to maximise the chances of finding her. I expect the police will be doing something similar, but, you know, there's always a better response if it's us doing the asking rather than them.'

Nods all around. Vanessa beaming. She likes to feel we make a difference. We all do, even if it rarely happens.

'I'm going over to Magaluf tonight, so I'll make a start,' I say. 'I'll ask Freddie to put the word about as well.'

Freddie's one of our success stories. Another former resident of the Centro Penitenciario. In his case, it was a serious drug habit that led him into petty crime. But he was smart. He got out, started a business and now runs a café in Magaluf with his sister, with a nice sideline in giving paid advice to tourists who get into trouble. Helps keep some of the workload off us. He knows everyone that's anyone in Magaluf.

'But this is a Palma Nova thing,' Vanessa says. 'Wouldn't it be better to start there?'

They look at me now, like I've said something stupid. Rodrigo starts to grin.

'I know exactly what you're saying, Vanessa, but in my experience, when something like this happens, it almost always ends up leading back to Magaluf.'

Slow nods all around.

'Fair enough,' Vanessa says.

We file back out to the main office, where there is a persistent buzz from the front-door intercom. Soraya heads over to it and unlocks the door. It's 8am when we open to the public, and there's already half a dozen confused-looking Brits waiting to come in from the corridor outside.

I pick up my mobile and scroll to Freddie's number. It's a while since I've spoken to him. In the event, my call goes to voicemail. I tell him something's come up that I could do with speaking to him about, and say I'm heading to Magaluf later and that I'll try to call in and see him.

When I've finished, Soraya is looking at me like a lost puppy.

I force a smile.

'Can I help?'

'There's a lady outside,' she says. 'Wants to talk to you.'

'I've got a few things that I need to...'

She interrupts me.

'She's one of Michelle Fraser's friends. Steph. She says it's important.'

We use Interview Room 2. It's small and charmless. No pictures, no sofas, no windows, just the obligatory beige consular colour scheme, a table and three hard chairs. We take two of them.

Steph is nervous. Her shoulders are rounded and hunched and she frequently checks to her left and right, as if someone might be listening to us. Her hair is unwashed and she's not wearing any make-up, which means her drained skin and the dark patches under her eyes are on full display.

'It's my fault,' she says, and her face starts to crumple.

I stand up and walk round to her side of the table. I put my arm round her shoulder and do my best to comfort her.

'Don't worry. It'll be all right.'

'No, it won't,' she says. 'It'll never be all right. She's dead, it's fucked and it's all my fault.'

More tears, great heaves of the shoulders as the sobs come one by one. I stroke her back gently and squeeze her encouragingly.

'What happened to Michelle is no one's fault except the sick, deeply disturbed individual who killed her,' I say. 'It cannot possibly be your fault.'

'No, no,' she says, shaking her head vigorously. 'You don't understand. The reason for the fight that night – it was my fault.'

Tears again. More stroking, more squeezing.

I pop out to the kitchen, grab some tissues and a plastic cup of water and take it back to the interview room.

She wipes her eyes, sips the water, then gathers herself.

'So we'd all been out on the Saturday night – drinking and dancing and that,' she says, concentrating, staring at the floor.

'Who's all of us?' I ask.

'Me, Kai, Ben, Michelle and Kerry. And we were at this bar, I don't remember what it was called. Shots were two for one, so we were working our way through a few, having fun. And then me and Kerry want to go on to Kiss. That was always the idea. It's what you do in Magaluf, right?'

'I'm sure,' I say. She hands me a used tissue and I screw it up and put it into my pocket to dispose of later.

'But Michelle doesn't want to go, right? Says she's tired, which is fair enough because we've been at it since the moment we got here – full on, you know. So she wants to give it a rest for a night, recharge her batteries she says. Cos that's her, isn't it? She's got boring. Used to be a big party animal but now, since she had Dylan, she's just not that fun. Tends to duck out early. Anyway, Ben doesn't want to go home. That's her boyfriend, right?'

She looks up at me and I nod but don't interrupt.

'He says he wants to go on to Kiss with the rest of us. So they have a bit of a... well, not a row as such, but, you know, frosty words I guess. He's saying she should come for a bit. She says she doesn't want to pay twenty euros to get in and only stay for half an hour. Then Kai says he's not that fussed about it tonight and that he'll go back with Michelle. But Ben doesn't like it, right, cos, he knows Kai's got a bit of a thing for Michelle, cos all the boys do, cos she's pretty and that. But he doesn't say anything, says it's fine, but you can see he's not happy: doesn't like that Michelle's going home, doesn't like that Kai's going with her, and doesn't like the fact she doesn't seem bothered that he's going on to a club without her. Cos it's like she's not all that jealous, right, that he'll be out partying with loads of other girls, cos it's like she's not that bothered about him, right? And she never is and that winds him up chronic.'

Nothing to do but nod. She's rabbiting at a hundred miles an hour, no let-up in the flow now she's started.

'So they go off home, Kai and Michelle.'

'To the hotel?' I ask.

'That's right, and the rest of us go to Kiss. And Ben's still livid, keeps going on about "fucking Kai" and what a creep he is and how if he tries to touch her he's going to kill him and all that. Anyway, we have a dance and a bit to drink and we...'

She looks around, left and right again.

'It's okay,' I say, 'anything you tell me goes no further than these walls.'

'Well, you know, it's Magaluf and that, so to keep it going we have a bit of a pick-me-up. Nothing crazy, just a bit of coke and that. Well, me and Kerry just have a line each, but Ben does a bunch of other stuff. So everyone's loving it and we just party, you know, and things just happen.'

She starts to cry again. I sit there, letting her get it out of her system. She blows her nose into another tissue.

'Where was I?' she asks.

'You were saying that things happened,' I say as gently as I can.

She nods.

'Yeah, things happened that I ain't proud of in the cold light of day. So at one point Kerry's up in the main room and me and Ben are down in the VIP lounge, and I'm just feeling really good cos of the drinks and the coke and everything, and we're having fun and that's when Ben just grabs me and kisses me and I know I shouldn't have, I know it's really wrong, but it just felt so right then, and I kiss him back. Fuck,' she says and the tears flow again.

'It's okay, it's okay,' I say over and over again. 'These things happen. It doesn't mean anything's your fault.'

Vigorous head shaking now.

'It fucking does. So we go back to the hotel and we fuck, don't we? Fuck in me and Kerry's room because he's angry at Michelle and wants to get back at her, and I've always fancied Ben and he suddenly shows an interest in me and it just happens, doesn't it? And we don't give a shit cos we've taken a bunch of coke and we're wasted and by this stage neither of us cares. And then we pass out and Kerry comes in and sees me and Ben in bed together and she goes mental at us, starts screaming and shouting. So we're trying to calm her down before she wakes the whole hotel up. And eventually we calm her down and Ben leaves, goes back to his room, his and Michelle's room, and it's just me and Kez and we talk for a bit and she says that if I don't tell Michelle, *she* will, cos it's just not right. And I agree that I'll tell her so she leaves me alone.'

A pause now. Deep breaths to get some air back into her lungs.

'And you told Michelle?'

She nods. Just a small one. The tears are over now.

'Next day I get up and I feel terrible. Absolutely fucking awful. My head hurts, every bit of my body hurts, I feel sick and tired and just shit, right? Kez has gone somewhere, so I get up and go to the loo and I've got his stuff coming out of me and I realise I'm not even on the pill and he didn't use a condom, didn't even ask, and I let him cos I was so wasted I didn't care and I'm just in a state.'

Another pause, more staring at the floor.

'So I throw up and feel a bit better, then I have a shower, take some Nurofen, drink a bit of Pepsi, head downstairs. There's no one about, so I ask at reception where there's a pharmacy and they tell me, so I go looking for it, but I can't find it for ages and when I do, it's shut for lunch. And then I get myself some food, manage to keep it down, have a beer, start to feel a bit more alive. It must be early evening now, so I go back and the pharmacy's open, so I get a morning-after pill, swallow it down. I'm feeling like shit again, so I go back to my room and have another lie down. When I wake up, Kez is back. I'm hoping she's forgotten our discussion and we can all just pretend the night before didn't happen, but she's right on it the second I'm awake. "Either you tell her or I will". So I'm like, all right, I will, but I only want to do it when it's just the two of us, cos I want to explain properly how it happened and that. Kez agrees and it must be like... I don't know, eight or nine by now, and we go down and meet the others for a pizza, and it's really awkward cos they're all there. Ben and Michelle being all lovey-dovey, Ben acting like nothing ever happened last night, so that pisses me right off as well. So I'm in a huff, just saying nothing, and they all know to leave me alone when I'm in a mood like that. But eventually we get up and go over to Donovan's, have a couple of shots and start on the beers again, and eventually me and Michelle get together in a corner and...'

She breaks down again.

'Hey, hey,' I say, but my sympathies are beginning to wane. 'These things happen,' I add.

'That's what I thought she'd say. I don't know, I sort of expected her to understand. I sort of thought she was going to go, "Don't worry, you were both wasted, one of those things." So I tell her, plain as day. "I'm really sorry, but me and Ben got wasted last night and we accidentally slept together." That's what I said. Those exact words. And she just looks at me, gobsmacked, and I realise, shit, she's not going to say "don't worry". And her face just breaks up and she bursts into tears and then it all just hits the fan. She freaks out and starts screaming at Ben and he's like, "What have I done?" Then he realises I've told her and he starts screaming at me, and we're getting looks now from the other people in the bar. Then he's trying to talk to Michelle, but she's screaming that she doesn't want to talk to him, and Kai starts comforting Michelle and Ben's like, jealous, and telling him to get his hands off her and it's just awful. Eventually, the bouncers kick Ben out, and Michelle goes off as well, says she wants to be on her own, and me and Kerry and Kai end up in another big row, them having a go at me, until I go off in a huff. And that's the problem, because obviously, at some point, Michelle's like, "Fuck him, I'm going to go and have some fun", and she ends up at Kiss and, of course, Ben goes looking for her, and that's why he gets in a fight, cos he's jealous she's chatting up some other bloke. If all that hadn't happened, if I hadn't shagged Ben, then they wouldn't have argued and she wouldn't have ended up with some other bloke, the bloke that killed her. That's why it's all my fault.'

She's crying hard again, so I hand her more tissues and squeeze her tightly.

'It's not your fault,' I say. 'No one could have known. No one's behaviour can be blamed for what happened to Michelle. It's a sick and deranged individual's fault, not yours. Don't beat yourself up.'

She leans into me, wanting me to hug her. I do my best but I'm aware of the time. I'm meant to be seeing the boy from the car crash in forty-five minutes.

Eventually, I break off, go and get her the box of tissues and tell her not to worry, that it's in no way her fault. That people make mistakes, but that doesn't make anyone responsible for what happened to Michelle other than the murderer. I tell her I have to go, but that she can sit and wait in the room until she feels ready to go home.

I leave her staring into her tissues, intermittently crying and blowing her nose.

~

Hospital Universitari Son Espases.

The island's main hospital.

My second home.

Virtually.

I'm sitting in the waiting room of the Atocha Ward, waiting for clearance from Nurse Ariza to go and see Riley Thomas – the boy from the car crash. Nurse Ariza, an intimidating matron with a strong Majorcan accent, disappeared a couple of minutes ago to see how he was and to let him know I'm here.

I sit and wait, idly thumbing through my emails, my conversation with Steph going around my mind. Is it significant? In a murder inquiry, it can't be insignificant that the victim's boyfriend recently cheated on her. It certainly accounts for why Michelle would be at Kiss on her own, and why things were so fraught between her and Ben. But as a motivation for murder, for rape, does it change things? Just more evidence of the bizarre, moral melting pot up there on the strip that night. Drugs, sex and murder.

Magaluf.

Shagaluf.

The nurse reappears, looks at me suspiciously, then says Riley's happy for me to go in, but that he's very tired and is on strong painkillers. She asks me not to spend longer than fifteen minutes.

I thank her, walk past the nurses' desk and through to his room. There are six beds, of which four are occupied. A limp arm is raised from the furthest bed, and I head towards it.

Riley is propped up against a pillow, his legs looking elephantine underneath a blanket. A mass of cables and tubes poke out, linking up to a series of monitors, drips and machines.

'Riley?'

He opens his mouth, but finds it easier to just nod.

He has short dark hair cropped tightly to his skull, but grown back to perhaps a centimetre's length all over. His left cheek is covered in sticking plaster, but the yellow bruising creeps out from its edges. There are scratches to his left cheek, which is already pitted with acne.

'Best if you speak into this ear,' he says weakly, pointing to the left side of his head. 'Ruptured,' he says, gesturing to his right ear.

I pull up the single-wheeled chair and sit down next to him.

'I'm Elaine from the British consulate,' I say. 'I'm very sorry about what happened to you.'

A nod.

'How are you feeling now?'

A small shrug.

I nod back, give him a couple of seconds. The blanket is thin and Riley quite slight, which puts the massive bulk of his covered legs into some context.

'Can I ask, what's the latest on your injuries?'

He takes a big breath, starts to speak, then stops and coughs, a painful exertion for him. He gathers himself and points to the jug of water on the side table next to him.

I half-fill a beaker from the jug and bring it towards him.

He shakes his head.

'Straw,' he says, and flicks his eyes towards the jug again.

There's a small packet of coloured straws, so I pull one out, add it to the beaker and pass it back.

He holds it in his right hand and sips carefully. He winces as he does so, then hands the beaker back and I put it on the table.

Another long breath.

'I'm okay,' he says.

Breath.

'Don't exert yourself,' I say. 'That's the last thing I want. Let me do some talking.'

He nods.

'I just want to let you know who I am, who we are and what we do. As the British consulate, we represent the UK Foreign Office here in Spain. When a British citizen is unfortunate enough to end up in hospital, we try and visit to offer what assistance we can. I can help put you in touch with your family if you like, and to some extent, I can liaise with the hospital authorities. If the police are involved, I might be able to help explain some of the processes involved there too.'

He nods his way through my list.

'If it's easier,' I say, 'you can just nod and shake your head while I ask you a few questions.'

He nods.

'Is anyone out here with you? Friends or family?'

Nods.

'Friends?'

Nods.

'Are they here for much longer?'

Shakes head.

'They're flying back on Saturday?'

Nods.

'Is anyone coming out to see you from your family?'

Nods.

'Soon?'

Nods.

'Mum and Dad. Tomorrow,' he says, voice croaky.

'Good. Do they have flights and accommodation?'

Shrugs.

'Are you happy for me to call them? To check they're okay?'

Shrugs again.

'Your injuries, just so I'm clear... you've broken your legs?'

Nods.

'I can see you've also got some cuts and bruises to your face.'

Nods.

'And you've mentioned the burst eardrum.'

Nods.

'Were there any others?'

Nods.

'Hip,' he says, pointing to his left leg.

'Broken too?'

Nods.

'Ribs,' he says, lightly stroking them under the blanket.

'Broken?'

Nods and holds up four fingers.

I nod.

'Have they said how soon they think you'll recover?'

He starts to laugh, then winces, then coughs. I instinctively put my hand on his left arm, and he winces again.

'Sorry,' I say.

He looks at me, eyes wide open and wet.

'They don't know if I'll ever walk again,' he says. 'Still waiting on scans,' he adds, and winces once again before angrily wiping the tears away from his cheeks.

I nod slowly, as understandingly as I can.

'Please don't upset yourself,' I say. 'What I can tell you is the treatment you'll get here will be as good as anywhere in the world. If anyone can get you up and running, it will be these guys.'

He gives me a heavy-lidded look as if to warn me off patronising him.

I clear my throat and shift in my seat.

He's looking straight ahead now, staring at the wall opposite, no longer searching for eye contact.

'Can you remember much about what happened?' I ask.

He shakes his head, then turns towards me.

'Haven't got a fucking clue,' he says, then coughs again.

I nod.

'Look, maybe this isn't the best...'

'I was hammered,' he says, speaking still an effort, but determination in his voice. 'Been out drinking a load. Taken some coke, MDMA, crystal, a bit of ketamine. Lost my friends in the club. Couldn't find them. Gave up. I remember walking outside, saying something to the bouncer. After that, can't remember a thing.'

He collapses into coughing now, jerking his chest with effort, his face red and eyes bulging.

'But you think you were hit by a car?'

Shrugs.

'Hit by something,' he says.

'The police think it was a car?'

Nods.

'There was metallic paint on my clothes.'

I nod.

'And you've lost your passport as well?' I say.

He nods.

'You had it on you when you were out?'

'Must have,' he croaks.

'We can get you emergency travel documents, which will enable you to get home. I know you don't know when that will be, but it's probably a good idea to start the process. What I'll need from you are passport photos and a police report. But you will need to be up and about to get those.'

He looks at me, eyes narrow, a mixture of tears and hate in them, and I realise my last comment was a bit insensitive.

Then he's coughing again. He splutters and sends a mixture of yellow-and-red catarrh out across his blanket.

I stand up, unilaterally deciding I've outstayed my welcome.

'The nurse has allowed me only fifteen minutes, and I think that's about up, so I'm going to leave you now,' I say, placing a business card on his side table and pointing it out to him. 'You can ring or email me any time. Please be assured, we're here to help. We're based just up the road in Palma, and as long as you're here and happy to see us, we'll be in touch every few days, okay?'

A nod, then more splutter.

'Okay,' I say. 'Look after yourself, get lots of rest, and take your time to get better. There's no rush with these things. I've seen a few injuries like yours before, and I've not known anyone who wasn't up and running within a few weeks.'

Not true, but I know how important positivity is at this stage.

He nods, and gives me a thumbs up.

I begin walking away, then turn on a whim.

'Sorry, Riley, just one last question.'

He nods.

'The club you were in?'

Nods.

'Kiss?' I ask, but I know the answer before he manages another weak and painful nod.

It's just past 6pm by the time I finally get to Santa Catalina, the gentrified neighbourhood around the old fish market, find a parking space on the narrow streets and work my way up the stairs of Miriam's building, before ringing the bell for her apartment.

She buzzes me in and I go up another two staircases to get to the attic flat that doubles as her practice.

She greets me at her front door, looking like a healthy forty-something professional in culottes and a brown linen blouse.

She takes me through to the bedroom she's converted into her study. It's lined with bookshelves, lending it a reassuring air of academia.

She gestures for me to sit in the leather chair, then disappears to her kitchen, from which I soon hear water heating up and the clink of cups and spoons.

A couple of minutes later she returns with a camomile tea for me.

She knows me too well.

She hands me the cup.

'How have you been since last time, Elaine?' she asks.

'So-so,' I say.

I don't have to lie with Miriam. Don't have to make anything up. Can just tell it like it is.

'Along with the usual trials and tribulations,' I say, 'work's got pretty stressful.'

'High season?'

I nod.

'We've had a girl murdered.'

'The girl on the beach?' she says, and I nod. 'But they've got the guy,' she says.

I let out a weary sigh.

'Or that's what they said on the news,' she adds.

'They've kind of got the guy,' I say. 'That's sort of the stress.'

She nods and gives me a smile, realising, perhaps, that I'm not here to discuss work. She crosses her legs, adjusts her glasses and opens her notebook.

'Last time, I thought we made some real progress,' she says. 'Would you agree?'

Another sigh. My head making a so-so gesture.

Last time we discussed Jonathan.

Again.

We always discuss Jonathan. I wonder, deep down, if that's the real reason I'm paying for these sessions: I have no one else to discuss Jonathan with. It's too difficult with Nick, too upsetting for both of us. Also, too difficult with my daughter, Arianna, when she's around rather than on her international travels. And the rest of my friends and family are all too terrified to bring his name up around me. Which just leaves Miriam.

'Do you find you're still thinking about him a lot?' she asks.

I nod, slowly this time.

'It doesn't change,' I say. 'I can be doing almost anything – working, driving, shopping, sleeping – and no matter what else I'm thinking about, he pops into my mind and I start to feel sad again.'

She nods now, alternating between making notes and maintaining eye contact.

'Which Jonathan is it?' she asks.

'It varies,' I say. 'Sometimes he's very little. A toddler or at school. Other times, he's in his early teens, adolescent, or like he was towards the end, all grown-up in body, if not in mind.'

She nods.

'Just the same then?' she says.

'It doesn't change,' I say.

It's her turn to make a so-so gesture now. She looks disappointed, like I've rained on her progress parade, but I'm not here to make *her* feel better.

'And things with Nick?' she asks.

This time, I laugh.

'Worse,' I say.

She nods again.

'The drinking? Or just generally?'

'Generally,' I say. 'And the drinking.'

'Have you tried talking to him about it? Raising the issue? Asking him to see how his behaviour is affecting you?'

'Sort of.'

'Sort of?'

I shrug.

'Sort of, not really. It's hard to talk to him when he's drunk, and he's drunk most of the time. Most of the time I'm home, anyway.'

'You know, you could bring him with you to a session,' she says. 'I do quite a lot of couples therapy and it can be very effective.'

I swallow at the thought.

'I can't see Nick being up for it, somehow,' I say.

She shrugs again.

'He might just need to get used to the idea,' she says. 'Most long-term marriages develop patterns of non-communication on tricky issues. Joint counselling's got a strong track record in breaking the cycle.'

I nod and tell her I'll think about it.

'Going back to Jonathan,' she says, 'talk me through the last time you were thinking about him.'

# 8

I go home feeling better, like an hour with Miriam has lifted another small chunk of the weight.

It always helps, even a little.

Just someone grown-up to talk to.

Someone to listen to me for a change, rather than the other way around.

I feel better, happier, refreshed, which is good, because I've made a decision.

Tonight, I'm going to go to Magaluf.

Karim says he's innocent. I don't know if I believe him.

But I don't want another Glen Mills on my hands. The thought of him doing a twenty-year stretch because of a simple check I couldn't be bothered to do, is more than I can take.

There should be CCTV of him leaving the club. Miguel says there isn't. Karim says that's because the police will have made it disappear.

It's not my problem. I shouldn't care. Consular officials do not investigate crimes. That's the police's job. Don't get involved. It's a can of worms.

But I'm sick of sitting idly by. I promised Karim I'd at least check.

So Magaluf it is.

There's not much point in getting to Magaluf early. It doesn't really 'open' until gone 10pm. Plus, I want to have a shower, change my clothes and see what state my husband's in.

When I get home, Nick's acting like nothing ever happened; all bright and breezy, apron on, cooking up tapas and listening to music.

'Hello, love,' he says when I arrive. 'Good day?'

He gives me a kiss and I stare at him in disbelief.

'You're feeling better then?'

'Any better, you'd have to arrest me,' he says, before ducking back into the kitchen. There's a small half-drunk bottle of supermarket beer on the work surface. First of the day then. No wonder he's chirpy.

'I'm cooking mackerel,' he says. 'Your favourite.'

'Right,' I say, watching as he chops up some herbs. 'Nick, I'm really sorry, but I've got to go out again in an hour or so.'

He looks at me, his face dropping.

'Really?' he says.

'We've had a twelve-year-old girl go missing. Everybody's desperately searching for her. I need to help out.'

'Right,' he says, still staring at me, looking like a child who's just had his best toy taken off him.

'I'm sorry. I'd love to stay. I think we need to have a talk.'

'A talk?' he says. 'What about?'

I shrug, not sure I can face this right now.

'Just about us.'

'What about us, love? We're good, aren't we?'

'Are we?'

He screws up his forehead, looks at me, quizzing me with his eyes.

'Nick, would you come with me to see Miriam some time? Just to talk with her.'

'Your therapist?'

'She's a counsellor, Nick. I find it really helpful to talk to her. I think you might as well. Talk about us, this,' I say, pointing to the beer bottle on the work surface. 'Talk about Jonathan.'

'I don't know,' he says, and looks away, back at his cooking, tired, deflated.

'If I made an appointment, for both of us, would you come? If you didn't like it, you wouldn't have to stay.'

He carries on cooking, doesn't answer me immediately. I give it a minute.

'Nick?' I say. 'Well?'

He turns around, the wooden spoon in his hand.

'Whatever you like, love,' he says, then turns back to his fish.

It's dark by the time I arrive in Magaluf. I say dark, but Magaluf's never really dark. Not in the main streets and business areas. Not on the strip. It only gets truly dark in the outer reaches of the beach.

I drive in on the MA1 and make my way down the Cami Porrassa to the town centre. I find a place to park not far from the main drag, grab my bag and make sure to lock the little SEAT.

First stop is Home Café.

Freddie's café.

It's late but there's a handful of people sitting at one of the half-dozen tables in the front courtyard, eating their way through gloopy-looking curries, burger meals and fish and chips.

A young girl asks me if I want a table and I say I'm here to see Freddie. She takes me out to the kitchen where he's hard at work at the ageing white cooker.

He smiles when he sees me, flips a burger on a hob and asks how I am.

'You never answered my call,' I say, doing my best to look miffed.

'There's only me on today and we've been run off our feet. What was it about? Something bad, I presume.'

He pulls a wire basket of chips out of the deep-fat fryer, shakes the grease off and leaves them on the side to cool down.

'A twelve-year-old girl's gone missing in Palma Nova. I wondered if you'd heard anything, or if you could keep a lookout.'

He picks a chip out of the tray and eats it cautiously, trying not to burn his mouth.

'You got a photo?' he asks.

I take my phone out and show him.

'She's never twelve,' he says.

'Thirteen in a couple of weeks,' I say.

He shakes his head.

'No one I know, but I'll keep 'em peeled.'

I tell him I'll forward the photo and ask if he'd mind putting a few up locally.

'You know me,' he says. 'Always on hand for the British consulate.'

He gives me a wink, and I leave him to it.

I work my way towards the bottom of Punta Ballena. There are British bars and cafés dotted sporadically around the outlying roads as I walk up. It's nearly 11pm and they're busy but not rammed. They're the old-school ones, with names like the Red Lion and the White Hart, the ones that have Union Jacks posted prominently on them and still advertise British fry-ups and egg and chips. These days they're almost museum pieces in themselves – slices of Anglo-Spanish life from the mid-1980s. They attract the older clientele: pot-bellied men with shaven heads who've come here every year since their twenties, their saggy-bodied partners sitting next to them as they chomp their way through greasy servings of spaghetti bolognese or steak and chips.

But once you're past them, you get into more up-to-date Magaluf territory, the heart of the party town, where giant pubs litter the area. And it's then you know you've made it to Punta Ballena, better known to all and sundry as the strip.

It's a short road, perhaps half a kilometre, snaking up the hill, with ugly, low-rise buildings on both sides – cafés, restaurants, fast-food joints, pubs, bars, amusement arcades, nightclubs and strip bars.

The second I step onto it, I start to feel vulnerable. I don't look like the kind of person who should be on the strip. I'm wearing baggy linen trousers and a floral blouse. The people spilling out of the bars, cradling plastic pint glasses and jugs of cocktails, are wearing far less clothing than me, and showing a lot more flesh.

There is light everywhere, streaming out of doors and windows, all the bars in competition to outshine each other in the fight for custom. There are special offers advertised everywhere: two for one on drinks, happy hours, first drink for free, half price for ladies.

I make my way up. A group of lads standing outside the Queen Vic bar stare at me as I head past them. One of them whistles at me.

'Show us your cunt, love,' he shouts, and his friends laugh.

I ignore him. Head on.

It's still early for the strip, but already it smells of fried food, beer and vomit.

Outside the Pineapple Lounge, a man is being restrained by

two bouncers. One of them holds his arms behind his back, the other takes aim and punches him in the face. Blood gushes out of his now broken nose as they throw him into the street. His friends rush out to help him. One of them says something that the bouncer doesn't like. The bouncer moves towards him and he backs away fast.

There's a siren behind me and I turn to see a Policia Local squad car coming up on one of its patrols. A few people turn to look. Most ignore it. I step out of the road and let it go past. Emergency vehicles are the only type allowed on the strip after 8pm.

The squad car stops by the bouncers and two uniformed officers get out, rearranging their equipment belts. They speak to the bouncers. There's a rapid exchange, some shoulder shrugging and then some laughter. One of the officers heads over to where the boy with the broken nose is propped up against a wall between two bars. The officer asks if he's all right. His friend remonstrates angrily. The policeman shrugs.

'He's drunk, take him home,' he says in English.

The boy's friend calls the policeman a 'spic bastard'. The copper stands to his full height and reaches for his truncheon. The friend backs away and puts his hand up to apologise. The policeman smiles and walks back to his colleague. They get in their car and continue their patrol.

I continue on my way too. Outside Rooney's, two girls dressed in bikini tops and miniskirts are being chatted up by half a dozen men dressed in togas. A stag do. It all looks convivial enough, until one of the men goes behind one of the girls and unties her bikini top without her permission. She shrieks and uses one hand to save what she can of her top, while using the other to slap him across the face, hard. The man catches her wrist and spits in her face. She's getting upset now, hysterical, shrieking obscenities at him. He laughs and lets go of her wrist, and the girls walk away. He catches my eye.

'Fuck are you looking at?' he says, Yorkshire accent, words slurred.

I ignore him and walk on.

Four men walk into a strip club that advertises 'private dances *and more*'.

Two boys walk out of it, rosy-cheeked, smiling.

Finally, halfway up the strip, there's a vast warehouse-style building set back from the street like an otherworldly spaceship landed in a suburban high road. A massive-lettered sign proclaims Kiss.

It has a wide, steep staircase leading up to the main entrance. There's a man in a crumpled suit standing outside it, a laminated cardboard sign hung round his neck: *Jesus Will Save You.* He rattles off a mixture of Bible verses about sin, excess and Sodom and Gomorrah. A couple of girls eye him kindly.

The Preacherman.

He's a local landmark.

Must be high season – he only ever appears in June through to August. Always trying to save a few sinners who have lost their way.

I don't have high hopes for his success rate.

In front of him, there's already a queue forming to get into Kiss.

I walk past and head for the front of the club. There's a shout behind me.

'Queue-jumping bitch.'

I ignore it.

A bouncer is holding people back behind a black rope, letting ones and twos in occasionally. He's a large, Slavic-looking guy, possibly the same guy Karim was talking about. I ask him, in Spanish, then in English, if I can speak to the manager.

'Who are you?' he asks.

'I'm the British Vice-Consul,' I reply, and show him my identity card.

He looks at it, looks back at me, tells me to wait, then goes inside.

~

The manager, Alejandro Lopez, meets me at the door and waves me inside in a cloud of designer cologne dominated by the scent of sandalwood. At first glance, he looks like his punters – tight black T-shirt, clean blue jeans, expensive-looking white trainers – but, looking closer, you can see hints of his age. In the darkness of the club he could pass for his early thirties, but by the time we're in the back office, under ordinary ceiling lights, you can see the flecks of white hair at the roots that even a pricey dye job hasn't managed to eliminate.

He speaks to me in English to begin with. Treats me like a schoolmarm. Patronising. Polite. Too polite. Like he's overdoing the helpfulness to cover up for something.

I launch at him in rapid Spanish, a haze of job titles, responsibilities, name-dropping the ambassador, the mayor, the deputy chief of police. He listens to bits of it, nods, looks at me, then away, then at me, then away, desperately searching for something to distract him, interested but not interested. Sure he'd far rather be working out his bar takings. He won't look me directly in the eye. Keeps staring at my shoulder. Nervous. Uncomfortable. Doesn't want officials sniffing round his club.

I get to my point.

'A British citizen has been implicated in the murder. He's asked if I could double-check the CCTV, which should prove he left here at the time he says. Would it be possible to see it?'

He thinks for less than a second. Relief seems to creep

through his face and he manages a bit of a smile. Gets his mobile out.

'Would you like a drink?' he asks. 'Beer, cocktail?'

I shake my head.

'Maybe some water,' I say.

He nods and disappears through a side door. A minute later, he wafts back in. Sandalwood and blue jeans.

Asks me to follow him.

We head off down a weakly lit corridor, through an anonymous door, into a wider, darker corridor, and then the music hits. Pounding, beating, so loud I almost put my arms to my head to protect myself.

We're in the club proper.

We walk down the corridor, illuminated only by subdued LED lights in the floor and bright-green fire-door signs.

Alejandro sets a fast pace and I have a job to keep up.

At the end of the corridor are two sets of double doors. Like an airlock. Pushing through them, we come into one of the main dance floors and the noise is even louder, the giant speakers all around the room pounding my head like a stiff breeze.

The lights have a life of their own. Spinning, flashing and sweeping around like choreographed dancers. I stumble after Alejandro, doing my best not to rub against any of the sweaty bodies that surround me.

It's still early by Magaluf standards, so the place is only just beginning to fill up, but there must already be several hundred people throwing their arms around to the music. Men, mainly, but a fair number of girls too. Maybe a 60:40 ratio.

I know nothing about dance music.

Not my thing.

But here it's king.

The DJ changes the track slightly. Possibly a key change and the speed increases. There's a high-pitched repetitive note that the dancers respond to, and now the arms are pounding away, great legions of youths shouting their approval.

It's not my first time in one of these Balearic superclubs. Not even close. We make regular visits when one of them wants to show off its new, improved security systems, or explain how it's doing its bit to clean up Magaluf.

Tonight, the main room's a sea of people, but it parts as Alejandro forces a way through, up to the front, where there are crowd barriers and black T-shirted security officers keeping some distance between the revellers and the DJ, a big black guy in a plain white T-shirt. He stands on a raised platform, in a booth behind a mixing desk, visible to all, headphones on, concentrating on what he's playing.

Alejandro gestures at one of the security team, who unhooks a barrier and lets us through. He nods at me and I say thank you, but it's lost in the music.

Alejandro walks behind the DJ booth. He turns to me, sticks his head so close to my ear I can feel the spit when he shouts into it.

'Dante,' he says, 'one of the top twenty DJs in the world.'

He smiles, and I notice one of his pre-molars is gold. He nods his head to the music, looking proud, like he's watching his son in a school play.

Alejandro shouts something at Dante, but in the noise I can't make out what he says.

Nor can Dante.

He looks down at us, Alejandro first, and then me.

Alejandro raises his hands and does a theatrical clap to show his appreciation.

Dante nods slightly, his face impassive.

Alejandro looks at me again, grinning.

I lean into his ear.

'He's very good,' I say.

Alejandro smiles and nods, then remembers what we've come for, touches my upper arm to lead me behind the DJ booth through a black curtain at the back. There's a soundproof door and we walk through, up a flight of stairs and into a long, dingy corridor, then another, then another. We're somewhere at the back of the club, in the service corridors that snake around the main dance areas. Huge pipes and vast bunches of cables litter the floors, walls and ceilings. It's the engine behind the machine – where the smoke and mirrors come from – the real deal, twenty-first century, super-club experience.

Finally, he shows me into a windowless office. Inside is a bank of CCTV monitors and a man and a woman dressed in black T-shirts with Kiss logos on the front. They're perched on tables, vaguely keeping an eye on the screens, walkie-talkies crackling with occasional bursts of Spanish. They eye me suspiciously, looking stern and unamused. The man looks like a local – neat, short hair, olive skin and stubble. She looks Anglo, British or possibly German, her long hair tied back in a no-nonsense ponytail.

'This is our main control room,' Alejandro says in Spanish. 'It's where we monitor everything and everybody. We've got over seventy cameras and we can review them just like this.'

He leans over, pushes a few buttons on a keyboard and uses a mouse to turn one of the monitors into a collection of twenty or thirty different camera shots. He selects one: it's a close-up of part of the dance floor we were just on. A girl and a boy are dancing closely together. He puts his hands on her hips. She turns round and twerks in his groin. Alejandro clicks away to a more respectable camera shot.

He looks at me expectantly and I force a nod of approval.

'We've got probably the best security set-up in the Balearics,' he says, this time in English. 'Keeping our customers safe is our number one priority.'

Mission statements and PR puff.

'I'm impressed,' I say, and he seems satisfied.

He introduces me by my job title to Sergio, the duty security manager, and Kirsten, his deputy. They both look at me, eyes narrowed, brows creased. Sergio shakes my hand and Kirsten gives me a short nod of the head and a weak handshake.

'These two will be here all night, checking everybody is okay,' Alejandro says.

They nod.

'Safety always comes first,' Sergio says.

More PR.

'That's great to know,' I say.

There's a knock on the door and a nervous-looking Spanish teenager comes in, obligatory black T-shirt.

He has a tray with two bottles of mineral water on it. Alejandro takes the bottles, thanks the boy and watches him leave.

'Your water,' he says, handing it to me. He opens his bottle and starts drinking.

'Of course, we can only monitor what happens in our footprint,' Alejandro continues, switching back into Spanish. I look at Kirsten, who seems to be following every word. 'Once the customer leaves our premises...'

He raises his hands in a 'what can we do' gesture.

I nod that I understand, open my bottle of water and take a swig.

'But while they are here,' he gestures to the camera shots on the screens, 'they are as safe as they can possibly be.'

I'm not here for a safety briefing, but Alejandro has switched into full marketing mode now. He's on a roll and I want to keep him on side, so I continue to nod and look impressed.

'We have a zero-tolerance policy to any fighting, or groping, or aggressive behaviour,' he says.

Sergio and Kirsten nod in unison.

'And we have absolute zero tolerance to drugs,' Alejandro continues.

A nod from Kirsten. The tiniest hint of a smile creeps into the corner of Sergio's mouth before he smothers it, saying, 'Absolutely.'

We stand there for a moment, four of us, staring at the image on the screen of several hundred young people dancing and gyrating together. Then Alejandro claps his hands and we turn to look at him.

'Mrs Martin is here about the night the girl disappeared,' he says.

Sergio and Kirsten frown.

'The girl found on the beach,' I say. 'The one that was murdered.'

Recognition on their faces. They nod.

'She would like to see our CCTV from that night to help one of her...'

He looks at me, unsure how to phrase it.

'Clients?' he asks.

I shake my head.

'Customers,' I say. It's what we're meant to call them. Get us in the right mindset.

'Right,' he says.

Sergio and Kirsten look at each other nervously – glance at Alejandro, then each other, then me, then back to Alejandro.

'Can we get it up?' Alejandro asks.

A pause. Awkward looks. A bead of perspiration on Sergio's forehead. Kirsten goes to speak, then swallows what she was going to say.

Finally, Sergio:

'I am really very sorry, but that is not something we can do,' he says.

Alejandro, cool, calm, unruffled.

'Why is that?' he asks.

'The Guardia Civil have already taken all the CCTV we have for that night,' he says. 'We no longer have access to it.'

Bullshit, I think, and Karim's words come back to me:

*If that CCTV exists, it'll never see the light of day.*

Sergio's eyes dance between the four of us. Alejandro, still unruffled, unfazed.

'Really?' he says.

'I'm afraid so,' Sergio says.

Kirsten, silent, implacable, staring at the door.

*You've got to help me, Elaine. I didn't do it.*

'You don't keep copies? A record on a hard drive?'

Of course they do. We're a long way from VHS tapes and DVDs.

Sergio shakes his head.

Alejandro turns to me, his face all apologies.

'It appears not,' he says. 'But you could ask the Guardia Civil.'

*If that CCTV exists, it'll never see the light of day.*

I want to call them out, get them to show me now, on these very monitors, that there's nothing on their drives from that night.

But how can I? I have no statutory powers, no right to demand, no legal basis on which to ask for it. I'm here through their goodwill towards a job title based on a 200-year-old idea of diplomacy.

I stifle a yawn. It's late. I sneak a glance at my watch. Just after midnight. I'm beginning to feel my long day and late night from the previous evening. Tingles of exhaustion run through my body. This is getting me nowhere.

'Of course,' I say. 'I'm in touch with them. Now I know it's with them, I'll ask them directly.'

'A very sad case,' Alejandro says. 'This girl. Awful. But, thankfully, so very rare here. We have over a million British people come to Magaluf every year. When you think of the numbers, a dreadful incident like this really is very unusual. It's actually a very safe town.'

Bullshit.

'Of course,' I say. 'Safer than you'd think.'

Alejandro walks me back out to the front of the club. We take a behind-the-scenes route, keeping away from the dance floor this time, which is good because I don't feel like forcing my way through all those people again. Don't feel like it at all, in fact. Don't know if it's the long day or everything that's happened just catching up with me, or the effects of the pounding music and jarring lights, but I'm not feeling good. At all. Tired, lethargic, edgy.

We reach the main doors and Alejandro gets the same Slavic bouncer I saw earlier to let me out. The queue is now three times the length it was before. One in, one out. A group of queueing blokes are in full cry, singing and shouting. A group of girls near the front giggle in response. Three men have painted themselves blue to look like Smurfs. One has blood dripping from an open wound on his head.

I thank Alejandro, head towards the stairs and work my way down them, careful to hold the handrail, because my legs now feel a bit unsteady. Weak. Like they're not all that keen on keeping me upright.

At the bottom of the steps, I'm back on the strip. It's now in full swing, peak Punta Ballena. High season and rush hour is upon us. Bodies stretch out all over the road, groups of men, groups of boys, groups of girls in different states of undress and drunkenness.

I take tentative steps down the street, back in the general direction of my car, but my legs seem to be wading through treacle. Things are starting to blur now. Images rush at me: two men, arms around each other, shouting for joy, shouting at me, encouraging me. Two girls, holding a third up as she tries to walk, legless, wet marks down her dress. A man and a woman, arm in arm, him lifting her top up, showing her breasts to a group of guys on the side. Two men, just in swimming trunks, arms around each other, having a kiss to the delight of a group of girls.

I feel myself about to fall.

I move over to the side, between a bar and a café, put my arm against the wall for support.

Something's not right now. Definitely not right. Not tiredness or late nights or some kind of sickness. Something else, something I've taken, some drug working on me and I don't know what it is. Sweat breaking out on my forehead and all over my body. Feel hot, like I'm sitting next to a radiator in the middle of the noonday sun. The lights dance around me, accentuating colours, greens and blues mainly, interspersed with white flashes.

'You all right?'

I look up.

A girl is sitting at a table outside the café, eating some chips, while her boyfriend throws up next to her in the street.

No, I'm not all right. Someone's slipped me something. Spiked my drink. God knows what. God knows what it could do. Could I overdose? Christ, I don't even know what it is. Sharp prickles now, running down my right arm. Just my right arm. Hard pins and needles. I try to rub them, but stumble and have to cling on to the girl's table to keep upright.

'You sure you're all right?' she asks.

'Fine,' I say, in more of a slur than a word.

I push myself off, and walk on. Just want to get away from this place, this hellhole. I stumble, bump into a guy.

'Easy,' he says, helping me to stand. 'You all right?' he asks.

Haven't got the strength to answer.

'Get your tits out,' his friend adds.

I push myself away, stumble a bit further. No, legs don't want to do that. Just want to sit.

I drop to the tarmac. Sit, something approaching cross-legged. Heart pounding now, cold sweats and nausea all over me. Shivering, the sounds all blurring into one another.

Try to relax. Whatever it is, relax and it will be better.

I listen to the sounds of people walking and shouting, grunts and calls and urges.

A scuffle breaks out somewhere. Someone's calling someone a 'cunt'. Jostling and shouting, pushing and arguing. There's an impact and the sound of bone. Then sirens and a patrol car. People moving around me now, just avoiding me.

Laughter.

'Check her out.'

Someone laughing at me.

A girl's voice:

'Must have wandered out of her old people's home.'

A man's voice:

'I would.'

I bury my head between my legs, try to control my breathing, deal with the sounds and the lights and the vibrations and the smells. Stenches and scents, sweat and deodorant, dry ice and cooking oil, beer and vomit, tarmac and sandalwood.

~

Sometime later.

Don't know how long.

Arms grip me and pull me to the side. I stir slightly. Still smell chip fat. Still hearing footsteps.

'Jesus loves you,' a voice says.

I try to open my eyes. Really try. Screw my face up really hard to get the muscles working, but they don't want to wake up.

'If we confess, He is faithful and just to forgive us our sins, and to cleanse us from all unrighteousness,' he says.

I try to sit up, but my back doesn't like it. I slump. Better that way. Nicer that way.

Arms try to sit me up. My back against something hard, something firm, something good.

'For all have sinned and come short of the glory of God,' he says.

*Preacherman?*

I try my eyelids again.

No, nothing. My mind's eye sees a place I want to go. Deep, down there, where it's warm and cosy and I can sleep.

Angry, sharp pain across my cheek. He just slapped me. Slapped me.

'Lady? You hear me?'

A voice. His voice.

*Preacherman.*

I try my eyes again, but they're tired. Leave them be.

Sharp pain again. Another slap. My face stinging again.

'He did it. This is him,' he says.

I shake my head, put my arm up to stop the slaps.

'It's him, it's him,' he says.

Shaking me now, arms on my arms, shaking and shaking.

'You see him? You see him?'

I try the eyes again. Jolting and juddering. They open slightly.

*Preacherman.*

Shaking. Shuddering.

'You see him? You see who did this?' he says. 'Who? Tell me. Who?'

I shake my head. People shouting now.

'Got a problem, mate?'

'Leave her alone.'

I shake my head. Put it back between my legs.

'It's him,' Preacherman says. 'The man with the hood.'

# 9

I'm waiting for him.

The school gates.

We're all waiting for someone.

A line of mums.

Me, waiting for Jonathan.

Endless streams of everyone else's kids come out, in a crocodile line through the one open gate, into the arms of their mothers.

But not Jonathan.

I try to crane my head, looking for him over the teacher's shoulder.

No sign.

One by one the other parents greet their children, give them a hug, take their bag, hold them by the hand, then lead them away.

But not Jonathan.

I ask around the other mums – have they seen him?

Blank looks, blank stares.

I go over to the teacher. Does she know where Jonathan is?

It's okay. It's all right. He'll be out any second. I just have to wait over there.

I walk back, behind the gate. Stand and wait.

After a minute, I see a shape emerging from the door. The shape of a little boy. He walks into the light and I can see it's Jonathan in his school uniform, forest-green sweatshirt with the school crest over his little polo shirt, dark-grey trousers worn and crumpled after a day at school, backpack slung around his shoulder.

He walks a couple of steps towards me, then stops.

'Jonathan,' I call.

He looks scared, worried.

'Jonathan?' I say. 'Everything all right?'

His face drops. I look at the teacher for support. Her face is blank.

I step towards him and the teacher barks at me.

'Behind the gate,' she says, followed by a reluctant, 'please.'

I step back, drop to my haunches, open my arms wide.

'Jonathan, it's me, Mummy.'

He stands there, looking at me, as if he's trying to work something out.

Just stands there watching, as a tear falls down his cheek and he starts to cry.

I wake in a hospital bed. It's a ward and my bed's one of six. Only two are occupied, including mine. It's a ward I know well. Room 713, block G at Son Espases.

I'm usually the one visiting.

As I sit up I sense some wires moving with me.

There's a cannula in my wrist tracing a path up to a drip on the right-hand side of my bed.

Sore all over, joints aching, a sharp pain in my right elbow that makes me draw breath when I touch it. I'm cold, yet I can feel a layer of sweat over my body. I have little spasmodic shivering fits every few seconds as my body tenses up, painfully, then releases. The soft tissue all over my body feels alien and dead to me, like it might fall off my bones at any moment.

And then there's my head.

If I try to move it, a burst of pain erupts like there's a great big concrete block in it, shifting this way and that.

I slump back. The block moves again. Agony.

I'm sweating. Sweating all over. I feel terrible, like someone's been in and sent a scourer through my veins.

Try to think back, work out what happened. I'd been on the strip. Been to Kiss. Had made my way out and then something I'd taken took effect. Except I didn't take anything. Which means someone must have given it to me. Spiked my drink with God knows what. It must have been, can only have been, someone at Kiss. The water bottle. The only thing I ate or drank while I was there. The fuzzy head, the confusion, the smell of sandalwood.

I reach over and see a call button. I press it and wait.

A few minutes later, a nurse appears. She's a kindly-looking woman in her fifties, her hair a cheap dye job scraped back with a scrunchie. Big, 1980s-style glasses.

'We were wondering when you'd come around,' she says in English, picking up a clipboard hung on the side of my bed and making some notes.

'What happened?' I ask.

'Ambulance picked you up in Magaluf. Punta Ballena. Usual story. Think you might have overdone it a bit. Can you remember what you took?'

I try to shake my head but it hurts too much.

'I didn't take anything,' I say.

She gives me the look I imagine she saves for the young,

wasted Brits that turn up: eyebrows raised, a smile dancing around the corners of her mouth.

'At least nothing I know of,' I say. 'I think someone must have spiked my drink.'

She doesn't say anything, just nods, long and slowly.

'I wasn't there for fun. I'm not on holiday. I work here.'

I slip into Spanish.

'I work for the British consulate in Palma. I'm up here a lot. I was in Magaluf working. I drank nothing but water. Someone must have spiked it.'

She looks at me differently now, as she senses that maybe I'm not just another drunk Brit. She studies me, trying to work out what's not right about me. Deep furrows in her brow.

'Why would anyone want to do that?' she asks. 'You could have died.'

I try to sit up again.

'What was it?'

She shrugs.

'Some sort of opiate. Hard to know for sure.'

I breathe out hard, and feel the pins and needles in my body again.

And then I feel the cramp in the pit of my stomach and know I've only got seconds. I wave at the woman, who understands instantly, grabs a nearby cardboard bowl and hands it to me.

I vomit copiously, great spasmodic retches, followed by thick yellow sick.

After a minute or so, I finish, my stomach now empty.

The nurse takes the bowl off me, hands me a fresh one and a cup of water. I sip it slowly, worried I might have a relapse. The pain in my head is ferocious.

'You're lucky,' she says. 'If that was your first time, it could easily have killed you. I've seen plenty of others who didn't make it home. You're fortunate someone found you.'

Someone?

'Who?' I ask.

She shrugs.

'They rang in, said you'd been taken ill on the strip. Said you needed urgent medical attention. Stayed with you till the ambulance arrived. Might very well have saved your life.'

*Preacherman.*

'You need to be careful,' she says. 'Up there, on the strip, it's a jungle.'

She gives me a stare like I'm the same sort of street trash she sees every day, and takes the sick bowl off for disposal.

I lie back on the bed, feeling half dead, and fall asleep again.

I don't know what time it was that I was sick, so I don't know how much later it is when I wake up again, but I feel a bit better.

The concrete block's still weighing heavy in my head, and my elbow screams any time I move it, but the fever's died down and my body doesn't feel like it might pack it in at any moment.

I pull myself up in bed and look around. It's still daytime and the sun is streaming in through the large windows on one side of the ward room.

I turn my head to my bedside table. There's nothing there but a jug of water, some paper cups and a box of tissues.

Somewhere around here must be my clothes.

I sit back against my pillow and try to make sense of it all. Someone tried to spike my drink. Someone tried to kill me. It can only be someone at Kiss. Alejandro? The sandalwood smell. Or one of the security team? The people in the CCTV room? The bouncers?

That young kid who brought my water? Why would they bother? All I asked for was some CCTV that they had an easy excuse not to provide. What possible benefit can it have been to poison me?

Unless they meant to scare me.

Warn me off poking around.

If they're willing to spike my drink, then what else might they be capable of?

I look around. The other person who was sharing the ward with me has gone, leaving me the sole occupant. There's a clattering of footsteps as I hear someone walking down the corridor. Steady, heavy footsteps. One person. Walking with purpose. It sounds like men's shoes.

They reach the door to my ward room.

And walk past.

I breathe out. The fug in my head is beginning to clear.

I do my best to swing my legs off the bed. Every movement is agony and comes with icy tingles and muscular aches. I do my best to stand, using the bed to support me, and tiptoe towards the wardrobe unit. I open it and see my belongings: clothes, shoes and handbag.

I change as quickly as I can, which isn't easy with the way my body's hating me right now. I take my hospital gown off and struggle into my underwear, trousers and blouse.

Shoes next.

Then I grab my handbag and make for the exit.

I'm halfway down the corridor, heading towards the lifts, when there's a shout behind me.

'Hey.'

I keep walking, don't want to stop.

'Hey!'

A woman's voice. Louder this time.

I take a risk, turn around.

The nurse is staring at me, an angry look on her face. She walks towards me.

'You're in no fit state to be going home. We need to keep you in for at least forty-eight hours for observation. We need to make sure that everything that's entered you has worked its way through your system. There's still a chance you could have blood poisoning.'

My eye itches and I reach up to rub it. Then I fix her with a stare.

'I'm fine,' I say. 'I really just need to go home.'

I turn on my heel and walk away.

I grab a taxi from the steady stream of them that's depositing ill and injured people at the emergency clinic, and ask the driver to take me to the outskirts of Palma. I don't really know where I'm going, but I do know I don't feel safe in Son Espases, that my car is still parked in Magaluf, and that I can't afford a taxi all the way home to Santa Luisa.

His taxi, like all Spanish taxis, smells of cigarettes and air fresheners, each part making the other worse. His rosary jingles as he pulls out.

'Beautiful day,' he says.

A talker.

'Yes,' I say as brusquely as I can.

I reach into my handbag and search through it for my phone. It's still there. I look in my purse. I only had about thirty euros on me, and it's all still in there.

I bring my phone to life. It's now nearly 5pm. There are two missed calls and two texts, one each from the office and from Nick.

I deal with the office first. A text to Louise to say I'm not feeling well and won't be coming in today. I can imagine her fury, what with the workload they've got on, but deep down I know I'm not in a fit state for the office.

Then it's time for Nick. After a few rings, he answers.

'I've been worried sick about you, love,' he says.

For the first time in a very long time, it's a pleasure to hear his voice.

'I'm okay,' I say, and then it all just comes out and I start crying profusely. I can hear his voice but can't make out what he's saying for the tears. The taxi driver asks if I'm all right and I nod that I'm okay.

'I'm sorry,' I say, speaking over whatever Nick's saying. 'I've had a bit of a shock. Bit of a nasty experience.'

'Oh, darling, what sort of experience?'

'I'll tell you later,' I say, not desperate to run through everything in front of the taxi driver.

'Look, can you pick me up from Palma?' I say. 'My car's still in Magaluf. I've got no transport.'

'Oh, I'd love to,' he says. 'But, you know, I've had a couple of beers.'

And then I can hear it in his voice. The very slight slurring of his C's and S's. The edge of alcohol on the vowels.

'That's all right,' I say, trying hard not to start crying again. 'I'll work something out.'

I go through my phone contacts until I get to Miguel.

I wait for Miguel in a dying old café on the edge of town, by the Carretera de Valldemossa roundabout, where I asked the taxi driver to leave me. It's ugly and anonymous and, hopefully, the last place anyone would think to look for me. It's also the fastest way out of town to my home.

I sip a coffee and a bottle of water and watch the window, scanning for anything, anyone suspicious.

The coffee wakes me up and gives me strength. I notice my hand is shaking and I feel a sudden, vast hunger.

I buy a packet of crisps and a small ham pastry.

A couple of ageing workmen enter and order beers. They eye me, then ignore me.

Ten minutes later and a marked police car pulls up in the little parking bay opposite. Miguel gets out and enters. He's on his own. Not many deputy chiefs of police would drop everything to drive thirty miles to meet a friend.

I feel the obligation building.

He comes in and there's a clink as the other people in the café stop what they're doing and stare. It's not often they have a uniformed police officer here. Even stranger that he's meeting the strange old foreign lady.

He greets me, barks at the man behind the counter that he wants a coffee, and sits next to me.

'Are you okay?'

I try and speak but nothing comes out.

Instead, I start to cry.

Ten minutes later and we're in his squad car, driving back to Santa Luisa. On the way, I explain what happened: the visit to Kiss, the request to see the CCTV, the collapse, waking up in the hospital, the lot. He listens, nods occasionally, doesn't say a word till I've finished.

'I'm sorry,' he says eventually.

'You're sorry?'

He shrugs.

'Sorry that it happened. Not nice. You want to make a

complaint? You'd have to make a statement, but I could then get one of our guys to look into it.'

I don't even think about it, just shake my head. I know I don't want to go there. Don't want to invite the attention, the baggage that comes with it, explaining it to my boss. And also, deep down, I know there are dangerous people involved, and I don't want to provoke them.

Which means, whoever they are, they've won.

'You're sure?' he says, although I suspect he already knows my answer.

'I'm sure,' I say.

He looks at me, then pulls the car over. We're out in the sticks now, off the main highway, on the side of a quiet, dusty back road.

He puts his hand on my knee and looks me in the eye.

He presses gently.

'You're worried,' he says.

Not worried, terrified.

'Maybe a bit,' I say. 'This sort of thing doesn't happen to me.'

More pressure, more squeezing. Reassurance? Or something else?

He moves the hand away.

'I can speak to my colleagues out here and in Palma. I know a few of them. If you're worried, they can run a patrol car past your house and past the consulate. Might make you feel safer?'

'That's very nice, but I don't think so,' I say.

He shrugs, then turns the engine back on.

We drive in silence the rest of the way, Miguel inscrutable behind his aviator shades. I wonder if this is wise – going back to the house. Can't be too hard for those who want to, to find my address. Am I a target? Was it just a warning? Do I leave it all alone now? Leave Karim to his fate? Is there anything else I can do to help him?

I just want to go home, go to bed. Think about it in the morning.

I look over at Miguel.

'Is there any news on Kayleigh?' I ask.

He raises his eyebrows and screws up his mouth to say 'maybe'.

'We found her on CCTV,' he says. 'And guess where she was?'

I'm too tired to do any thinking, so just shake my head.

'Wandering down the strip about midnight.'

'On her own?'

He nods.

'On her own, yes. She then joins the queue for Kiss. Gets in and goes clubbing.'

Twelve years old and gets into Kiss.

'Did no one ID her?'

He shakes his head.

'She's twelve years old, for God's sake. How could no one ID her?'

The shrug.

'This is Magaluf, and she's a very... grown-up twelve-year-old.'

A very slight smile at the edge of his mouth. I feel a chill crawl down my skin.

'Do you know what happens next?' I ask.

He nods.

'CCTV shows she leaves Kiss about 3am.'

'The main entrance?'

'That's right. Heads off, takes a right down to the beach. That's the last we have of her. We think she was heading to the beach to maybe walk home along the front.'

'So if something has happened to her, it would be on the beach between Magaluf and Palma Nova.'

He nods.

'She would have had to cross Torrenova at some point, but we've been through all the CCTV there we can find, and she's not on it.'

Torrenova: the bit of headland between Magaluf and Palma Nova, made up largely of hotels for partygoers. Which means she didn't even make it as far as Torrenova.

'We're combing the beach and all around for her,' he continues. 'It doesn't look great.'

His face is serious, focused. For once, he might just mean it.

'Is there anything more we can do?' I ask.

'Get your newspaper reporters to go home?'

My best sarcastic smile.

'So she went to the same club as Michelle Fraser on the same night: one winds up dead, the other's disappeared. Is there a link?'

He shrugs.

'Ask Karim,' he says.

He does his best to look me in the eye, but soon looks away. A smirk. My heartbeat's up again, the heat rising in my cheeks, and I have an urge to tell him what I really think.

Deep breath, take your time. Don't give him the satisfaction.

'So you've seen all the Kiss CCTV then?'

He nods.

'Any sign of Karim leaving?'

He looks over at me.

'No. He doesn't leave on any of the footage. I've told you that already.'

'Care to let me have a look at it?' I ask.

He laughs.

'My dear Elaine, much as I love discussing cases involving British citizens with you, I'm afraid I can't let you have access to police evidence. But then, you already know that. You're the British Vice-Consul after all.'

*If that CCTV exists, it'll never see the light of day.*

A few minutes later and we pull into Santa Luisa. I direct Miguel and he pulls up outside my front door.

Before I can say goodbye, he turns to me.

'You need to be careful with Kiss,' he says. 'There's a lot of money there, a lot of people making a lot of money from it. They won't like you sticking your nose in, and God knows what goes on there behind the scenes. I'm not trying to scare you, not trying to freak you out. It's just a murky world in Magaluf, a feeding frenzy. I think you're perfectly safe up here, and in Palma, but when it comes to the clubs and the bars out there, just leave it to us, okay?'

He takes his shades off and leans in closer, smiles.

'Right?' he asks, eyebrows raised.

'I understand,' I say, opening my door to get out.

I enter the house.

Nick's drunk.

Impossibly drunk.

He starts off all concerned, wanting to know what's happened, why I didn't come back, what this 'nasty experience' was that I mentioned to him. But it's all a bit OTT. He kneels in front of me, taking one of my hands in his and rubbing his cheek on it, and I know he's in a world of his own – his own little place where only he and the booze can live.

I can't face the truth.

Not here. Not right now.

Instead, I tell him there was an abusive customer in the

consulate, who threatened me. Tell him that the security guard, Fermin handled it. It was all fine, just a nasty shock.

He gets himself into an Islamic prayer position and swears to be my faithful protector forever and a day, genuflecting up and down, a miserable, pitiful sight.

There's a smell of burning and he suddenly stands up, nearly falls over again, then rushes into the kitchen.

Burnt chicken casserole. Inedible.

He says not to worry, claims he can salvage enough for two portions.

I tell him I'm going for a shower and a rest, and he doesn't object.

I tramp my way upstairs, lie down on the bed and pass out almost immediately.

The knocking is long and persistent. It grows in volume: just a tap, tap, tapping to begin with, then a knock, knock, knocking, then a full-on hammering on the door, and I'm awake.

I sit up in bed. I'm naked and sweating, but in one piece. The pain in my head is still there, dull, and so is the darting pain in the elbow, but the rest of my body seems to be more or less back to normal.

Knock, knock, knock.

Someone at the door.

I get up, shout that I'm on my way, and look for my dressing gown. I find it, tie it around myself and head down to the front door.

The knocking's stopped now.

Nick's still lying on the sofa, passed out, snoring. Two plates of burnt chicken casserole lie on the coffee table, uneaten. There are half a dozen empty beer bottles dotted about the room.

A liquid dinner then.

I make my way down the hall and look at the antique clock we bought from the Palma antiques market when we first moved out here.

Half past midnight.

Who? Why? At this time? Out here?

I have no spyhole or security camera. I won't know who it is till I open the door.

If they wanted me dead, why would they knock?

I turn the latch and pull the heavy old door open.

A figure turns towards me, dark jacket, long hair in a ponytail.

'Can I come in?' Kirsten, the security girl from Kiss, asks.

She brushes past me before I can answer.

# 10

'Sorry,' she says, not sounding apologetic. Her eyes are fidgety, whipping around, establishing her surroundings, making a note of everything, then darting back to me.

She's in a black leather biker jacket, hot for the weather, but probably about right for this time of night. Her gaze is intense, her weight shifting from foot to foot, like she doesn't want to be here any longer than she has to.

Heart going now, beating fast, butterflies dancing, little thrills of adrenaline stabbing through me.

Senior security person from Kiss, in my house, right now. Kiss. The bottle of water. The strip. My legs going, the lights, the sounds, the loss of control. Vomit. Shouting. Sandalwood.

Why?

Ring Miguel. Phone. Damn, it's in my bedroom.

No alternative. Style it out, act unconcerned while getting ready to scream blue murder.

'Kirsten, right?' I say, for some reason extending a hand. She studies it, like it might contain a noxious substance, decides it's okay and shakes it limply.

'That's right,' she says, stepping down the hall, 'do you have internet?'

I follow her, steering her away from the living room where Nick's sleeping, and into the little study I keep at the back of the house with the intention of one day working from home, which, as yet, hasn't happened once.

'Of course,' I say. 'It's not superfast, but I can get Amazon and eBay.'

Nothing, not a nod, wink, smile or any other acknowledgement of humour.

'This it?' she says, gesturing to the ageing desktop I call my work computer.

I nod.

She sits down and brings it to life.

'Password?' she says and I hesitate.

'I don't really give...'

'You do it,' she says, turning the keyboard in my direction, stepping away and looking out the window at the back.

I stare at the keyboard. Realise I don't remember my password. Hardly ever use the machine. Have a note of it. In my handbag. In the kitchen.

An excuse as well.

'It's in my bag,' I say, my voice shaking, hoping the guilt doesn't show on my face.

She stares at me. Raises her eyebrows.

'Want to get it, then?'

She has a snotty, patronising look on her face which suddenly gets to me.

'Sorry, but what the hell are you doing here?' I say, with as much fortitude as I can muster.

'Get online and I'll show you,' she says. 'I think you'll want to know.'

I nod and shuffle nervously out to the kitchen. My handbag,

the red leather one my daughter, Arianna, gave me two Christmases ago, is sitting on the kitchen table. I grab it, then head to the sink, the knife rack just to the side of it. I pick one out. The short ceramic one. My favourite to chop with – as sharp as a razor.

I push it into the side pocket of the handbag, then head back to the study.

I walk over to the keyboard, pull the notebook out, flick through to the list of passwords that I shouldn't, but do, keep at the back, and tap in the nine digits.

'Done,' I say, turning the keyboard back to her. She takes over again, clicking and tapping.

'Sorry, but how the hell do you know where I live?' I ask.

She looks up and frowns, like it's obvious.

'Rang the consulate,' she says. Turns back to the screen and taps away.

She takes her jacket off. Underneath is a black vest. Her arms look thin but strong, like a rock climber's, all stringy, long muscles.

I put my chances of a successful getaway at slim to zero.

'We don't give out that sort of information,' I say. 'As a matter of policy.'

'Yes, you do,' she says, without looking up.

We don't. Yet she seems so confident, so sure. She looks up at me briefly, sees the confusion on my face.

'I said I was the mother of the dead girl and I needed to speak to you urgently,' she says, eyes still trained on the computer screen. 'They gave me your mobile, your home number and your address.'

Louise? Duncan? Probably Rodrigo. Much as we like to appear professional, too often we can still be a fairly amateur operation.

'I want you to see this,' she says, beckoning me over.

I walk around to her side of the desk. She opens a file from an email and a small video window springs to life onscreen.

'When we told you we'd given the CCTV of that evening to the police, that was bollocks,' she says, enlarging the player window. 'We gave them some of it, but not all of it.'

It's a shot from a camera trained on the outside of the main entrance of Kiss. I can see the front doors, the head of the queue to get in, and the pair of bouncers monitoring it. The time code shows it's two in the morning. Not much is happening. People in ones and twos are being let in. Occasionally, people come out.

Kirsten fast-forwards for a few minutes then, at 2.14am, she stops.

A group of men are attempting to come out of the main doors, scuffling. I look closer and can see that at least three of the men are wearing the black security team T-shirts: bouncers. They're manhandling two other men. One is thrown to the ground at the top of the steps.

'That's the boyfriend,' Kirsten chips in.

I nod.

Ben.

A second man being held by the bouncers is then thrown to the floor. He trips and stumbles down the stairs.

'That's your man, Karim,' she says.

'He's not my man.'

She shrugs.

'Keep watching,' she says.

I watch as Karim sits up and gets to his haunches. He's standing when Ben makes it to his feet, catches his eye and then charges at him, fists and feet flying. The bouncers watch, not interrupting. It's not on their property anymore – they don't care.

Karim is trying to bearhug Ben, blunt his attacks, doing his best to protect himself – just as he told me. Ben's like a wild animal, fighting on pure emotion, no method, just raw hate.

There are onlookers now. Most of the queue are staring. Some look worried, others are smiling. No one looks away. And then a car pulls up, lights flashing. Cops. Two officers get out. Then a police van comes and more get out. They seize the two men, separate them. Three pull Ben to one side, four more get Karim. Ben's wrestling wildly, trying to get free. There's no sound, but I'd bet anything he's screaming like a banshee.

Karim is speaking to the officers now, quietly controlled. The police have produced cuffs but are holding off from cuffing him as he tries to talk them down. They seem to recognise him. The other officers drag Ben to the opposite side of the plaza. He's resisting – struggling hard. They take him and force him into the back of a police van. The door's slammed shut. Karim chats to a couple of the bouncers, and then he's let back into the club. So far, it matches the version of events he gave me to a tee.

Kirsten reaches in front of me and pauses the video.

She closes the window and opens another video file.

'This is about an hour later, the camera on our west door. One of our service entrances.'

West door?

'I thought the east door was the service entrance?'

'There's another one,' she says, 'although, not many people know about it.'

The shot is high up and shows a stretch of what I assume is the wall of the club facing out into an alley. It's a wide shot – wide enough that I can make out the fronts of some of the businesses on the far side of the alley, open in the day but shuttered at night. Occasionally, people stroll past the camera, arm in arm, walking and stumbling depending on how much they've had to drink. Then the wall of the club starts to move, as a small doorway I hadn't made out before opens and three men appear from it. I recognise two of them as bouncers: the big Slav and the smaller, Spanish-looking one, I assume to be Simon, the one Karim mentioned. Between them is the slimmer but unmistakable figure of Karim, hands held behind his back, body twisting as the bouncers push and pull him outside. Their faces are clearer now, closer to the camera, so I can make out their expressions. They push Karim up against one of the shuttered shops, hard. His face bangs against it and I can see a look of pain. The big Slav holds him by his arms, keeps him pushed up against the shutters.

He produces some leather gloves from a pocket and works them onto his hands, first with his fingers, then his teeth.

The Spanish one takes an extendable baton out of his pocket, takes aim and cracks Karim hard across the backs of both knees. Karim's mouth opens in a gasp of pain and he goes down on his knees. Then the bouncers are onto him. The one with the baton works his body and arms, sending repeated blows and jabs across his torso. The other uses one hand to hold Karim's arms behind his back while he uses his free hand to punch him repeatedly in the face.

The two bouncers look at each other, one makes a gesture with his hand and points at the camera. The Slavic one walks out of frame, while the other one stands, leans forward, does a couple of swallows, then spits onto Karim's back. He then takes a step back and launches a further kick into Karim's ribs. Karim's body doesn't even respond this time, just lies limply on the floor.

Then the camera goes dead. The time code reads 03.17am.

'They switched it off?' I say.

Kirsten nods.

Beaten black and blue.

The punch to the face, the kick to the ribs. The body limp on the floor.

He never said a word to me about it, not one word about the bouncers, about the beating.

'Have the police seen this?' I ask.

'They don't even know we have a west door.'

'You're kidding me?'

She shakes her head.

'It's used by the bouncers. For "special occasions".'

'What's that supposed to mean?'

She pushes herself back in her chair, takes a breath and looks around the room, trying to find something to focus on.

'You know how I got into this job?' she says, but doesn't wait for an answer before continuing. 'I came out here for one summer, aged twenty-three, not a clue what I wanted to do with my life, £200 in my pocket and desperate to have some fun. Got a job at Kiss, behind the bar. Worked and partied for six months. Saved enough money to see me through the winter. Then, next spring, they needed a woman to do door checks on the girls coming in. Got me to do it. That's how I started on the door teams. After a couple of years, they got me to help monitoring the cameras. And do you know what they said to me? Day one, watching the screens: "You're here to watch out for the three Fs", they said. "Any fighting, any fucking, any fires, raise the alarm. Anything else, let it go". You know what they were getting at?'

I stare at her blankly, then slowly shake my head.

'Turn a blind eye to the dealing. "That's what pays your wages", they told me the one time I raised it with them. So I have. Ignored it. They don't want to know about it because they're running it. The bouncers. That's their main job. Get the stuff sold quietly, cleanly and discreetly enough that no one worries too much.'

Drugs.

The oil that keeps the Magaluf machine running.

'Which is where the west door comes in,' she continues. 'It's where they're supplied if they're running out. It's their quick getaway if there's a chance the police might raid the place. It's their secret passage to safety in any awkward situation. Which is why they keep it secret. From the outside, you wouldn't even know it's there. Connects up with a service corridor out past the boiler room at the back.'

I nod slowly, repeatedly, trying to think things through.

'So what's Karim done to get such a beating?'

She laughs, the first sign of amusement tonight, then looks at me, furrows her brow.

'You don't know?'

I can imagine, but decide to play dumb and shrug my shoulders.

Now she's shaking her head.

'That's what I like about you. You wear your honesty on your sleeve.'

She leans back into the seat again, crosses her legs, gets comfortable.

'He's a dealer, Karim. One of the permitted ones. Anyone selling inside Kiss does so with the bouncers' approval. They give the bouncer a pre-agreed cut, they're allowed to trade. Except your man, Karim, he's a bit of a loose cannon. Doesn't always pay on time, so every so often he's kicked out until he finds the cash and gets allowed back in. Like that night: he's still owing, so he's not meant to be there. Then he gets in a fight and they all realise he's got himself inside anyway, working when he's not supposed to. So they let him back in, have a word with him, and when he still doesn't pay, they decide to take him for a chat through the west door.'

The west door.

'So what, they just left him lying there?' I ask.

She shrugs.

'That's all I've got. No idea what happens once the camera's off. The others don't know I have this footage, and I need it to stay that way.'

'It's just that, if we had footage that showed Karim walking away, that showed that he didn't re-enter the club afterwards, then that might help put him in the clear.'

'Like I say, they pulled the camera at that point.'

I'm meant to respond but can't think of anything much to say. Throat's dry. I feel dirty, like I want a shower and to change my sheets. Feel like waking Nick up and getting him to put his arms around me. To hold me tight, the way he used to.

'Glass of water?' I say, getting up and not waiting for a response.

I fill two glasses from a bottle in the fridge, drink one standing there in the kitchen, refill it and carry them both through to the study.

Kirsten is sitting in the desk chair, leaning back, swivelling slightly left and right. I hand her a glass.

'The police need to see this,' I say.

She sits there impassively, says nothing.

'I mean, God knows what else is on that camera. If you rewind it, it could show how Michelle Fraser left the building. Might show who she left with.'

'It doesn't,' she says. 'I checked. She doesn't leave on this camera. Not before it gets turned off at least.'

'Even so,' I say, 'the police need to know about this door. For God's sake, this could make the difference between Karim getting a life sentence or walking free.'

She's shaking her head.

'No point.'

I frown at her.

'What do you mean?'

'They're all in on it,' she says. 'Nothing happens on the strip without the police knowing and approving of it,' she says. 'The cops run this place. Of course they do. You see their little cars going up and down, patrolling it every ten minutes. Nothing happens without their approval. Everyone knows everyone in Magaluf. You couldn't clear as much stuff as gets sold at Kiss without their blessing. Hence they're all friends. They nod it through, take their cut, keep a lid on things, leave the rest to us.'

'You mean the Policia Local?'

'Most likely,' she says. 'Don't think the Guardia Civil are too bothered either, but they leave the strip to the local guys, unless they have to step in, like with this murdered girl.'

'What do you expect me to do about it?' I ask.

The shrug again.

'Just do something,' she says.

I realise how tired I am. I want this woman gone and this footage out of my house. I'm a Vice-Consul, not a chief of police. This has nothing to do with me.

Or at least that's what I keep telling myself.

I slump down to the floor, put my arms around my shins, wait for her to go.

After a while, she speaks:

'This whole place is rotten,' she says. 'Magaluf, Calvià, Majorca, all of it. It's warped to the core. You must have noticed?' she asks.

My turn to shrug and look away.

She's quiet for a minute, staring at the screensaver on the computer. It's of some Mayan or Aztec ruins, framed by mountains and a brilliant, cloudless sky.

'So you're not in on this whole drugs thing then?' I ask.

'Like I say, I turn a blind eye. A few of us do. We're kept away from most of it. We're well paid and just keep our heads down and get on with it, the acceptable face of Magaluf door security. We all know the consequences if anything gets out.'

'So why are you telling me this?'

She leans forward and has a sip of her water for the first time, then puts the glass back carefully on the desk.

'Because you're not a cop and you're not from the town hall or some corrupt local official. You're different from them. You're interested in what happens to young British people here. And you came and asked for the CCTV.'

Looks me in the eye. Brown pupils boring into mine, a hint of desperation creeping into the corners.

'No one's ever come and asked for the CCTV before. Except the cops. They ask for it. Quite a lot. And they get it. Well, some of it. But no one else.'

She looks away now. Mayan ruins again.

'Just thought you might want to know,' she adds.

I rub my eyes. Really tired now. Need my bed. The baton, the beating, the blood. Karim's body lying prostrate.

'I'm grateful you came to me,' I say.

It's a lie.

Worst thing ever to fall in my lap. A nightmare of epic proportions, practical and moral.

'I am somewhat limited in what I can do,' I add.

'Show it to the ambassador. Show it to president of the Balearics. Show it to the newspapers. I don't know. Just get it out there, somewhere, that these cops are a law unto themselves.'

The ambassador. The president. The newspapers.

Right.

I nod slowly.

'Can I ask you a question?' I ask.

She shrugs.

'The other day, when I came to Kiss to ask for the CCTV, someone spiked my drink. Don't know what it was. Doctor said an opiate of some kind. I collapsed on the strip. I could have died. Must have been someone at Kiss. D'you know who would have done it?'

Her face remains impassive, but she doesn't speak straight away. Takes a moment to think. Then she stands up, as if she's about to leave.

'There's some nasty bastards at Kiss,' she says. 'Could be any number of them. Their idea of a bit of fun, and a warning at the same time to keep your nose out of it, I'd guess. I'm sorry,' she adds.

'What about you?' I ask as she begins to leave.

'I'm getting out,' she says. 'Like I say, keeping my mouth shut. It's well paid and I've saved up enough to make a new start. Got a flight booked at the end of the season, back to the UK.'

Heart beating again now. Perspiration in my armpits, a sheen on my skin.

'I'll see what I can do,' I say.

She opens her mouth to speak, then stops and nods instead.

A quick handshake. A very brief 'thank you' from Kirsten. A scribbled mobile number, then she's down the hall, out the front door and away.

I pad up the stairs, back to my bed, my head on the pillow.

I try to sleep, but it just won't come.

The baton, the beating, the blood.

# 11

The jaunty little polka once again. Quiet at first but persistent, until it's like an overhead helicopter in my ear.

I wake up, grab the phone and answer it. A man called Carlos Angel Blanco identifies himself as a welfare officer at the Centro Penitenciario. He has news about an inmate, Karim Ansari. Tried to take his own life. 'Intentó quitarse la vida.' Last night, after lights out.

He was unsuccessful, 'fortunately'.

One of their regular guard patrols caught him hanging from the window bars just a moment or two after he'd tied the sheet round his neck. 'Prompt intervention,' he says. 'Found alive. Rushed to the sick bay. Getting attention from medical staff and mental health workers.'

As if I should be somehow grateful.

The sound of arse-covering. Of not wanting a bad word to get back to the mayor from a respected foreign mission.

'Fortunately.'

I tell Blanco I want to see Mr Ansari as soon as possible. He says he'll check with medical staff and let me know when I can come in. I tell him that's not good enough. That he's a vulnerable adult liable to self-harm again if he's not given appropriate support and that we are, effectively, his next of kin. He grunts that he understands, says he'll call me back and hangs up the phone.

I reach over to the little wooden bedside table for my watch. It's gone 6am: too early to go into work, but too late to pretend I'll be able to get back to sleep.

The consulate opens to the public at 8am, and I'm in there by 7.30. We start with the regular morning meeting. Everyone's there, even Rodrigo. There's a lot of concern for me, why I wasn't in yesterday, why I hadn't contacted anyone. I explain I was in Magaluf till very late the previous day, chasing up the missing girl. I don't tell them about being drugged, or the hospital, or the CCTV. Don't see the point. Louise will only worry. Rodrigo will only smile.

They ask me what the latest is on Kayleigh. I say she's still not been found, but that, off the record, they have traced her last known movements and she was at Kiss that night. There's a few stifled gasps. Louise frowns, thinking hard. I add that the Policia Local are still concentrating all their resources on finding her, and that if they hear anything, they're going to let me know. I promise I'll chase up Miguel this morning.

They fill me in about things from their point of view. It was predictably bedlam at the consulate yesterday. Louise spent most of the day fielding calls from the UK press, who were desperate for updates on the missing girl, then, when there weren't any, demanded everything from the chief of police's mobile number to our assistance as a translation service. At least three newspapers now have reporters on the island, with others using local stringers. Half a dozen television crews have also arrived, all of whom are sniffing around Magaluf, looking for something to fill the gap until there's any news. One of them's already offering a £100,000 reward for information leading to Kayleigh's discovery, 'alive' that is.

The last official police statement was dated one in the morning, and said 'searches were ongoing'.

Helen and Mike Walsh, the mum and dad, have moved hotel. Officially, it's to get away from the hordes of reporters, but unofficially we've been told it's because they've taken a £25,000 down payment from a newspaper for their exclusive story, which will run, according to Louise, 'whenever Kayleigh's fate is confirmed'. The newspaper's also gone public with a £10,000 reward for information that helps find her.

While Louise's been dealing with that, there's been no let-up in the rest of our work, with Duncan, Soraya and, amazingly, Rodrigo here till ten o'clock last night, catching up on paperwork. Twenty-five lost passports yesterday, two broken legs, a heart attack, three arrests in Magaluf and a premature baby.

The waiting room's already filling up by the time the meeting finishes. Duncan and Soraya get busy dealing with it.

I go back to my desk and start working my way through the emails I've missed. I scan my inbox.

Nothing from Kirsten.

Nothing from Miguel.

Do I show him the footage?

I should.

I know I should. I can trust him.

I've always thought I could trust him.

Can I trust him?

*The cops run this place.*

*Everyone knows everyone in Magaluf.*

*The baton, the beating, the blood.*

I email Miriam. Ask if I can bring Nick over for a couples session. Suggest tomorrow evening. She replies straight away that that's fine and suggests a time. I'm just imagining breaking the news to Nick when there's a cough next to me and I look up to see Louise standing over me, looking concerned.

'What's wrong?' I ask, looking over at the front desk. There's a young man standing there, white, in his late twenties possibly, wearing a big peaked baseball cap, with a closely shaved chinstrap beard and tattoos showing on his arm where his white T-shirt stops.

'He's come to pick up emergency travel documents for someone else,' she says.

I frown.

'We can't give them out to someone on behalf of someone else.'

'I've explained that to him,' she says. 'But he's not accepting it.'

He's looking at me now, eyes narrowed, furtive look on his face. We make eye contact and it's like he's calling me out for a fight.

I tell Louise I'll deal with the situation and go up to the window. I press the microphone.

'Can I help?' I say.

'Who are you?' he says, a 'street' accent from somewhere in or around London.

'I'm Elaine Martin, the British Vice-Consul.'

He nods slowly, then smiles, revealing recently whitened teeth.

'I'm here to pick up a passport,' he says.

'We don't give out passports, only emergency travel documents. Is that what you mean?'

'Them, yeah.'

'My colleague says that you're here to pick them up for someone else, is that right?'

'That's right,' he says, nodding.

'I'm afraid, sir, we can't give out emergency travel documents to anyone on behalf of other people. They have to attend in person to receive them. It's a security thing.'

He leans into the microphone.

'That's what *she* said,' he says, nodding his head in Louise's direction. 'But you don't know who it's for.'

'You're right, I don't, sir, but it won't make any difference.'

'It's for Dante.'

He takes a step back from the counter for emphasis.

I look at him, narrowing my eyes, before it registers with me, and the image of the big black DJ in the white T-shirt comes into my head.

'I'm afraid it doesn't matter who it's for,' I say. 'We only give out emergency travel documents in person.'

He leans back in now, his eyes flickering.

'He hasn't got time to come in. He's a busy man. So just give me the documents and I'll be on my way, right? I'm telling you, I ain't got time for this.'

'Sir, I've told you twice and my colleague has told you once, we only give out travel documents to the person named and photographed in that document. It's so we can prove the document is going to the person it's intended to go to. It doesn't matter whether you are Dante, the prime minister or Prince Charles. Whoever's document it is will have to attend in person. So if Dante is a very busy man, then I regret to inform you that he will have to forgo his travel documents. Or he will have to arrange a time to come and get them. Our office hours are on the door.'

I step back, take my finger off the microphone button and watch as the news sinks in.

He looks left, looks right, thinks, scowls, then smiles in a menacing way.

'Lady, you're making a big mistake,' he says.

I put my finger back on the button.

'It's not a mistake, it's simply the rules, the way this whole system works. But we have the documents ready, so any time Dante would like to come in, he can collect them.'

He looks at me, nods, puts his finger up and points at me, nods again.

'I'll be back, lady,' he says.

'I look forward to it,' I say, as I watch him strut his way through the waiting area, making eye contact with some of the people sitting there, before walking past our security guard, Fermin, looking him in the eye, and walking out of the building.

I go over to Louise, who's been waiting by my desk.

'Charming guy,' she says.

'I didn't know that DJ had lost his passport,' I say. 'When was that?'

'Came in Wednesday.'

'Did he say how he'd lost it?'

'No. Just said it had gone missing two nights earlier.'

'The night of the fifteenth?'

'That's right.'

'The night the girl was murdered.'

'I guess so,' she says.

I'm about to make a comment, to say something about a coincidence, when I'm interrupted by more noises. A raised voice. Someone unhappy. Duncan doing his best to appease them: 'I'm sorry to hear that, sir.' 'That doesn't sound right, sir.'

It's the man with the fawn-coloured shirt again. The man with the 100-year-old mother. He's in with his family this time – a wife and some teenage kids.

'If you don't fucking sort this out, I will personally write to my MP and the fucking Foreign Office and explain to them the fucking shambles that is the British consulate in Palma, Majorca.'

I walk over, push in front of Duncan and lean into the microphone.

'Mr McLellan, what seems to be the problem?'

There's a flash of recognition in his eyes. He's subdued. Slightly.

'It's you,' he says. 'Good. Perhaps you can explain to me where my fucking card is. It's my mother's birthday next weekend. I've spent over two grand setting up this party for her, flown my whole family out, and you lot still haven't sorted out my card from the fucking Queen. What's a 100th fucking birthday without a card from the goddamn Queen?'

'Just give me a moment,' I say, and turn off the intercom.

Duncan looks sheet white. I lean into his ear.

'Where *is* his damn card?'

He looks at me blankly, then leans into my ear.

'I haven't a clue.'

I look over at Rodrigo. He's on the phone: talking, joking. I walk over to his desk and stand there, looking at him. He registers me, swivels his chair to face the opposite direction. He's talking to his friend, the former deputy mayor of Palma: golfing buddies. He's saying something about sailing off Soler when I cut the call.

He turns and glares at me furiously. He's about to say something when I cut him off.

'Where's the damn card?' I ask.

'What card?'

'The 100th birthday card. From the Queen.'

Something flashes across his eyes. A moment's recognition. A tinge of guilt.

'I ring the palace, I order it. We are waiting.'

'Waiting?'

'Yes. They are sending it. We are waiting.'

'How long did they say?'

'They didn't.'

'And did you pass any of this on to the gentleman at the counter?'

'It's not my job to keep him informed of everything–'

'Look, just deal with him,' I say, and walk back to my desk.

I sit at my computer, raging, staring at the screensaver of the Foreign Office coat of arms, until I finally calm down.

I check my inbox and there's an email from the prison. I can see Karim at visiting hours, from 5pm this evening. I'm just replying when my desk phone starts ringing.

I pick it up. A woman speaks, breathless, nervous.

'Elaine Martin, please,' she says.

'Speaking,' I say, waiting for the inevitable tale of woe: a break-in at her hotel, a lost passport, her son assaulted, one of the usual stories.

'It's Laura Neil here. You rang me a couple of days ago, about... what happened to me. A few years ago. In Majorca.'

Heart racing now. Muscles in my arms stiffening.

I sit up, pull my notepad over and pick up a biro.

'Laura, hi, thanks so much for calling back.'

I sound like a holiday rep.

'Is it him?' she says.

Pause. Try to think through my next answer.

'I don't know,' I say finally. 'I'm sorry to contact you, Laura, sorry to dredge over old ground. I know it's probably the last thing in the world you want to think about ever again.'

I wait to see if she responds. She doesn't. I take it as a cue to continue.

'What it is, well, it might be absolutely nothing to do with what happened to you. Might not be linked at all. I just want to be absolutely clear, right at the start.'

Holiday rep voice again. I wince, but push on.

'We had a girl who was attacked a couple of nights ago. As I say, it might be nothing, but there are a few similarities to what happened in your case. So I just wanted to see if you would be willing to talk about it. It might just help, in case there is a link.'

'What similarities?'

No emotion. Matter of fact.

'It happened on Magaluf beach. In the early hours of the morning. The victim, I mean woman, in this case, had been at Kiss club. The perpetrator used a knife.'

I pause, and so does she. I can hear her swallowing as she goes to speak, stops, then finally starts.

'Was he wearing a hood?'

'I'm afraid we don't know. I'm very sorry to say that the woman in question, the girl, didn't survive the attack.'

'Oh, Christ,' she says. 'Oh, I'm so very sorry.'

Change in her voice. Different timbre. Emotion coming through. Then I can hear her sobbing at the other end. She tries to apologise. Tries to say 'sorry' a couple of times, in between sobs and sniffs. Finally, she recovers her composure.

'It's terrible, isn't it, but it takes someone to be murdered to realise that I got lucky, really. It could have been me. I could have been killed.'

Her last line tails off as she starts to cry again. I give her a few seconds.

'Listen, Laura, would you like to call me back when you've had time to think about things. I can see this is very emotional for you. I didn't mean to just, you know, drop it on you like that.'

More sniffs. Sounds of her wiping her nose with a tissue.

'No, no, it's fine. I totally get why you're calling. It's just a shock, you know. After all these years. You think about it every day, sort of put it in a box in your head. It's just a thing that sits there. But no one else ever speaks about it, or even mentions it. And then you get a call and, well, anyway. I'm glad you called. I'm happy to speak. Do they have anyone for it? Suspects?'

Karim. The denials. The suicide attempt.

'That's partly why I'm ringing,' I say. 'Look, Laura, you've obviously been through an experience that I can barely even imagine. All I feel I can do is be honest with you.'

'Of course,' she says.

'What happened to you, what's happened to this girl, well, it's rare. Even in Magaluf. Which is partly what made me think of you. And, well, in this latest case, the police do have a suspect, a British guy in custody. He denies it. Says it was nothing to do with him. Well, I suppose he would say that. The thing is, what happened to you, well, *that* can't have been him because he was in prison at the time. Drug-dealing charges. That's what he is... was: a bit of a petty crook. Swears blind he's on the straight and narrow now. Anyway, I don't know either way if this guy's innocent or guilty, but I just thought, if your case is linked to this latest case, then we know the guy they've got now isn't the man they're after. So I just thought I could run through what happened with you, see if there are any other similarities, anything different, just see if it leads anywhere. I don't know. I'm jabbering a bit. But do you see?'

'I understand,' she says, a slight quiver in her voice. 'Totally. We all want to see the right person behind bars.'

'Absolutely,' I say.

Louise's making a 'T' sign at me. I mouth 'water' and she goes off to the kitchen.

'I'm a bit surprised the police haven't called me,' she says. 'I hear from them periodically, when one of them goes back to review the case. They give me a call, run through what happened, then I never hear from them again.'

'Well, the latest attack has only just happened,' I say. 'And they think they've got their man.'

'But you're not so sure?'

Another pause. Walking on eggshells.

'Some of it feels like wishful thinking at the moment,' I say.

'Okay, well. With me, you probably know the basics. I was out here for a week with some friends. Normal sort of thing. Young girls wanting a week of hassle-free sun, sea and sex. All girls' nights and giggles, party all night, sleep in the day sort of thing. That night, we went to Kiss. Met some guys. Got talking. Had a bit to drink. I think someone produced some coke at one point and we all had a bit. Sounds wild, but it's just what you did. To be honest, that night was one of the quieter ones. I met this guy.'

'Matthew?'

'That's right. Didn't know his name till after it all happened. Never bothered to ask. You don't sometimes. That's just how it works in Magaluf. We had a bit of a dance and that. He seemed really nice. Had a bit of a kiss and a cuddle. Decided we wanted some fresh air. Went for a walk, down to the beach. Sun, sea and stars. More than a bit tipsy. Christ, I think I was actually sick on the way. Anyway, we get to the beach and we start having sex, and that's when it happened.'

She pauses. Reluctant.

'I know it's difficult, but could you talk me through exactly?'

'We're lying down on the sand, Matthew on top of me. Then, over his shoulder, I see this figure emerging. It's horrible. It happens so quickly, I hardly understand. He just starts stabbing at Matthew. Stab, stab, stab. A bit of me's thinking it's one of his friends. Some sick Halloween stunt, using one of those fake knives. Then I feel the blood and I realise, oh Christ, this is real.

I'm screaming, and the attacker's got one hand on my mouth to shut me up. And he's wearing this hood. Really crummily made bit of sacking with eyeholes and a hole for his mouth. He pushes Matthew off, turns me over. Ties me up. Then... well, you probably know most of the rest. He rapes me. Might as well call a spade a spade. I just lie there, praying for it to end. Not sure what I can do. And at the end, when he's finished, I feel the knife on my neck and I presume it's all over for me. But to get the knife in position, he's had to move a bit, so I make one last effort to try and shift him. I move my whole body, and it throws him a bit and I'm screaming again now, and there's a voice from somewhere, and he panics and gets off me and runs away.'

'What can you remember about him? His build? Voice?'

'Big guy. Strong. Heavy. Can't really remember much about his accent. He didn't say much. Just kept calling me horrible things – a slut, a whore, a bitch, that kind of thing. Probably British. English. Southern, I think. Not cockney but, you know, down that way. Deep voice. Older, I think.'

'Older, like, in his thirties? Or in his fifties?'

'Could be either, I think. It was all so long ago.'

'What makes you think older?'

'Just his voice. It was deep. Like someone who'd seen a bit of life.'

'So he could have been anywhere between thirty and fifty?'

'Look, I can't be sure. Sometimes I doubt every detail of that night, wonder how accurately I remember it. I remember thinking he was older. More like middle-aged, but I wouldn't want to put a year on it.'

'Are you still in touch with Matthew at all? It would be useful to talk to him too.'

She's silent for a moment and I can hear her swallow.

'It's terrible but I didn't stay in touch with him. I'm a bit ashamed of that really. But, well, I'd only just met him and, you know, it was just going to be a sordid, one-night Magaluf thing, wasn't it. And then we were both in hospital but having different treatment regimes. He was in a much worse way than me. He got flown back to England and the police told me he had survived and was recovering well and that's the last I know, I'm afraid. The cops might be able to help you find a number?'

'Oh, don't worry,' I say, looking down at my mobile which is buzzing.

It's flashing Freddie's name.

'Thank you, Laura,' I say. 'I know it can't have been easy. But you've been really helpful.'

'Just make sure they get the right bastard,' she says.

I put the desk phone down and grab my mobile.

'Elaine,' Freddie says as I answer. His line is crackly with street noise and wind. 'Got a bit of news for you.'

Cold shiver. Not sure I can handle any more 'news'.

'Go on,' I say non-committally.

'You know that missing girl you were after? The little one?'

'Kayleigh Walsh?'

'That her name, right. Well, I think I might have found her.'

Matter of fact. Just like that. A small piece of good news, like his football team's won a match or he's scooped a tenner on the lottery.

'Are you sure it's her?'

'Well, I can't be sure, no, because she's not saying anything and I can't really see her face but how many other young girls in Magaluf are likely to be hiding under swimming pools?'

'Swimming pools?'

'Well, between the pool and the pump room. It's a bit of a complicated arrangement.'

Then his voice becomes a touch more distant as he talks away from his phone:

'You just stay there, love, help's on its way.'

'Have you told the police yet?' I ask. 'The family?'

'I thought I'd try you first. Don't want to give the filth all the glory, eh?'

I'm running out of the consulate, nearly tripping over Fermin on my way out, going as fast as I can to get to my car. Jump in the driver's seat, get Freddie on hands-free and start heading to Magaluf, fast.

He talks as I drive. He got a call from one of the hotels on Torrenova. They thought they had a drugged-up English girl hiding in one of the service areas under their main public swimming pool. She was refusing to come out. Not making the connection to Kayleigh, and not wanting to upset customers by causing a scene, they called Freddie first because everyone on Magaluf knows he helps out British tourists in trouble.

Freddie arrives, goes round to the back of the pool, where the bins, the gas canisters and the emergency generator live, and the public don't go. He crouches down and can see that, hiding under the pool, in a space barely big enough for a cat to crawl in, are two eyes with a body attached, and it's moving. Breathing. Not a lot, but enough to show it's alive.

So he tries talking to it in English. Explains who he is. Explains that he can help. Sits there trying to talk this thing out for the best part of half an hour.

Nothing.

He's about to leave and tell the hotel management to let the police deal with it, when it occurs to him that this might be the missing girl and that there's a reward.

Which is when he rings me.

I'm there in twenty-five minutes, breaking the speed limit on the MA1, swerving through traffic, wondering whether to call the police and have done with it, or check it's her first.

I park on a side street and head to the Marina Hotel. It's famous, one of the landmarks of the area. The main entrance is opposite a restaurant called El Sombrero, which is crowned by a twenty-foot sign saying 'Tex-Mex', with a neon sombrero on top – just in case any holidaymaker might be unsure as to what type of ethnic cuisine they're likely to get inside.

I head across the road and enter the hotel grounds, walking up to reception. Nobody stops me. It's early morning, so quiet. At the back is the pool. It's a big, kidney-shaped affair with a Hawaiian-style bamboo bar in the middle. Two people are asleep on sunbeds, fully clothed with a half-empty tequila bottle and a used condom lying to the side.

I walk past them and make my way around to the back.

Can't see Freddie.

I call. He answers and starts directing me: tells me to head for a row of leylandii trees, to go around the back of them, then walk along and down a slope. He meets me at the bottom and walks me around to the left, to the service area. The back of the pool.

'She's in there,' he says, and points to a space about a foot and a half high, underneath a big concrete block that's jutting out above the ground – the base of the swimming pool above.

I crouch down and look in. At first, it's just dark but I take my sunglasses off and my eyes begin to adjust. At the back, squashed against the wall as far as it can go, is a shape. Hard to make out what. And then there's a quick, sudden movement and I see the flash of two small reflective things: the girl's eyes.

'I bought her these,' Freddie says behind me.

I stand up. He's holding a plastic shopping bag with some packets of crisps, chocolate bars and a couple of small bottles of water.

'I threw her one of the chocolate bars but she's not touched it.'

I nod, then crouch down again. I'm virtually lying on the ground now. I feel a button tear on my blouse.

'Kayleigh,' I say.

Nothing.

'Kayleigh, is that you?'

Still nothing, but I can see the eyes now, wide open, intense.

Terrified.

'Kayleigh, love, my name's Elaine. I'm from the British consulate. I can help you,' I say.

Still nothing but I can now make out the shape of a head, with long hair and a body underneath it. She's staring at me, listening, making calculations in her head.

'Kayleigh, love, there's lots of people looking for you. Your mum, your dad. I've met them. They're worried sick. Why don't you come out and I can get them for you.'

A flicker in her eye. A tiny bit of recognition. A movement. Head turning.

'Would you like some food, Kayleigh? You must be hungry?'

Eyes disappear for a second, then return.

I turn to Freddie and get him to give me one of the packets of crisps.

'I'm going to throw you some crisps, Kayleigh. If you're hungry, eat them. They'll make you feel better.'

I do my best to throw them in her direction. They make a soft, scuffing noise as they land.

No movement.

I give it a minute. Still no movement.

She has to come out. At some point, she has to come out. She needs medical attention and to be reunited with her family. I weigh up calling Miguel, getting the police in. I will have to, eventually, but I can't see all the sirens and flashing lights helping to coax her out somehow.

There's a shuffling and clawing noise. I crane back down and can make out a bit of movement. Some scratching at the ground. Then some rustling.

She's eating the crisps. Eating them fast. I can hear crunching and the rustle of the packet.

'That's good, Kayleigh,' I say. 'That's really good. Do you want a drink?'

I listen intently. No reply. I take the bottle of water from Freddie and roll it towards the shape anyway. I hear her pick it up, unscrew the top and drink. I can hear her swallowing. A trickle of water rolls its way towards me from where it's been spilt in her rush to consume it.

'We've got more food,' I say, 'and more drink out here. Why don't you come out and we can give it to you. You must be starving.'

Nothing. Just the slurp of her drinking followed by silence.

'Kayleigh,' I say. 'I don't know what's happened to you or why you're in here, but I can help you. I can get the police here, I can get a doctor to help you and I can get your parents here. I can make things better for you, I promise. We're only here to help, but I can't help you unless you come out. Now I'm going to wait here for a few minutes. It's just me and my friend Freddie. We're going to sit here and if you come out, we'll do everything we can to help you. But if you don't come out, then I'm going to have no choice but to call the police and tell them you're here and then it will all get really loud and busy and you might not like that so much.'

I stop speaking and listen. It's quiet. I stand up and look at Freddie.

'What will be, will be,' he says.

I nod and look at the floor. We stand there in silence,

listening for any indication she's moving. Hoping she'll just appear. Thirty seconds, a minute, two minutes. I take my phone out, scroll down to Miguel's number. Three minutes, four minutes, five minutes. I get ready. What else can I do? Six minutes. And then, there's an almost imperceptible scuttling sound, like a mouse running across a kitchen floor. It gets louder, a crackling and a crinkling. I look down and a dirty, filthy foot appears in front of me, followed by a second one.

She pushes herself out, legs-first.

I crouch down and wait for her to come out.

She appears, face covered in dirt and grime, long hair filthy and matted, crop top torn, skin on her arms and legs badly scratched. Eyes bright and wild.

Despite all the filth on it, it's unmistakeably the same face as in the prom photo.

I break into a smile as I make eye contact.

'Oh, Kayleigh,' I say, like I've known her for years.

She says nothing, but tears form in her eyes and she collapses into my arms.

~

We sit there like that for a good few minutes, in a kind of trance. She sits on my lap, sobbing, I hold her close to me, my hand running through the mess that is her hair, stroking and patting.

We rock gently to and fro, her body heaving gently as she sobs, my voice doing its best to reassure: 'There, there... it'll all be better now... nothing to worry about.'

After a few minutes, Freddie clears his throat to remind us of his presence and whispers to me, 'I'll go and get my car.'

~

We take her back to Freddie's café, with her sitting on my lap all the way, wrapped in my arms, burrowed into my flesh.

There's a group of lads at the front of the café, working their way through a breakfast curry when we arrive. They look wired, still coming down from whatever they've been doing over the last few hours, pints for each of them on the table. They look at us as we carry this girl, wrapped in a blanket, into the café, then turn back to their meals.

Freddie shows us to the storeroom at the back. It's small, loaded on all four sides with tins of cooking oil, boxes of dried foods and huge plastic containers of rice.

Freddie clears some space and puts a hard school chair in the middle. I sit down, Kayleigh on my lap.

'There, there. Nothing to worry about now.'

I can hear her gentle snores. Freddie looks at me.

'What do we do now?' he asks.

'She needs a doctor,' I say.

'Any sign of injuries?'

I shrug.

'Few bruises and scratches is all I can see at the moment. Externally at least.'

Bile in my throat. I swallow some coffee, wipe the acidity away.

'She's still not said a word,' he says.

I shrug.

'The main thing is she's alive,' I say. 'Time to call the police.'

# 12

Son Espases, 4pm. I've been waiting for over an hour for Miguel to emerge from the ward where they've taken Kayleigh.

He came fast once I'd called him. Brought himself, a female officer and a sympathetic ambulance crew, who did what they were told and waited outside, without sirens, until we were ready.

I explained what had happened, then Miguel helped me carry Kayleigh to the ambulance. We put her on the bed in the back and I rode with them to the hospital, holding her hand.

Kayleigh didn't stir in all that time.

Miguel, the crew and a doctor took her off to the intensive care unit, as a precaution.

Mike and Helen Walsh arrived an hour later and went straight to her room, faces flushed and tense.

I've been outside ever since, waiting for news.

A blue shape comes around the corner – Miguel heading my way, looking serious. Gone is the bonhomie and high spirits, replaced by a steely focus.

'You want to get a coffee?' he asks, and I nod. 'You might want to visit the bathroom first,' he adds.

I look at him, raise my eyebrows, but all he does is smile.

~

I go to the bathroom, look in the mirror and realise why he was smiling. My blouse is ripped and part of my bra is visible where the button has been pulled off. I look a state. My skin is drained, bags under my eyes, clothes filthy from crawling under swimming pools. I splash my face with water.

Back outside, we go and get two stodgy-looking brews from a vending machine by a staircase, and Miguel starts sticking his head into rooms, trying to find an empty one.

Eventually, he's successful: an examination room with no one in it. He turns the light on and I follow him in. Boxes of latex gloves, wipes, spatulas and syringes line the walls. He gestures to the bed and I sit on it, while he takes the single chair opposite.

'Doctor's sedated her,' he says, once we've had time to settle. 'She's badly dehydrated and malnourished. Doesn't look like she's eaten for the best part of five days. She appears to have got some water from somewhere, but until she starts talking, we won't know where. Even so, they've put her on fluids. She has a few scratches and bruises but nothing serious. Physically, at least.'

He looks agitated. Fiddles with his plastic cup, running his thumbnail up and down the ridge.

'Has she been...'

I leave it there, hoping Miguel will pick up on what I'm hinting.

He doesn't.

'Has she been interfered with?' I ask.

He cocks his head slightly to one side.

'Hard to know for certain,' he says. 'There's no sign of anything... untoward. No bruising, or ripped underwear, but she's not saying anything so...'

I close my eyes and mutter something like a prayer, I'm not quite sure who to.

'We're working on the basis,' he continues, 'that she was walking home from Kiss, something frightened her, and she took refuge pretty much where you found her. But we won't know until she's in a fit state to talk to us.'

He drains his coffee and his shoulders slump, the adrenaline of this morning's excitement wearing off.

What could frighten a girl so much she'd hide for five days in a gap underneath a concrete swimming pool, too scared to emerge?

*Coarse, sacking over his head, two holes where his eyes should be.*

'Have you spoken to her parents?' I ask.

He nods.

'They're obviously delighted she's safe. Not saying much either, just sitting there, holding her hand.'

'They must have been worried sick.'

'You'd hope so,' he says, not looking convinced.

'The press?' I ask.

His face changes and he scowls.

'We'll need to put something out.' He looks at his watch. 'Which is what I'm going to be doing next.'

He takes another gulp of his coffee, makes a face at the quality of it, then pushes it away.

He stands up and starts to walk slowly towards the door.

'How's it going with the Michelle Fraser case?' I ask on a whim.

He looks at me and shrugs.

'Guardia Civil still investigating,' he says. 'Not looking too good for your friend.'

It's my turn to scowl.

'Why's that then?'

He makes a face.

'Still their main suspect, isn't he? Dread to think what the Guardia Civil are finding out about him.'

'I thought you hated the Guardia Civil? A bunch of pumped-up adrenaline junkies who'd frame their own grandmothers if it closed a case?'

He shrugs.

'Something like that,' he says.

'You're weak, Miguel. You know that, don't you? Weak and easy. Easy to buy, easy to fool.'

He stops, turns to face me. The frown again.

He thinks for a minute, sizes me up, then nods. He opens the door, then turns back.

'Thanks for your help with finding the girl,' he says, before walking away.

I swallow and do my best not to cry.

It's early afternoon. As I'm in Son Espases, my thoughts turn to Riley. I was due to pay him another visit this week anyway, so it seems to make sense to do that now, before I head home.

At the Atocha Ward, the officious Nurse Ariza is on duty again. She's no cheerier or politer than the last time, but at least she sounds more positive about Riley. He's much improved, apparently, back on solid food and beginning to start using both arms again.

I'm relieved.

She also starts telling me that he's beginning to get mobile again, when there's a 'hey' from behind me, and I turn to see him being wheeled into the ward by a porter.

He's looking much better, some healthy colour back in his face, the sticking plaster on his right cheek much smaller, the bruising almost disappeared.

I say hello and he nods, but doesn't smile.

'You can wheel me to my bed,' he says, so I stand up and push his chair into the ward room. The porter and the nurse follow and both help to manoeuvre him onto his bed until he's sitting up, his legs straight out in front of him in heavy splints. He thanks them both and they leave us to it.

'Can't even go for a shit without someone to wipe my arse,' he says, and smiles. Gone is the croaky, breathy voice from before, and instead, I can make out his accent, somewhere from the north-west I think, Manchester or thereabouts I'd guess.

'That won't be forever,' I say.

'No. Which is the good news. The scans are all back and there's no damage to the spinal cord, or spinal canal, so I won't be a vegetable.'

A warm feeling rushes through me and I feel my muscles relax.

I put my hand on his right arm.

'I'm genuinely delighted to hear that,' I say. 'That's really good news.'

He nods.

'Just three months of intense recuperation and physiotherapy to go then, but at least I'll be wiping my own bottom at the end of it.'

I laugh, then ask how his family is.

'Dad's gone back. Mum's staying here, to see me through the op. They've got to take some metal plates out of my legs and screw a few more back in. Shrapnel, my dad calls it.'

'When's the operation?' I ask.

'Tuesday next week,' he says. 'Then it's a couple of days for everything to settle and then I can start the physio properly. Apparently, it hurts like hell, but it's worth it in the end.'

I nod and smile. I'm starting to like Riley.

'Got to be worth it to get back on your feet,' I say, and pour water into two beakers before handing him one. 'Are you going to stay in Majorca for treatment?'

He shakes his head.

'Once I'm through the op and everything's back together, I should be able to fly home. Going to kick off the physio here, then pick it up again back in Stockport.'

'Have you got medical insurance?' I ask.

He shrugs.

'Didn't bother. Shit call that was, eh?'

It's my turn to shrug.

'You're not on your own with that one,' I say. 'Too many people don't when they come here. Think it's all taken care of by the EHIC card, but that's not the case.'

'Tell me about it. Nurse said if I'd had it, I'd have got a private jet home. It's going to be Ryanair for me. Still, you live and learn.'

'Do you know when you're likely to be going home?'

He nods.

'This Saturday. Got a midday flight, paid for extra leg room and priority boarding. Going up in the world.'

'Saturday,' I repeat, mind working hard. 'You'll need the emergency travel documents I was telling you about.'

He looks at me, searching through his memory, not a lot registering.

'I did speak to you about it before.'

He snorts.

'I was so jacked up on morphine, I don't remember a lot,' he says.

'You lost your passport?'

He nods.

'To get to the UK, you'll need special documentation to let you fly. Which is what we can help with. But if I'm to get you them in time for Saturday, there are a few things we need – passport photos and a police report.'

'I had a copper visit,' he says, 'asking about what happened. Would he have a report?'

'I don't know, but he might be able to get you one, and that could save you a trip to the Policia Nacional in Palma. Do you remember his name?' I ask.

'He left a card,' he says. 'Should be somewhere in that drawer.'

'You mind if I look?' I ask. 'I know a few of the officers round here.'

'Knock yourself out.'

I open the drawer and start trawling through it. There's the contents of his wallet, an English car magazine, a few well-wishers' cards.

I find the card at the bottom. It has the Policia Local crest and the name Inspector David Galvan on it.

'Thanks,' I say. I hold the card up so he can see it and point to the name on it. 'Does he know you're flying home?'

'I've not told him,' he says. 'Bit too busy trying to learn to walk again and all that.'

'Of course,' I say. 'Just in case they track down the driver who did this to you, they might need to speak to you some more. But don't worry, I'll get in touch with him, see if he can send us a report.'

He nods and sniffs hard.

'That okay?' I ask.

He shrugs.

'Suppose so,' he says.

'It's just a report,' I say. 'Without it, you won't be able to get on your flight.'

'Whatever,' he says. 'What about the passport photos?'

I look over at the wheelchair, folded up and propped by his wardrobe.

'If that nurse will help me get you back into this, there's a photo booth near the main reception.'

We head down the main corridor, Riley looking grumpy in his wheelchair, me pushing him, people eyeing me like I'm his mum.

At the end of the corridor, we reach the lift. I press the button and push him inside.

The lift starts its descent.

'I've remembered a bit more,' he says, looking up at me. 'About the accident.'

'Go on,' I say.

'It's not a lot more, but a bit. Last thing I remembered was saying something to the bouncer, then leaving the club. After that, it was all pretty blank. Well, I remember now that he, the bouncer, was asking if I was going to be coming back in and I said I wasn't and I made my way out. Then I remember thinking that I'd like to sit on the beach for a bit, so I went down the side of the club, passing a few couples, and then it sort of fades away again into a haze.'

'Which alley?' I ask, perhaps a bit too quickly.

He shrugs.

'Screwed if I know. One at the side of the club.'

'To the right or the left as you look at the front of Kiss?'

He takes a moment to get his bearings from the night. That night. Sunday the fifteenth.

'Right,' he says, and I nod.

'And you can't remember anything else?'

He shakes his head.

'Still a blur. Don't remember any car, any collision. With what I'd taken, even without the crash, I'm not sure I'd remember too much.'

'Have you told this to the police? To Officer Galvan?' I ask.

He shakes his head.

'I try not to speak to cops unless I have no choice.'

I frown.

'Why's that?'

'Cops don't like me,' he says. 'I don't like cops.'

'This stuff is important,' I say. 'Quite a lot happened in Magaluf the night of your accident. You never know, it might help the police fill in a few holes.'

He looks at me, his eyes narrowing, brow furrowing.

The lift stops, there's a beep and the doors open.

'This might be us,' he says.

I nod, and wheel him out into the brightly lit reception area.

## 13

I call the consulate to let them know Kayleigh Walsh has been found. Louise answers and I run through things, keeping it vague, not going into specifics. I let them know there's going to be a police press release issued imminently, which should get the press off our backs. Louise lets out a huge sigh, before asking how Kayleigh is and what might have happened to her.

Right now, her guess is as good as mine.

I tell her there's no further progress as yet on Michelle Fraser.

I explain that finding Kayleigh should ease everyone's workload. Then I check my watch, see I'm running late for Karim, and make my excuses.

The Centro Penitenciario is a new, purpose-built prison in the middle of the island, surrounded by desert.

There's a reason they built it here.

As I arrive, it's early evening and the shadows are lengthening while the fierceness of the sun is starting to dissipate. A large flagpole rises above the reception area making the whole complex look like a Foreign Legion fort.

I head into reception, go through the X-ray machine, hand in my phone and wait while a sour-looking, middle-aged woman gives me a pat-down. Then a male member of staff, tall and slight, with salt-and-pepper hair thinning at the crown, takes me through the empty courtyards that lead to the visitor room.

I'm shown to a big room split in half by a glass partition, itself separated into Plexiglas booths. The dividers are there to mute the various conversations that take place during visiting hours. Except today, I'm the only one here.

A few moments after I've taken my seat in one of the booths, there's activity on the other side of the glass. A uniformed prison officer shows Karim into the room, points at me, and leaves us to it.

Karim sees me, smiles, gives a slight wave, walks over and takes a seat. His face is drawn and his skin looks the palest I've seen it. He's thin, much thinner than before, cheeks gaunt, and his crisp white shirt, straight out of the prison laundry, hangs over him like a sheet on a coat hanger.

I press the 'talk' button on the intercom that connects the two sides of our booth.

'How are you, Karim?'

Something between a nod and a shrug.

'Been better,' he says.

I fix him with a stare. Serious face. The one I used to scold Jonathan.

'I heard what happened,' I say.

He looks away. Part embarrassment, part shame.

I continue:

'Karim, you mustn't ever do that again. You must promise me...'

'You've got to get me out,' he blurts, tears filling his eyes, colour coming into his cheeks. 'I can't cope much longer in here. Can't do a twenty-year stretch. You know me, Elaine. You know I can't do it.'

Tears now on his cheeks. His hand wipes them away.

'I know, Karim, I know, but you must stay strong.'

My face again stern.

'I'm doing everything I can, Karim, but you must bear with me. I'm working with the police and I've been speaking to people up on the strip. This is way beyond what I'm meant to be doing for anyone, but I'm doing it for you, okay? I don't think it will be very much longer. I'm turning up things that could get you free, but there's no point in me banging on doors in Magaluf, asking questions if you're in here tying sheets together.'

The look away again. The embarrassment. He turns back and nods slowly.

I lean in and hold his gaze.

'Why didn't you tell me that the bouncers beat you up, Karim?'

He narrows his eyes, acting surprised.

'Those cuts and bruises you turned up with at the consulate, they weren't from your fight with Ben. I've seen footage of it,' I say. 'CCTV. They took you out of a side door and laid into you. Why didn't you tell me?'

He shrugs, looks away, mutters something.

'I can't hear you, Karim.'

He looks back at me, a snarl on his face.

'Shit happens. Didn't seem important.'

'For God's sake, Karim, of course it's important. It shows your whereabouts on the night you're being accused of murdering another girl. It's important. Things like that could help me get you out of here.'

The shrug again.

'Is it because you were dealing? Are you worried you're going to get done for that? Because you'll get a much longer sentence for murder than for anything to do with drugs.'

He's shaking his head, smiling, laughing to himself.

He stares at me, a look approaching pity in his eyes.

'Don't be such a fucking headmistress, Elaine.'

'Don't patronise me,' I say. 'I'm the only one in this whole goddamn world lifting a finger to try and get you out of this. Do you know what I've put on the line for you? The shit I've had to deal with, am dealing with, to get you out and you sit there, lie through your teeth and call me a headmistress.'

He looks down at his shoes, which I can hear scuffing up and down under his side of the booth.

'Now, I've got evidence that could very well get you out of here. You want me to take it to the police, you damn well tell me why you were dragged out of that door and beaten.'

He continues staring at the floor, head going left and right, like a kid with ADHD trying to concentrate. Then he looks up at me, stares me in the eye.

'Why do you think, Elaine? Stuff gets sold, just fun drugs, party drugs. They let everyone have a nice time on holiday, you know. I'm doing a service in there. I owed some people money, people that get the stuff, but I'd spent it all, so they wanted to make their presence felt. No big deal, happens all the time.'

'I know all that, but why didn't you tell me?'

'Because they're dangerous. I can't give them up. What's the point of me getting out of here only for them to get me? You've got to keep them out of it, Elaine. You can't go telling on them to the police.'

I'm shaking my head now, staring at him, wondering what he ever did to charm me in the first place.

'And where did you go after they'd finished with you?'

'You know where. Just went home.'

'What direction?'

'What do you mean?'

He's screwing his face up, not sure what I'm getting at.

'Did you head out towards the beach, or back to the strip to get home?'

He shakes his head, still not sure why it matters.

'I can't remember. I'd just taken a kicking. Could have been either.'

'You must remember. It could be important. If I'm to find footage of you that proves you walked away from that place on your own, it will help your case no end, but I need to know which direction you went.'

He pauses for a moment, the gears in his head on rewind. Then he speaks.

'Beach, I think.'

'Thank you,' I say. 'That helps.'

'How much longer?' he asks.

'I don't know, Karim, I just know I need you to be strong. Stronger than you've ever been before. You think you can do that? Hold on in here for me? Give me a week or two?'

He sniffs, and I can hear him pulling the mucus back into his throat. He rubs his eyes and manages something approaching a smile.

'I'll try,' he says. 'I'll really try.'

# 14

Magaluf. 5pm. Back in fun town. But it's very different from Magaluf at 5am.

The strip is almost empty. A few people are enjoying early pints in the baking sun, sitting at tables in front of the pubs, just like it's England, except it's not far off thirty-five degrees.

A few more stragglers wander down, heading for the beach shops at the bottom to buy blow-up lilos, sun cream, flip-flops and T-shirts.

And then there's me: aged fifty-four and walking up the strip in a ripped blouse and baggy trousers. On edge. Looking this way and that, checking whether anyone's watching me or following me. Remembering my last trip here. The bottle of water, the smell of sandalwood, Preacherman.

They wanted to scare me. They succeeded.

They wanted to scare me off. They failed.

I need to find proof that Karim left Kiss on his own after the bouncers turned the camera off. The police have been concentrating on the east door. They didn't know about the west door, where Karim came out. There were other businesses in that alley, clearly visible on the CCTV. They were shut at night but at least some must have security cameras. Do they show where he went? Show what happened to him? Because I'd bet a month's earnings, the police haven't bothered checking.

I walk past the pubs and a string of fast-food joints. Still quiet. A few people munching their way through burgers and chips. One skinny guy in a wide-brimmed sun hat looks the worse for wear. He pokes at a kebab, unsure if he wants to eat it or not. The girl he's with has her head on the table, asleep.

A police car slowly drives past me. Normally, its presence would make me feel secure.

Not now. Not today.

It comes to a stop by a man lying asleep against a wall, in a small patch of shade. An officer gets out and tries to rouse him, shaking him by the arm. He starts to come to life. They have a brief exchange. I can't hear it, but moments later the man stands up gingerly and starts to walk away.

It's different from 5am.

The police are being nice. And no one shouts at me.

Then I see it, the massive bulk of Kiss rising up like a solitary skyscraper in the business district of a Third World city.

I feel a tingle, like a finger tracing its path down my back.

*Dry ice and vomit, tarmac and sandalwood.*

No queue in the plaza out front today. No bouncers, no revellers. No Preacherman. Just an empty square with tatty club flyers blown gently around in the breeze.

I walk past and take a right down Carer Roser alley, where the west door leads to.

The businesses that were shut that night, a Wednesday, are now open. There's a minimart whose sign has lost its 't'. A mother comes out holding the hand of her boy, about five years old, both clutching cans of Coke. There's a small amusement arcade with a few eager punters trying to prove their strength by hitting a punchbag as hard as they can. There's a strip club called Diamonds, which is closed, a kebab shop and, to my surprise, an estate agent.

I look in the window. There are photos of apartments to rent, and investment opportunities, all in Magaluf and Palma Nova. By Majorcan standards, they're cheap, dirt cheap. But who would want to live in Magaluf? I look up at the doorway. There's a CCTV camera.

Inside, a man and a woman, both Spaniards, both wearing suits, are sitting behind computers. The woman, probably thirty, smart and businesslike, looks up and smiles. She asks me, in English, if she can help.

I reply in Spanish.

I explain who I am and why I'm there. It's about the murder of the young British girl down on the beach. A British citizen involved in the case has asked me to check if there's any CCTV from that night which might help him establish where he was.

The woman looks at the man. The man looks at the woman. They have a brief exchange. The man shrugs.

'Why not?' he says. He gestures that I should sit next to him. The office is air-conditioned, but poorly so. There's a fan recycling the warm air. The man smells of aftershave and sweat.

He opens up a web page, types in an ID and a password, and a video window opens. It's the view from the camera above the shop door in real time. It's a tight shot, barely showing any more than the step in front of the entrance. He rewinds it a few seconds to show me entering, then asks what date and time I'm interested in. I tell him and he types it into a search box. A new window opens with the same view of the shop on that night.

He shows me how to rewind and fast-forward and leaves me to it, walking over to an empty desk and logging himself onto a different computer so he can continue working.

I begin scrolling through. I can see the door with the shutter, and a couple of square metres in front of that. I start to fast-forward – twice normal speed to begin with. It's 2am in the shot and not a lot is happening. At 2.03am a man walks past, looks at the shop window, presumably at the property cards, and walks on. Then nothing for an hour. At 3.12am, when Karim was being beaten-up by the bouncers, there's still nothing. At 3.17am, when the Kiss footage cuts out, there's still nothing. The shot's just too close to capture anything of interest. I watch on for a further hour or so, fast-forwarding at four times normal speed. Just after 4am, finally some action: a man comes into the doorway and urinates against the shutter before walking off.

Pointless.

I thank the man and woman for their help and leave.

I go back to the amusement arcade.

The group of people playing with the punchbag machine have left. A big burly guy in a pink polo shirt and shorts is firing a plastic computer machine gun at a screen in the corner. A shorter friend is watching and encouraging him. The shorter guy looks up at me as I come in, then turns back to the game.

A man with glasses is sitting behind a desk near the back of the room, below a sign advertising 'Change' in English. I walk over and explain the same things I told the estate agents. He studies me as I speak, trying to work out if I'm telling the truth, then, after a moment, he shrugs his shoulders and asks me to follow him into the back room.

The room's a mess, covered in box files, bits of wire and multipacks of crisps and fizzy drinks for sale to customers. I'm shown to an aged vinyl desk in a corner with a black monitor, keyboard and computer tower on it.

He types in some commands and brings up the CCTV programme. He clicks on the date I've asked for and it opens up a viewing window. As with the estate agents, I'm invited to roll through it at my leisure.

It's a better shot. It shows the front of the shop and a good shot of the street, including the west door to Kiss. As I watch, the recordings show people wandering up and down the alley as they head to, or spill out of, Kiss. At 3.12am, Karim appears, as before, dragged by the two bouncers to the neighbouring store and held against the shutters. I watch the attack again, in even closer detail. I see more of the bouncers' faces, gazes focused, exertion in their cheeks, pleasure in their eyes, as they administer the beating. I see more of Karim's face as first horror, then pain, then unconsciousness sweep across it.

Then the bigger bouncer leaves, apparently to turn off the CCTV, and from then onwards, on this street, at this time, we're into new territory: footage of moments not caught on any other camera.

My heart's pounding now, my body tense, full concentration on the 12 x 12cm pop-up window on the screen.

I watch as the other bouncer stands over Karim's body, checking for signs of life. He leans in, appears to say something into Karim's ear, stands up, gives him a prod with the toe of his boot, then walks off, back through the west door and inside the club.

The time code ticks on and I fast-forward. Five minutes, ten minutes, fifteen minutes. Karim's body just lies there, face down, immobile, lifeless. My mouth goes dry, so I reach for my water and take another sip.

A few more minutes of fast-forward, then a flicker of life. First the head, lifting ever so slightly, then fading back to the paving. Another minute, and a hand comes up to the face. Rubs it gently, then reaches round protectively to the back of the head.

Two people walk down the alley: a boy and a girl. She's in a short, tight dress, he's in a tight T-shirt and jeans. They walk past the body, stop, take a look. One of them seems to shout something. The hand moves to the face again.

The boy goes over, kneels down on his haunches, says

something. The girl joins him. They help turn Karim onto his back. Then the boy gets his hands under Karim's armpits and drags rather than lifts him into a sitting position, propped up against the shutters.

Karim's got his eyes open now. He feels his face with his hands. Conscious. Thinking. Talking.

There's a discussion with the boy and the girl. I can only imagine it. Asking if he's all right? Is he hurt? What happened? Who did it? Does he want them to get help? Get an ambulance? Karim's mouth opens sporadically, in short, staccato answers, yes and no, I'm guessing. The boy stands up, puts his arms around the girl. They say something else, followed by some more monosyllabic replies from Karim. The couple take a step back. Then another. Is he definitely sure he's all right? They can get him some help. Ring a friend. It's really no bother.

Karim shakes his head. Says something. Then the couple turn away and walk breezily down the alley towards the beach.

Karim stays sitting up, trying to get his thoughts together for five, six, seven minutes. Then he reaches up to the shutter, finds a handhold and pulls himself upright. He tries his legs. One pigeon step. He nearly collapses. Grabs the shutter again. Holds himself steady. Another pigeon step, just one hand on the shutter this time. Then another step and another. One, two, three more steps, then he pushes himself away from the shutter. Takes two more steps this time, no support, growing in confidence, runs his hand over his jaw, then up to his temple. He staggers on up the alley. At first, it's the same stuttering walk, then he finds a few strides. He heads on, away from the beach and the darkness. He's nearly out of shot when he stops and stands still. Has a think, then carries on and leaves the shot.

The time code says 3.49am.

I carry on idly fast-forwarding through the footage, trying to get my thoughts together. I want to check Karim doesn't go back in through that door, the west door, to show he doesn't go back into Kiss, so he couldn't have met Michelle Fraser and taken her back outside and down to the beach.

A couple walk down the alley, heading to the beach. They stop, have a kiss. He tries to put his hand up her skirt, she pushes it away, laughs, and they walk on.

I think about if and how I might tell Miguel. Can I trust him? Or is he in hock to Kiss and the bouncers, and everyone else on the strip?

Maybe I should avoid him, go straight to the Guardia Civil. Show them the CCTV. Inform them about the west door. Do everything I can to show that there's no way Karim could have committed this murder.

A group of three girls walk down the alley. The one in the middle is being held up by the two on either side. They carry her over to the wall of Kiss and hold her while she cranes her head and throws up copiously. I fast-forward more quickly and watch as they wipe her face, laugh, turn and walk back up to the strip.

I could press the nuclear button. Go and see the mayor or the deputy mayor. Show them the footage. Demand they take action. After all, I know the latter quite well. All the Vice-Consuls do. He throws regular drinks parties to keep us happy, keep things smooth, doing his bit to make sure the tourist dollars keep flowing.

But that would be betraying Miguel's friendship.

I know he'd never forgive me if I didn't go to him first with new evidence. Let him handle it from there.

Do I care?

There has to come a time when you draw a line, when you can't do personal *and* professional anymore.

And then the west door opens again.

Slowly at first, and a man appears. I can't see him clearly, but he's in a light-coloured T-shirt, baseball cap; big guy, well built.

He holds the door open and a girl follows him. Hard to make out too much about her. She's young, in hot pants, medium-length hair.

The west door closes, and I see their backs as they walk away from me. She's hanging on to him, barely able to walk, his arm around her waist, either too drunk or too high to walk properly. Both the hot pants and her T-shirt, tied up around her waist, are covered in paint.

Paint Night.

She stumbles, almost falls.

He does his best to stop her hitting the ground, gets his hands under her arms. She takes a moment, then he pulls her to her feet. He's looking at me now. I can see the bottom of his face, his jaw stubbled and tanned. His T-shirt has 'Superdry 72' written prominently across it. As he pulls her to her feet, I can see her as well. Young. Pretty. Brown bob, with lighter tinges at the ends.

*The blood, the face, the neck at that godawful angle.*

Sweat on my forehead. A feeling like someone's slapped me in the face. Heart pounding at my ribcage as if it wants to get out.

It's her. Spaced out, confused, just about smiling, but definitely her.

Michelle Fraser.

He pulls her up, puts his arm around her again and carries as much as walks her down the alley, on their way into the darkness at the end of the shot and the void beyond.

Whoever he is, he's not Karim.

# 15

I walk back down the strip, every muscle tight with nerves, body wired.

The man with the glasses in the amusement arcade agreed to copy the footage and email it to me. It's sitting there, in my email account, somewhere in the cloud, and it's important. It matters. It has the killer on it. It cannot be Karim. Although I don't have a clear shot of his face, this man is much bigger than Karim. He's bulked-out like a bodybuilder. Karim is not. Karim is tall and wiry, this man is stocky.

They are different people.

Another man walked Michelle Fraser down to the beach that night.

I walk on, adrenaline flowing, hyper aware of everything around me. There's a TV crew trying to film a reporter speaking to camera. He stands in an open-necked shirt while the cameraman sets up. A few stragglers stand and watch. He has sandy, floppy hair and skin the kind of white that shows he's newly arrived here, almost certainly having come to cover the story of the missing girl.

I head back to my car, passing Kiss on the way. I weigh up

going in to talk to Kirsten. Michelle came out of Kiss that night, headed down that alley with that man and was then found murdered on the beach. If I have this footage, she might be able to find the man in the Superdry T-shirt on the other cameras inside the club. She might have a clear shot of the man's face.

I need to talk to her.

But going into Kiss and asking for Kirsten could put her in danger. So instead, I walk past quickly. I get to my car, unlock it, slide in the driver's seat and take a long, deep breath. I turn the ignition on and drive off.

~

I should tell Miguel.

I have to tell Miguel.

Show him the footage.

Get Karim released.

But can I trust him? If his officers are wrapped up in the drugs trade here, if he's involved himself, how much help will he be? What was it he said to me?

*You need to be careful with Kiss.*

Or there's the Guardia Civil. The investigating judge.

I could go straight to them.

I need to think about it. Need to work out how to play it, who to show it to.

Karim's still in prison, still recovering from his suicide attempt. Any longer in there and he might try again with more success.

I have evidence that would very likely clear him.

I couldn't live with another young man's pointless death.

I need to make a call.

I've just got to the outskirts of central Palma. I indicate and pull off at the Porto Pi shopping centre. I park in its cavernous underground car park. It's only half full, being early evening, and a few mums and their kids scurry in and out, trying to escape the heat and glare of the sun.

I keep the engine running so my crappy air-con can keep going, pull out a note with Kirsten's mobile on it, and dial.

~

We arrange to meet in the car park at the rear of the disused theme park on the outskirts of Magaluf. It shut down ten years ago after three children were injured on one its rides. One of them never walked again.

The twisting steel spines of rollercoasters still tower over this part of Magaluf, but the rides are mothballed and the park entrances boarded up. At the front, the massive car park is open to the public. A roughly painted sign announces charges of five euros for a whole day's parking, or one euro an hour. A man in a small booth takes my money and I pull into a quiet corner.

Five minutes later, a woman arrives on a motorbike. She chats briefly to the man in the booth and convinces him not to charge her, then taxis her bike over to where I'm parked. She gets out, takes her helmet off and climbs into my passenger seat.

Kirsten.

She seems more energetic today. Her skin is bright and her manner is breezy and confident.

She says hello and I explain why I've called her. Explain that I wanted to see where Karim headed off to that night, so I went in search of more CCTV. Explain that I found material shot after the west door camera was turned off. How I was looking for Karim but found Michelle. How I think I might have found an image of the killer.

She listens to me politely, without any great reaction. Just nods to show she understands. I know she's just waiting. Waiting to see the footage.

I take my phone out of my handbag and bring up the email from the man in the amusement arcade. I open up the file and scroll to the relevant bit of the footage. I play it all, in real time: the two of them walking into shot, her nearly falling over, him picking her up, steadying her, his jaw, his T-shirt.

'Fuck,' she says when his T-shirt comes into shot. 'Jesus Christ,' as his jaw comes into view.

She looks at me, holds my gaze, as if to make sure the footage is for real.

'Fuck,' she says again, and this time smiles. Then her face changes, her eyes narrow, the shine in her cheeks disappears.

She reaches over, takes the phone off me, rewinds the footage and watches it again. She hands the phone back to me, then sinks into her seat, staring out of the windscreen.

She shakes her head.

'You know him?' I ask.

She doesn't react at first, then begins to nod.

'Santiago.'

She's silent.

I don't say anything for a moment, giving her time to think.

'You're sure?' I say.

She nods.

'One of our door team,' she says. 'Creepy as fuck, always perving on the girls, boasting about fights he's been in, people he's hurt, women he's screwed. Nasty piece of work.'

One of the team from Kiss. A rapist and a murderer. And my mind starts to wander. What else might he have been up to? How many drunken, vulnerable women might he have had access to over the years?

'How can you be so sure?' I ask.

She shakes her head, as if fighting off her own doubts.

'The T-shirt,' she says. 'He's got about three he wears regularly. This is one of his favourites. Reckons it shows off his muscles. I'd know him anywhere. The build, the shape. He's a bodybuilder. They all are. Well into his supplements and steroids. Helps him bulk up, he says. Funny thing is, he wasn't on that night, but he still came along. He often does. Likes to try and pick up girls there on his nights off. Chats them up with free drinks from the bar staff – they're frightened of him – everyone is.'

The head-shake again. She looks at me, no smile now, eyes wide open, pupils small.

'If he works there, and it is him that murdered her,' I say, 'he's taking a hell of a risk, walking the girl out like that. Someone might see them, recognise him.'

She shrugs, then turns back to the windscreen, staring out at the giant, faded giraffe above the entrance to the theme park.

'Overconfidence probably,' she says. 'Kiss. Magaluf. Normal rules don't apply here. Cops keep a lid on things and take their cut from the dealers. The dealers are run by the bouncers. Santiago thinks he's bulletproof. Thinks none of them would fit him up. Why kill the goose that lays the golden egg? After all, he's probably got enough shit on them to make sure they wouldn't be policing for very much longer. Whole place is screwed if you ask me. All these kids come out from the UK in their thousands, thinking they're in paradise: a fucking party island where the weather's amazing, the booze is piss cheap and you can dance your night away in a drug-fuelled fury. They don't realise what's going on behind the scenes, how dangerous it is. What a fucking corrupt, Third World war zone they're actually in.'

She looks at her watch.

'I need to get back to work,' she says. 'What are you going to do?'

I stare at her blankly.

'Haven't had a chance to think about it,' I say. 'Take it to the police, I suppose.'

She laughs.

'Be very careful which one you take it to,' she says and smiles. Then she puts her hand on mine. 'You *do* need to be careful, though, with this footage. They're not going to like it. You're prising the lid off something that a lot of people don't want opened. Just think carefully before you do anything.'

'I've got a kid in the Centro Penitenciario who might take his own life at any moment because the police think he murdered this girl. I can't afford to think for too long.'

She nods once before opening the door and putting a foot outside, onto the tarmac.

'Just, you know, do it sensibly,' she says, and climbs out.

She closes the passenger door and gets onto her motorbike, leaving me with a blast of hot air and the video on my phone.

I meet Nick at Plaça d'Espanya. He got a bus in, took him the best part of two hours all told – Santa Luisa is not blessed with great public transport – and he's in a grump. He looks worn out, stubble on his face and red around his eyes.

He looks desperate for a drink.

He gets in the passenger seat and I head towards Santa Catalina.

He's grumpy all the way, morose and uncommunicative in the main, except when it comes to Miriam.

'I don't see why we're going,' he says.

'We've been through this,' I say. 'Things need to change, and couple's counselling has a great record in achieving breakthroughs when people are having problems.'

He gives me a glare before turning to look out of the window.

We don't speak again for the rest of the journey.

'Do you think about Jonathan much?' asks Miriam.

Nick flinches visibly.

We're sitting on matching chairs in her studio room, me nursing a camomile tea, Nick slouching in his seat, refusing anything to drink, trying to stare out of the window at every opportunity.

He stammers something barely audible, looking at the ground, flummoxed and flustered.

'I don't know if you know, but Elaine thinks about him a lot,' Miriam continues.

Nick looks at me, brow furrowed.

I nod.

'All the time,' I say.

'Is it something you do as well?' Miriam asks.

Nick looks at her, staring and glaring, then turns to me, sticking his neck out with a jerk. Then he sinks back into the chair, trying to form words.

'Course I do,' he says finally.

Miriam nods, waits for him to expand.

He doesn't.

'What do you think about with Jonathan?' she asks.

Nick bends his head forward, looks at his shoes, rubs his hair with his hand, rubs his neck.

Then shrugs.

'I sense that you don't find it easy to talk about it,' Miriam says. 'About Jonathan.'

Nick looks up, gives her a fake smile.

'I wonder if a lot of the problems you're having are because of Jonathan. Because of what happened.'

'What problems?' he says, turning to me. 'We don't have problems. Nothing serious. Nothing we can't handle. I mean, I'm sure you'd like us to have problems. That's how you make your money, isn't it? But we're good, thank you.'

Miriam nods, takes her glasses off and puts them on top of her notebook.

'I'm sorry,' she says. 'I don't mean to upset you. I know some of this is difficult, but if we're to make progress in addressing some of the things that are affecting Elaine, and you as well, then it is important we can talk about things.'

He nods slowly for a few seconds, his eyes looking agitated.

'Whatever,' he says, putting his head in his right hand and staring back out of the window.

The session carries on in the same pattern. Miriam and I talk, travel over familiar ground. Nick sits there, pretending not to listen, doing everything he can not to engage beyond the occasional monosyllabic grunt. After half an hour, Miriam calls a halt and suggests we come back another time, after he and I have had a proper 'chat' about what we hope to achieve.

We don't talk on the journey home.

Another sleepless night. Computations and calculations spinning around my head. Anger and frustration at Nick. Stress about Karim and Santiago. Who to tell? What to do?

How do you inform on a police force that might very well be corrupt? There must be agencies. Anti-corruption departments.

I could take it to the press, as I threatened. Give them the footage, get them to take up the cause. But that would be my friendship with Miguel gone, and very possibly his job too.

I could try Miguel. Show it to him. Say that I'll send it to the press if he doesn't take immediate action: release Karim and arrest Santiago. See if he is as honest as he claims to be.

But then I run the risk of giving the police a chance to cover it up. Put myself potentially in harm's way. Give them a chance to tip off Kiss.

I look at my clock.

6.15am.

I get up, shower and change, then head downstairs to make myself a coffee. Nick's still asleep, passed out on the sofa again, beer bottles spread around him, a large wet patch covering his shorts at the groin and spreading onto the cushion.

I pick up my phone and text Miguel.

We need to talk.

~

I'm halfway between Santa Luisa and Palma when my phone goes.

It's sitting on the driver's seat, buzzing away, and I nearly plough into an articulated truck as I reach across to flip it over so I can see who's ringing.

Miguel.

I wait till I'm off the motorway, coming into the outskirts of the city, before I pull over.

I ring back and he answers.

'What do you want to talk about?' he asks.

'Michelle Fraser,' I say. 'There are things you should know about it. But we need to talk face to face.'

~

There's a police firing range halfway between Magaluf and Palma, part of a larger training complex out in the wastelands.

We meet there.

The security to get in is tight, but when I give my name to the officer in the booth by the entrance gate, he waves me through.

Miguel has called ahead.

When I park in front of the low-rise concrete box that is the centre, Miguel's waiting for me, leaning against a pillar and smoking a cigarette. When he sees me, he chucks the cigarette on the ground and grinds it out with his boot.

He greets me as normal, a kiss on both cheeks, breath stinking of recently ingested tobacco, then shows me through to the reception. I'm signed in, given a laminated pass, and swiped into the main building.

He briefly puts an arm around my waist, steers me to a room to the left. It contains a table and chairs, vending machines and newspapers, and a soundproofed picture window overlooking the firing range below. I can see half a dozen lanes with targets at the far end. Most are in darkness. An officer is practising in the one furthest to the left. The soundproofing means we can't hear anything, but can just about make out the targets flapping slightly as they're hit.

'Policia Morales,' Miguel says. 'Just hope your life doesn't depend on him. He's a good guy but a shitty shot.'

He shows me to a chair and offers me a drink, which I decline.

'So you want to talk?' he asks, a half smile fixed to his face.

'Michelle Fraser,' I say. 'I think I know who did it.'

His eyes narrow now as he tries to read me. He nods for me to continue.

'I should probably pass this straight to the Guardia Civil,' I continue, 'what with it being their case. But you're a friend, and I know how much you'd like this yourself. Problem is...'

He's nodding now, imploring me to continue. I can see a vein in his neck pulsing fast.

'I need to know I can trust you,' I say.

Two officers enter the room, ear mufflers in their hands, both carrying equipment bags of some sort. Miguel gives them a look. They read his expression, nod acknowledgement and leave.

'Why wouldn't you?' he asks.

Being difficult. Making me do the work.

I lean back, take a breath. My turn to smile.

'You know how this place runs. How Magaluf runs.'

His face changes, walnut-skinned forehead wrinkling, eyes narrowing.

'What are you getting at?'

I shrug. His turn to feel discomfort.

'The clubs, the pubs, the bars, the discos, nightclubs, strip joints. We all know what goes on there, in the shadows, behind the scenes. We all know the Policia Local can't police it all.'

He puts his hands up, palms out. Tacit agreement.

'I don't know what your officers let go and what they don't,' I say. 'I don't know where your guys draw the line. I don't know how involved some of them are. I don't know how far up the chain it goes.'

His face droops. Disappointed at me. Hurt even.

I lean forward, put my hand lightly on his wrist. Feel him shiver slightly.

'I think I can trust you, Miguel,' I say. 'I think you're one of the good guys. I think, deep down, beneath all your bullshit, you're an honest man.'

Little, almost imperceptible, nods.

'I think that,' I say, 'but I don't know it. Do you understand?'

He takes his arm away from the table, leans back in his chair, purses his lips as if he's about to whistle. Takes a breath. Gets ready.

'You know why I'm here?' he asks.

'On Majorca?'

'Here in Calvià. I've been here for ten years now. Deputy Chief of Police,' he says. 'Before that, I was in Valencia. Policia Nacional. Proper police force. Proper policing. You know why I left?'

I shake my head.

'There was a property development on the edge of the city. Hundreds of people sank their life savings into it. Then there were storms and the complex flooded. Three people died, hundreds more lost the life savings they'd invested in the building. I was a detective. They asked me to investigate. I found out the developer had bribed the mayor to ignore planning regulations to allow the building to go ahead on land that was a designated flood plain.'

He turns back to look at me, his eyes steely and grey.

'My investigation...' He laughs. 'I tried. But you know how it is. Documents go missing, witnesses who are onside one minute suddenly don't want to co-operate, graffiti starts appearing on my locker, saying I'm on the take. Then the mayor calls me into his office. Has a chat to me, quietly, off the record, offers to make me Chief of Police. Says I've worked hard and thoroughly deserve it. But if he does that, he thinks it would be a very good idea to maybe drop the property case. After all, it's costing a lot of money and not really getting anywhere. Can't see any real prospect of prosecutions, and even if there are, they're not going to bring any lives back, are they? Not going to help anyone's savings magically reappear. Gives me a weekend to think about it. I come back Monday morning and tell him I'm sorry, but I won't drop the case. And that's when it happens. The complaint goes in against me. From a female officer I'd worked with. Accusing me of sexual misconduct. That I'd had an inappropriate relationship with her. I'm suspended pending investigation. Property case is dropped. Then, a month in, I'm made another offer. There's a deputy chief job available in Calvià. Transfer there and the complaint gets dropped. What choice have I got? I have, at that time, a wife and family.'

I swallow hard.

'I'm sorry, Miguel. I had no idea. I didn't mean to bring up...'

He waves away my regrets.

'I'm not in this job to make friends, and I'm not taking money from any club or bar in Magaluf or anywhere else. That, unfortunately, is why I'm here in the first place: a dead-end job for a dead-end cop. What I'm saying is–'

'–is I can trust you,' I say, breaking in.

'Yes,' he says. 'You of all people can trust me. Look,' he says, leaning in, an intensity to his expression, 'I know what my department is like, I know the sort of guys I've got on my team. Most of them are good. Some of them less so. I know some of them are on the take. I often wonder why they're pulling up to work in new BMWs and Kawasakis. I know how the place works. I know it goes on. Some of it I have to let go. What choice have I got? I've got a hundred square kilometres and a quarter of a million people to police – I need men. But listen to me,' his hand on my wrist now, 'when it comes to the big stuff, when someone is hurt, or raped, or murdered, then, I promise you, I will turn the place upside down, whoever's involved. You understand?'

Concentration in his eyes. Urgency. Sincerity.

I nod slowly and reach for my handbag. I pull out my phone and open the file from the amusement arcade. Fast-forward it to the couple walking down the alley. Him, baseball cap and stocky. Her, stumbling, having to be held up. The T-shirt. The jawline. The build.

'Recognise her?' I ask.

He nods, his eyes focused on the picture.

'Recognise him?'

Shakes his head.

'Bouncer at Kiss,' I say. 'On his night off. Name's Santiago.'

Looks at me, eyes dancing, colour rushing to his cheeks, breathing fast.

'Karim wasn't the last person to see this girl alive,' I say. 'It wasn't Karim leading her down to the beach.'

One, two, three nods from him, then he begins to stand up.

'Where are you going?'

'To get him picked up,' he says. 'Sooner I do that, sooner your friend can be released.'

I stand up, reach for his wrist again.

'Santiago is likely to be...'

I pause, wondering how to phrase it.

'...known to some of my men?' Miguel chips in.

Three nods again. Thinking.

'We keep it simple then,' he says.

# 16

We're in Miguel's car, an unmarked Audi, service issue for his pay grade, beating a path down dusty minor roads to the outskirts of Magaluf. We pass half-built concrete houses, still empty from the property crash over a decade ago. Here and there we pass a warehouse or faded apartment block. There's little vegetation, just yellowed grass fighting for survival amongst broken sandstone and endless dusty earth.

Miguel doesn't speak. He stares ahead at the road, his eyes burning through the view, jittery but focused. At one point I touch his arm. He jerks, his muscles stiff. He looks at me, then turns back to the road.

I've never seen him like this.

He has an address. Got it with a swift call to his office. A search on Santiago Molina. He was arrested six years ago after beating a man so badly that the victim lost the sight in one eye. The man refused to testify. The case fell apart.

We start to pass bigger apartment blocks. Some are hotels, with names like Seaview, Oceanwave, Queens. They sound more like Eastbourne than Majorca. But that's Magaluf.

Miguel drives without a satnav, negotiating side streets only he knows. He grips the steering wheel so tightly that the fabric bulges next to each of his hands.

He pulls up by a tired-looking, three-storey apartment block built of concrete with red-brick infills.

He stops, says we've arrived and starts to open his door.

'You're just going to go in?'

He cocks his head to one side.

'No backup? No one to help?'

'If you don't trust anyone, best do it yourself,' he says, and gets out of the car.

He looks nervous. Focused but unsure of himself.

Goes to the boot. Opens it. Searches around and pulls out a navy-blue stab vest with 'Policia Local' on it.

I get out, too, and watch as he puts the vest on.

The rip of Velcro. Once. Twice.

Armholes go over one shoulder, then the other. Pats down the straps.

'This guy's a bouncer,' I say. 'A bodybuilder. He takes steroids. You shouldn't do this on your own.'

He puts his hand on the pistol in his belt.

I shake my head.

He ignores me, heads towards the main entrance to the building.

I shouldn't be here. Shouldn't be a part of this. It's outside my job description. Identifies me too closely with the police.

'I can't do this,' I say.

He nods, hands me the car keys and gestures back to his Audi. Then he turns and heads to the communal door.

I wait a moment, weigh things up, look at the air-conditioned car, then turn back to the apartment block and run after Miguel.

~

The main door to the block has a series of numbered buttons on it, and a larger one with 'Call' embossed onto the white plastic. No caretaker. No phone number to ring if you're the postman. Miguel starts pushing combinations of buttons. As many as he can. Hoping to get a response.

A voice crackles through the intercom.

Miguel explains he's a police officer and needs urgent access to the building. Demands they buzz him in, no ifs, no buts.

There's a buzz and a clunk, and Miguel pushes the main door open.

I follow behind.

The communal entrance. Rows of pigeonholes. Junk mail on the floor. A corridor ahead. There's a lift with a 'Fuera de servicio' sign on it – 'Out of order'.

Santiago's flat is number 36.

Miguel says nothing, just heads to the stairs and starts climbing.

Second floor.

Third floor.

Another corridor. Faded maroon paint. Tatty, peeling doors, some numbered, some not. 32, 33, 35.

36.

He stops outside it. Puts his ear to the door. Listens. Turns to me.

Nods.

I stay well back, at the end of the corridor by the stairs. I lean back into the alcove of a door. Able to duck out of sight if I need to.

Miguel's hand goes to his belt. Pulls out his service-issue leather gloves. Puts them on. Left hand, right hand. Tight. Hand back to the belt. Past the pistol to the baton. Pulls it out. Whips his right hand to extend it. Locks in place. Taps hard on the door with it. Once, twice, three times.

Calls out.

'Santiago Molina. Police.'

Eyes look at the floor. Hand grips the baton.

Nothing.

Looks at me. Smiles. Trying to look confident, but his eyes are jittery and nervous.

Taps again: once, twice, three times.

'Santiago Molina. This is the police.'

Nothing.

Takes a step back. Lifts his leg. Sizes up the door.

Kicks it.

It rocks. A chink of light from behind the door. The lock holds.

Lifts his leg again.

Then sounds can be heard.

A voice.

'Okay, okay. Wait a minute.'

Puts his leg down. Right arm out to the side, holding the baton.

The door opens, fractionally at first, then wider. Two inches, three inches. Santiago's face visible. The stubble on the jaw. A broken nose, reset at some point. Deep, tired-looking eyes meet Miguel's. He clocks the uniform. Relaxes.

It's only Policia Local after all.

Opens the door fully. He's stripped to the waist, his gym-honed chest, shoulders and biceps offset by a waistline that's just starting to creep over the top of his jeans, which are tucked into worn workman's boots.

'Santiago Molina?'

Nods.

Miguel's right hand whips round. A thud and a slap as he catches Santiago full in the stomach with the baton. Santiago doubles up, gasping for air.

Miguel swings round behind him, gathering up an arm in each hand, pulling them backwards as his left hand reaches for his cuffs.

Santiago is trying to recover his senses and his composure. He's in a half nelson, then a full one. Miguel is working the arms, trying to get the wrists close enough to cuff.

'Santiago Molina, I'm arresting you under the Law of Criminal Procedure in connection with the recent rape and murder of Michelle Fraser. You have the right against self-incrimination and the right to contact a family member about your detention.'

Then Santiago's thinking clicks into gear. His muscles visibly tense as he crouches with his legs, then pushes up hard, his back forcing itself against Miguel, catching him off balance, pushing him backwards.

There's another thud and a gasp, this time from Miguel as his back crashes against the wall and he slumps to the ground. Then Santiago turns fast, sees Miguel scrambling on the floor, lifts his foot, stamp, stamp, against Miguel's chest. Useless against the stab vest. Changes target. Stamp hard to the head. Miguel's cap is off. Stamp, stamp, stamp against the head. A shout and a grunt of pain. A cut opens up above the eye. Blood spurts, then trickles. Miguel's hands to his face, arms protecting it. Santiago takes aim again, swearing: dirty cop, mother's a whore, filthy cop bastard. Grabs Miguel's right arm by the wrist, pulls and yanks until it comes away from his face, holds it while he aims his foot again. Stamp, stamp, stamp on his face. More blood. Miguel's right eye now a twisted mess. Stamp, stamp, stamp. Miguel's body goes limp.

Santiago raises his foot again for one more, possibly final, blow. Looks left, looks right to check no one's looking.

I duck back into the alcove of the door.

He sees me.

He shouts.

'Son of a bitch.'

Places his foot back on the floor. Feels around Miguel's belt for the pistol. Unclasps it.

My muscles are stiff now, stomach sick, lactic acid burning my veins, limbs not doing what I want them to.

Santiago is working the pistol free. Miguel's a bloody mess on the floor. Opposite me, the stairs.

'Whore. Bitch.'

The stairs.

I dash across, through the fire doors. Don't look back. Down the stairs. Two at a time. Then three.

Hear the door opening above. Loud footsteps.

Workman's boots.

Second floor.

Keep going down. Three steps at a time.

'Whore. Bitch.'

First floor. Ground floor. Rows of pigeonholes. Junk mail. The communal entrance. Main doors in front of me. A touchpad for a key fob to exit. A keypad for a code I don't know.

I have no key. I have no key fob.

Crashing down the staircase now.

I step back a couple of paces. Then a couple more. I watch, lungs feeling like they'll collapse with the effort of breathing.

The fire door near me opens. He comes through. Chest glistening with sweat and blood.

Miguel's blood.

Miguel's pistol held up in front of him. Pointing. Pointing at me. The dark little circle of the barrel staring at me like a tiny black hole. I look at it, look at his face, his wild eyes, his breathing almost as heavy as mine, hatred on his face, adrenaline coursing through him.

Stands there. Pointing it at me. Five seconds. Six seconds. Seven seconds.

I want to close my eyes. Just embrace the blackness. Wait for the inevitable, but the lids stay wide open, transfixed.

Ten seconds. Eleven seconds. Twelve seconds.

I look at him, look at the gun barrel, look at him.

Suddenly I realise he's scared. Undecided. Unsure of what to do next. Trying to decide whether to shoot me or leave me. Working out the odds. Can he kill a harmless middle-aged woman? Kill her as she stands there, defenceless, half the size of him? Kill her in cold blood?

I stare at him, eyes imploring him to leave me, my hands up and to the sides to emphasise I've got no weapons, I'm no threat.

But can he leave me? After what I've just seen him do?

His eyes flicker left, then right. Checking. Thinking.

Then he smiles. Drops his arms down to his sides, his right hand still holding the pistol.

Takes a step towards me. Then another, till he's towering over me, ducking his head down a foot so his eyes are level with mine.

In my face.

'Whore, bitch,' he says, then drags the end of the pistol across his neck in a throat-slashing gesture.

He laughs, then pulls back.

One last stare. Eye to eye, a hint of pleasure, revelling in his dominance. And I see it: see the eyes of the rapist. See the hatred and the burning inadequacy that's led to it.

And suddenly I don't care anymore.

He turns and starts to move away from me, headed towards the front door and the outside world. His back is turned to me, his eyes on the door.

I surge forward, sweep my leg out, hook it round his standing leg and watch him lose his footing and go flying into the main door.

He tries to put his hands out to break his fall, pistol still in one hand. There's a crash as his head collides painfully with the metal handle of the door in front of him.

My hand goes into my handbag, rooting around frantically. I know it's in here. A sharp pain as my finger finds it. Razor sharp. Finger already bleeding.

Ceramic knife.

He's trying to scramble to his feet.

I fall on top of him. Catch him by surprise, my weight taking his arms from under him.

I slash at his hands, slash at his arms, slash at his back, slash at his face.

Razor sharp.

He gets an arm free. Gets it up to his face to protect it. I continue slashing at his hand, slash at his face.

*Whore. Bitch.*

*Murdering, rapist bastard.*

He tries to stand. A great force pushing himself off the floor.

Images of all the pain and misery that I've seen coming out of Magaluf, the fights, the injuries, the assaults, the rapes, the murders. This dirty, disgusting, miserable, hedonistic, hellhole of a place.

I slash at his back, his arms, his face. Slash and slash and slash.

*Murdering, rapist bastard.*

Suddenly my arms are pulled away from me. I resist. Arms stronger than mine pulling me off. Loud, hysterical man's voice shouting at me.

'Leave him, Elaine. Leave him.'

Miguel.

He hauls me off Santiago. Drops his knees in the small of

Santiago's back. Grabs his arms, covered in cuts, blood smeared from shoulder to wrist. Pulls the left arm to the right arm and puts the cuffs on him. Grabs the pistol from the floor. A crackle on his radio. A call out to all units.

Turns Santiago's body over. Blood is spurting from the neck. Two hands, Miguel's hands, push the two halves of a three-inch gap in his neck together with as much pressure as they can muster.

## 17

A junior officer pulls the curtain around the bed and hands me some tracksuit trousers and a white T-shirt with 'Policia Local' written on the right breast.

She nods and leaves.

I take off my blouse, the whole right side sodden with blood, too much for it to have begun drying yet, even now, several hours on from what happened.

I change my filthy trousers for the tracksuit ones, bundle the dirties into the 'hygienic waste only' bin, and return to my perch on the bed.

Finally, I give in to my exhaustion, lift my legs onto the bed, pull a pillow down and lay my head on it.

I put my hands to my face and try to think of something nice. Something to take my mind off things. Happier times. The day we got the house. Getting the antique sideboard for thirty euros in a junk sale in Soler. My wedding day. Nick's proposal, halfway up Helvellyn in a snowstorm. Glasses of wine with friends. Laughter and kindness. My daughter's birth. Making cupcakes together, back home in England. Jonathan, a little boy on my knee, making the sound of a tractor. Jonathan playing football with his friends. Jonathan coming home. Jonathan saying goodbye. Jonathan swinging from his belt by the bedroom light. Nick doubled up and weeping on the floor, refusing to believe it. Nick sitting on the sofa, vomit on his chest, a pool of piss darkening his lap. The girl's neck at that unholy angle. Santiago's eyes as he holds the gun at me. Santiago's hands as I slash and slash at his face.

'Hola.'

The curtain's pulled back six inches.

Miguel. A dressing on this right eye, medical tape and glue on two gashes to his cheek. Tape across the bridge of his nose and ugly black swellings under both eyes.

I sit up, swing my legs off the bed and walk towards him, putting a hand up to his cheek and running it softly over the bruising.

He holds it there for a second, then takes it away.

He lowers himself into the chair and I sit back on the bed.

We sit there in silence for a moment, then I remember the feel of the knife in my hand, my desperate slashing at Santiago's face. I turn to look at Miguel.

'Is he dead?'

He shakes his head.

'He'll never see through his left eye again. And he'll never raise his middle finger either. You severed the tendons there nicely. Other than that, nothing that won't heal. He's never going to be so pretty again though.'

'Good,' I say, and stare at my shoes.

Should be appalled. Should feel guilt.

I feel nothing.

'How's your eye?' I ask.

'It will work again.'

He puts a hand up to the dressing and runs his fingers over it.

'You should have seen his apartment,' he says.

He purses his lips, lets out an almost silent whistle.

'Messy?'

He shakes his head.

'Opposite. Immaculate. Everything lined up in size and colour order, clothes neatly pressed, every surface spotless. Guy must have OCD. Even his drugs were carefully laid out in order. Makes that part of the case a lot easier. Just had to follow the bottles alphabetically. Had a whole drawer of GHB.'

'What happens now?'

'He'll go in front of a judge tomorrow, followed by a trip to Centro Penitenciario afterwards. Then, with any luck, a trial and a much longer stay at the Centro.'

'Good.'

I turn to look at him. He's impassive, as ever.

'Has he admitted it?' I ask.

'Yes and no,' he says.

I frown, waiting for some more explanation.

'He admits he had sex with the girl. Doesn't see it as rape. Convinced she wanted it.'

'He doesn't see it as rape?'

Miguel shakes his head.

'Admits he gave her GHB but claims it was recreational – that she knew. Without her testimony, it's going to be hard to prove that's not true. Which is why the Guardia Civil are trying to get him on the murder.'

'Has he admitted killing her?'

He snorts.

'No. He's adamant on that one. Says he had nothing to do with that. Says they made love on the beach. That's the phrase he uses: "made love". That he left her to sleep it off and went home. I reckon he's gambling on his defending counsel agreeing something with the prosecuting judge. Thinks we'll get tired of trying to prove murder, he'll choke for the rape and get a lesser sentence.'

'Will you?'

'Not a chance. He's going to take the whole lot and everything else we and the Guardia can pin on him. They're running his DNA through the system now. Could be linked to God knows how many other offences. There's no shortage of unsolveds in Magaluf, particularly rapes. One-night, drunken, holiday assaults where no one can remember anyone's name. We'll see what comes up.'

I nod and sit there, thinking, looking at my shoes, studying my wounds, not saying anything.

'Thank you, by the way,' he says eventually.

'For what?'

'Stopping him. That was clever. Stupid, but clever. Saved me some blushes. Wouldn't have looked good if he'd got away.'

He doesn't mention that I probably saved his life just by being there. Doesn't mention that Santiago could have shot me dead.

'I won't ask why you had a ceramic knife in your handbag,' he says. 'Just tell the court you like to cook.'

'How about you?' I ask. 'You must be in some trouble, going out on your own like that, no backup, getting your pistol stolen.'

He shrugs, unfussed.

'I'm the Deputy Chief of Police – they're not going to do much to me. I've brought in a murderer, and half of my officers are so compromised, I can't see them kicking up much of a fuss.'

'What about Karim?' I ask, and a hint of a smile creeps into the corners of his mouth.

'He's in the process of being released,' he says, before crossing his arms and adding, 'on bail.'

I sit up, fix him with a stare.

'For what?'

'What we found in his flat. Plenty in there. Pills, powders and potions.'

'You can't be serious? You've just had the poor kid in jail for a murder he had nothing to do with.'

He looks away, thinks for a moment.

'We have to go through due process,' he says, eyes narrowing, face hard. 'Unofficially, I'll do what I can to try and get the drug charges waived, but ultimately it's not my decision.'

We sit there in silence for a moment, eyes looking past each other, thoughts elsewhere.

I break the silence:

'So it ends here?'

'It ends when he gets sent down. I just hope we get hits on his DNA. Guy's a nasty bastard. You should have gone for his jugular. Would have saved us a trial.'

He looks me in the eye. I'm looking for the usual twinkle.

There isn't one.

# 18

We begin with another meeting. It's four days on from that ghastly day and all seven of us are sat around the boardroom table, Vanessa on the video link, giving us her twopenn'orth.

Louise moans on about the workload. Rodrigo sits there, doodling and smirking. Soraya and Duncan listen attentively. For all they whinge, it's clear that things are beginning to calm down since the girl's been found and Santiago got picked up. The press have submitted their final copy, the TV crews have wrapped their reports and gone home. Bryony, brought over from the consulate in Ibiza to help with our workload, is preparing to go back there. Louise might be moaning, but we all know she'd rather deal with lost passports than the tabloid press.

Everyone wants to know about the arrest of Santiago. I've said nothing, but word has got out that I had a hand in it. Chinese whispers have suggested it was me who arrested him, that I nearly killed him with my own bare hands. I play it down. The good news is that he's off the streets and in custody. The good news is that we've found Michelle's killer. The good news is that her parents will now get some closure.

And closure for me, too, I hope. The killer found, safely under lock and key. The girls of Magaluf a good deal safer now. Loose ends tied up. Well, sort of.

There's still the Crude Hood, of course. We know that wasn't Santiago – clear that was a Brit – but that was four years ago. Not much we can do about that now, but at least the clear and present danger has passed.

Vanessa congratulates me on my close liaison work with the police – a great example of multi-agency working. There's some nodding around the table.

Then we move on.

Kayleigh Walsh is back with her parents now. She's still not spoken about what happened to her that night, and spends a lot of her time sedated. The doctors have brought in psychologists from Madrid to help her deal with the trauma. Police are hoping to question her soon. The main thing is that she, too, is safe and sound.

Vanessa says there's a new poster campaign coming, aimed at spreading awareness of the risks holidaymakers might face out here. It tries to encourage better behaviour, warns that Spanish jail sentences are just as harsh as our own. The plan is to put posters up in every bar in the main tourist districts. That means someone traipsing around a lot of places in Magaluf.

No one volunteers.

I suggest Duncan.

He glares at me as politely as he can.

The meeting wraps up.

It's almost 8 o'clock, when reception opens to the public.

We head to our desks as the first tired and sunburnt British citizens start to filter into the waiting room, carrying their bumbags, money belts and plastic carriers full of papers. The room stinks of sun cream and beer.

Soraya opens a counter window and gets to work. I'm just checking through my email when there's a thump against my desk. Louise apologises as she dashes past. She's in a fluster, trying to find something. I look over at the front desk. There's a big black guy there, must be at least six foot two, head shaved, his bulk extending to a big stomach that's imperfectly hidden by the plain, oversized black T-shirt. He catches my eye, looks nervous, glances around, then back to me. He smiles sarcastically, revealing two gold teeth on either side of his mouth.

It's a face I vaguely recognise.

Louise's back at the front desk, bounding up with an envelope in her hand.

'Sorry for the delay, Mr Williams,' she says.

I try to place the face, but the name Williams means nothing to me. Then the gold teeth click and I realise, it's the DJ from Kiss: Dante. Williams must be his real name. His first name is probably just as deathly dull as his surname. Brian or Kevin, or something like that. I start to google 'Dante DJ'. It comes high up in the search results. 'Dante, born Derek Williams, Wolverhampton, 1974.'

I look back at him. He's standing over the front desk, full height, assertive in a 'do you know who I am' sort of way – more Dante than Derek right now.

Louise opens the envelope, produces the cream emergency travel document, and passes it through the serving tray.

'It's valid from today and will get you home. Just show it to the border force when you arrive in the UK. They'll take it from you, but will let you through.'

Dante opens the document at the photo page, studies it, then briefly looks back up at Louise and nods.

'That'll be 118 euros,' she says, and he looks at her again. He reaches into his pocket, produces a roll of euro notes, counts some out and passes them back through the tray, not saying a word. Louise thanks him and runs off to get his change.

He looks towards me again, then narrows his eyes. I look away quickly, concentrate on my computer screen. I see the little icon for the Plato database, the one we use to check people's passport history when they're applying for a temporary one.

I know I shouldn't, but I open it up, type 'Derek Williams' and his date of birth into the search box, then wait for it to bring up the results. There's a full list of his travel history under that passport. It's lengthy. He's been all over the world. The USA dozens of times, Dubai, Australia, Turkey, Russia, France, Singapore, Canada, Japan, Iceland, Poland... the list goes on and on. Spain crops up numerous times too.

Dante, one of the top twenty DJs in the world.

Dante, who lost his passport, the night Michelle Fraser was murdered.

Something flickers in my stomach, a little buzz in my skin.

I look over to where he's standing – where he *was* standing.

Dante has gone. There's now someone else standing in his place: an older guy, in his sixties, red in the face, skin weathered by years of drink and Spanish holidays.

He, too, has been here before.

McLellan and the damn card.

I can hear him through the counter speaker.

'No, not you, her.'

He's pointing at me.

'Her,' he says. 'You. You're the only one with half a brain cell in this place. I want to speak to you.'

Too late, I've caught his eye. I nod for Soraya to stand aside and go over.

'Mr McLellan, how are you?' I say as breezily as I can manage.

'Pretty bloody unhappy,' he says. He's not shaved and his stubble has bits of food trapped in it from his breakfast.

'Is it the card?'

'Why else do you think I'd be in this shithole, talking to you lot?'

'Have you not heard anything?'

I look across the office for Rodrigo, but he's not emerged from the meeting room yet. He's probably seen McLellan and is keeping his distance.

'Let me find out the latest, sir,' I say, switching the intercom off before he has a chance to respond.

I walk through to the kitchen, where Rodrigo's standing studying his phone while nominally making a coffee.

'The card.'

He looks up, nods, then looks back at his phone.

'What about it?' he drawls, thumb scrolling his screen.

'The man who wants it is here. Again. Now I don't know where it is, or what your excuse is, but it better be damn good, because if it isn't, you're going to go out there and apologise both personally and on behalf of this consulate.'

He continues to look at his screen. Takes his time, as snide and disrespectful as he can be. Then he slowly looks up.

'It's in my desk drawer,' he says, and turns back to his phone.

There's a whistle from the coffee machine as it clicks to say it's done. Rodrigo turns around and casually takes his cup out.

I can feel my cheeks burning up, red. I don't want to be here, don't want to spend another second in this wretched man's company.

I stride back to the office. McLellan's watching me, piggy eyes narrowing, just waiting for an excuse to kick off. I hold a finger up to ask for a moment, go over to Rodrigo's desk, pull the top drawer out. There's an old computer mouse and some tired-looking stationery.

Second drawer.

A large brown envelope with a crest on it, already opened. I look inside. There's a second envelope, thicker, high-quality paper, another crest on top.

The palace.

I pull it out and walk over to the counter. I put it into the connecting drawer and slide it over to McLellan before pressing the intercom.

'Your card, sir.'

He pulls it out of the drawer, opens the end, studies the envelope. Stares at the crest.

'My apologies for the delay, sir, but we have been very busy. Now if you'll…'

'Thank you,' he says, and catches my eye, the pupils softening, the fury gone.

'That's absolutely fine, sir.'

Sometimes it's not all bad here. Sometimes there are nice moments. Those brief seconds that keep you going in this damned job.

He looks up.

'And will someone still be able to come and present it to her?' he says. 'You know, on behalf of the Queen. It would mean the world to her, it really would.'

I look at him, trying to read him, trying to understand how a piece of paper from an institution over a thousand miles away could mean this much to anyone.

'Of course,' I say. 'I'll come myself, sir.'

'Oh, that really would, well, that would be just perfect.'

*Sometimes, it's not all bad here. Sometimes there are nice moments.*

'When is it?'

'This Saturday,' he says. 'In Santa Maria del Cami. Just up the MA13 motorway. I can guarantee a good spread, and you being there would be just... well, fantastic.'

Saturday. In Santa Maria del Cami. What the hell was I thinking? Caught in the moment like a soppy old auntie. Can I get out of it? Surely an excuse.

The eyes soft and pleading. A grown man showing weakness.

'Of course, sir. I'll be there.'

He smiles at me, thanks me with a sort of half bow and makes his way out of the waiting room, envelope clutched tight to his body.

I go back to my desk and start going through my emails. Nothing spectacular. A man in Deià wants to marry his Filipina wife. Wants us to register it. Not something we can do. A Spanish citizen in Palma with a British mother wants to apply for a passport. He'll have to go direct to the UK passport office. A retiree in Soler has died. I make a note to take them off our database.

My mind drifts off. After everything that's happened, it's hard to come back to the daily grind of consulate life. Hard to get excited about it. Not that it was ever that thrilling. I could do with some time off. A week on Menorca maybe. Take Nick. Have some proper time together. Talk about... stuff. See if we can address a few things. Try to rekindle something.

If only we had the money.

I think of Santiago staring at me, the gun in his hand pointed my way, that strange mix of hatred and excitement, pleasure and uncertainty in his eyes. Is that how he looked at Michelle as he attacked her on the beach? Were they the same eyes in the holes cut out of that hood?

My mobile goes. I answer it. It's a woman, asks for me by name.

'It's Helen Walsh here. Kayleigh's mum,' she says hurriedly, voice moving quickly over the syllables.

'Helen, hi,' I say. 'How are you? How's Kayleigh?'

'Well, that's the thing, you see. She's okay. Much better, thanks. She's off the sedatives and speaking. Says she wants to talk, tell us what happened that night. But she said she wants to tell you. Says you'll understand. Wants you to be there. Says it's important.'

## 19

The Walshes are staying at the Hotel Parador, on the edge of their beloved Palma Nova.

*A good family place this.*

It's a move up in the world: a plusher hotel, with two outdoor pools, an all-you-can-eat restaurant, children's play area and putting green. It has its own nightclub, Infinity. Means parents don't have to leave the complex to party. They even offer a babysitting service. I decide it's best not to mention either facility to the parents.

Helen seems happier. The pallid complexion and bloodshot eyes are gone now. She looks rested, colour back in her cheeks, flesh back on the bones. Mike looks much as before: full of himself, his rotund belly indicating too much good living and too many extra-large meals.

They have a three-bed apartment in the 'Buckingham Wing'. Mike explains this is the most upmarket block in the complex, reserved for those willing to pay a little bit more.

When we get to the room, it becomes clear how they can afford it. There's someone else with them today. I'm introduced to a thirty-something, red-headed woman with a mean-looking, thickly made-up face, and green eyes that would be pretty if they weren't staring at me so intensely.

She introduces herself as Danuta Barnes, a senior reporter with the press association.

She's here for Kayleigh's story too. Kayleigh's agreed to speak, and Mum and Dad have agreed Danuta can have the exclusive. I don't ask how much she's spent to get it, or how Kayleigh feels about her presence. It's clear from Helen and Mike's demeanour that this is just the way it's going to be.

We sit in the main living room. It has a sofa, armchairs, big television and a well-stocked fruit bowl on a coffee table.

I'm offered a mango by Mike, but decline.

'She's very nervous,' Helen tells us. 'She's still struggling to come to terms with... everything. She's shy anyway, but, you know, with all this.'

She gestures around the room.

Danuta starts making notes.

'That why she wants you here,' she says, looking at me. 'Says she trusts you, what with everything you did to help her. Says she feels safe with you. Happier to talk if you're here.'

I feel myself blushing and I look at the floor. Danuta eyes me up, probably wondering if there's a story in it. The Vice-Consul who's helping keep us safe. She quickly looks away.

'Can we see her?' she asks.

Helen nods and stands up. Asks us to follow her.

'Just a moment,' I say. 'I really think the police should be here for this. Anything she says could be of material importance to a criminal investigation.'

A baleful look from Danuta, eyes closing heavily.

'Until she speaks, we don't know if there's anything the police will want to know,' she says, and then forces something approaching a smile. 'We haven't got a clue what happened to her. Could be nothing for all we know.'

'If it's nothing, why are you here then?'

Her eyes narrow at me. She looks at Helen.

'Who is this woman?' she demands. 'What's she got to do with any of this?'

'She found her,' Helen says. 'We owe her that.'

I stand up, clutching my handbag.

'Look, I didn't ask to be here. This is nothing to do with my job. I came as a favour to Kayleigh, but I'm not here to aid and abet a tabloid news story.'

I start making for the door. Helen's after me, grabbing me by the arm, turning me around.

'Please,' she says. 'Sorry. Kayleigh asked for you because you did so much for her. If you could just hear her out.'

I can't work out if the pleading in her eyes is about keeping Danuta on board, or me. Either way, the whole thing feels grubby, wrong.

'I just don't feel comfortable doing this without a police officer present,' I say. 'Something deeply worrying has happened to Kayleigh. A lot of police resources went into finding her: days of officer time. I just think they need to be the first to know. And neither of us knows what will happen to the information if she,' I gesture my head towards the journalist, 'gets hold of it first.'

She's about to respond when the bedroom door opens, and Kayleigh's head peeks out. She looks different. Washed and scrubbed, younger now, with hair pulled into a neat ponytail. Much more like her actual age: a little girl doing what little girls do.

She doesn't smile, just looks at us, studying us nervously. Then she sees me, blinks and smiles.

She comes over to me, takes my hand in hers.

'I've been desperate to thank you,' she said. 'You were amazing.'

There are tears now, running down her cheeks. She moves

forward and embraces me. I put my arm around her and hold her close. I can hear a tapping behind me. Danuta is taking photos of us with her phone. I glare at her and she fakes another smile.

'Kayleigh, take a seat,' Helen says.

She leads her over to the sofa and Kayleigh curls up on one side. Danuta sits opposite in a maroon armchair. She opens a voice-recording app on her phone and places it on the table.

'I'm going to record this, all right?' she says, starting it off before anyone answers. 'Now I know you've been through a lot,' she says. 'No one wants to put you through any more stress.'

Yeah, right.

'We all want the best for you.'

She looks around at the four of us, checking we're on board, bringing us all into her conspiracy.

If I'm going to object, I need to do it now.

If I don't want to be a part of this, I need to say something now.

If I don't want to be present while this happens, now's the chance to walk away.

I sit still.

Danuta nods to Kayleigh and she starts to speak.

'The day before, we was on the beach,' she says.

'Before what?' Danuta interrupts.

'Before it all happened. We was on the beach. Me and Stace, Marie and Kerry. All just hanging out, you know. Sunbathing and messing around, doing a bit of swimming and that. Anyway, we get talking to these guys, me and Kerry did. Stace wasn't there. Just us two and them. And they seemed really nice, right. We played a bit of football with them and chucked a Frisbee around and it was like a giggle, right.'

Helen's nodding and Dad's looking disinterested. Danuta is leaning in, listening closely to every word.

'What guys, Kayleigh? Can you tell us any more about them?' she asks.

'There was about five of them. There was Sean and Taylor, they're the only ones whose names I remember. But there was a couple more of them. Nice. Sweet. I got on well with Taylor. He was really sweet to me. Seemed to take a real interest in me.'

'They were English then? White?' Danuta interrupts.

'Yeah. Most of 'em. One wasn't, you know, wasn't white, but they was all British.'

Danuta nods and Kayleigh continues.

'So we was playing and getting on well and we all got talking and, like I say, I was getting on really well with Taylor. I think he kind of liked me cos he kept talking to me, asking me loads of questions about what I liked doing and that. And I thought he was cute and that.'

She starts to blush and I remember again how young she is.

'And then we get talking about what we're doing later, and Taylor says they're all going to Kiss and if we want to, we can go with them. Well, I'm quite keen but Kerry, she doesn't fancy it. Bit scared of things like that. But I really want to go because I like Taylor and, you know, it sounds like fun and that.'

She looks at her mum: 'But I know you'll never let me go someplace like that.'

'Christ's sake, Kayleigh, course not. You're only twelve.'

'That's right,' Mike says, the first time he's spoken.

'But I think, if I don't go, he's not going to be interested in me.'

'How old was he, love?' Helen asks. 'And how old's he think you are? Inviting you to nightclubs.'

'I don't know. He's like, eighteen or nineteen maybe.'

'So what happens then?' Danuta says, impatient, trying to bring Kayleigh back to the story.

'So, I know I shouldn't have cos I know you wouldn't want me to, but I really wanted to go.'

She pauses, tears forming again now. Helen puts her arm around her. Danuta's face is getting tauter with every interruption.

'So?' she says, with a studied attempt at softness.

'So I decide I'm going to try and go, right. So I wait till you've gone out and me and Stace are in our room. And I wait till she's asleep, and then I get up, put some clothes on and I open the window and go out that way. It's facing out the front, so I don't have to go past reception or nothing.'

Helen is shaking her head again, playing the dutiful mother now.

Kayleigh continues:

'So I go to Kiss. Go looking for Taylor and the others.'

'You got in?' her mum asks, the eyebrows raised again.

Kayleigh nods.

'They didn't ask how old you were?' Danuta asks.

A shake of the head.

'Didn't ask to see ID?'

Another shake.

'Didn't question why you were there on your own?'

More shakes.

'Where d'you get the money from?' her dad asks.

Kayleigh makes a face.

'I spent what I had. Only had to pay the entry, and it was Paint Night, so half price for girls.'

It's now Helen who's shaking her head. More overt displays of disgust. Danuta is looking twitchy again.

'So you go inside,' she says.

Kayleigh nods.

'And then what?'

'I went looking for Taylor and the other lads. Took me a bit of time. It's proper dark there, even in the main rooms. So many people. But I found them and said hello and at first they seemed nice and that. So we had a few drinks and they... well.'

She looks at her mum nervously. Helen's eyes are narrowing and Kayleigh's hesitating, checking what she's about to say. Danuta spots this and leans in. I can smell her now, a mixture of designer perfume, fags and chewing gum.

'What else, Kayleigh? It's really important you tell us everything.'

Kayleigh looks at Danuta, then at her mum, then back to Danuta.

'Did they give you something, Kayleigh?' Danuta asks, putting her hand on Kayleigh's in an attempt at reassurance.

Kayleigh starts to get upset again. Face cracks up and cheeks red. Her mum pulls her in for a hug. Mike's forced to lean back.

'Don't worry, Kayls,' Helen says. 'Just take your time.'

I lean forward, look Kayleigh in the eye.

'You don't have to tell us anything you don't want to,' I say. I can sense Danuta's eyes boring into the back of my head. I glance at her and she stares daggers. I look back at Kayleigh.

'It's important you feel comfortable. We can take a break. Come back another time.'

Danuta again:

'Might be best to get it all off your chest now, Kayls,' she says, my skin shivering as she copies Kayleigh's mum's nickname.

'There, there,' Helen says.

Kayleigh sniffs hard, and I can hear the mucus rattling in her nostrils. She wipes her face with her sleeve.

'They gave me some shots. Don't know what they were. I know I shouldn't have, but I didn't want them to think...'

She breaks down again, and her mum's in tears now too. Mike looks away in disgust, then turns back and shakes his head. Tries a new tactic.

'It's so important you tell us things like this, Kayls,' he says. 'The more we know, the more we can help you. If people are doing bad things, we need to know.'

The sniff again. Some more hugs and more 'there, there's from Helen. Then, Kayleigh's ready again.

'They gave me something. Not sure exactly what it was, but they were all taking it, so I did too. Put it in my drink and told me to drink it. And at first it was all right, but then, I don't know, they sort of stopped talking to me. Kind of lost interest. And then Taylor was talking to this other girl and he sort of avoided me. And I got upset, so I went to the toilet and when I came back, he'd gone off somewhere. I tried to talk to his friends, but they just ignored me pretty much. So I was just stood there, on my own, and I was upset, and then I started to feel a bit funny. Don't know if it was what I'd drunk, but I felt sick. So I went to the toilets but there was a queue with all these girls, and I couldn't wait, so I was just sick there, and it got on some of the girls in the queue and they were screaming at me. Really horrible. And that made me cry and I felt awful. Then the bouncers came and they weren't happy at me cos of the puke and that, so they told me to leave and I got upset again, which they didn't like. One of them gets me by the arm and takes me to the front door and tells me to go home and get some sleep. They ask me if I'm with anyone, and I say no. They ask if I want to ring anyone and I'm just thinking of your face, Mum, and I'm like, the last person in the world I want to ring is you cos I think you'll go mental at me.'

And she's in tears again, the two of them clutching each other, exorcising their demons jointly. Danuta is scribbling furiously now, the story probably forming in her head already: 'Twelve-year-old girl given drink and drugs in party town where anything goes'. Another round of soul-searching, another push by HM Government to try and get the message out there about the risks of partying abroad.

Kayleigh stops sobbing and asks for a drink of water. Her mum looks at her dad, who heads off to the kitchen.

'You're doing really well, Kayls,' Danuta says, not even looking at her. 'It's so important that you tell us this,' she repeats, channeling Mike from earlier. She looks calmer than she has since I've been here – happy that she's beginning to get her money's worth.

'So what happened after you left the club?' she asks.

The water arrives and Kayleigh takes a long drink from the glass. She focuses again.

'So I leave and all I want to do is get home. I'm not exactly sure of the way and I'm still feeling a bit funny, but I know that if I follow the beach all the way along, I'll get back to the hotel, cos that's the way I've come, right? So I head down there, down a side street, can't remember which. By now my legs are starting to feel really, you know, like they don't work too well, and my head's hurting and I just want to get home. I get to the beach...'

Her eyes are wide now, straining with the effort of remembering. She reaches out for her mum's hand and grabs it, squeezing it so hard it starts to go white.

'And I have a bit of a sit-down, you know. Just need to get my breath back, work out where I am, get up the energy to get myself home. And I'm sat there on the beach, in the darkness, and after a while I see a shape sort of coming towards me, and I start to get a bit worried at this point, but then I see who it is.'

She coughs and Helen encourages her to drink some more water.

Danuta is leaning so far forward, I think she's going to fall off the sofa.

She's trying to catch Kayleigh's eye, nodding at her to keep going.

'As they get a bit nearer, I can see it's a girl. She's got brown hair and a blue dress on and she's walking towards me, a bit funny.'

'Funny?' I say.

'Yeah, she's sort of stopping and starting, going this way and that a bit.'

'Can you remember anything else about what she looked like?' I ask. 'Her face, her clothes?'

She shakes her head.

'It was really dark, so it was hard to see, and that's the thing, cos as she got a bit nearer, she was coming towards me and that's when the man appeared.'

She swallows now and starts to cry again, burrowing her head into her mum's lap. Big, heaving sobs, her body shaking, terrified.

Danuta stares at her in silence. Her dad just gawps, his eyes wide open, pupils like dinner plates.

We all sit and wait in silence. I'm about to suggest we come back later when she sits up again and wipes away the tears.

'He just came at her from behind,' she says.

She takes a deep breath. Steadies herself, then continues.

'He just grabs her, round here,' she says, demonstrating with her own arm around her stomach. 'And he drags her. I didn't know what was going on. I was just so shocked, and then he's just pulling her, dragging her, further down the beach. And he like hits her or slaps her or something. Hard. It must have really hurt. And then he's got her, dragging her further onto the beach. And I can see something against her neck and I know it's a knife. And he pushes her down, face in the sand, and I can barely breathe and he's sitting on her back or something. And I see him take the knife away cos he needs both hands now. He's got her wrists and he's trying to do something with them. And he's pulling at her skirt, pulling it up and trying to get at her knickers, and he's pulling at his trousers, getting his, you know out, and I can hear him saying things to her, horrible things. I don't know why at this particular moment, but I just screamed, and that's when he looks around and sees me and that's when I see, for the first time...'

Her eyes are wide again, pupils vast, staring ahead at the memory.

'There's this sack. This sort of hood thing over his head with two holes for eyes. I see him pick the knife up and he puts it to her throat, and then he looks back at me and I realise if I don't do something, he's going to come and hurt me. That he ain't right. That he's evil. So I just get up and I start to run.'

She looks at me, then to Danuta, then to her mum, then back to me. We each nod, trying to read her thoughts.

Eyes wide. Pupils dilated.

'I run away. Just leave her. My legs aren't feeling all that good and I'm slipping a bit, then he just hits me from behind, absolutely smashes me into the sand, his weight on top of me, grinding me into the beach. And then he's got my arms and he's trying to put this plastic thing on them, tie them together, and I can feel the knife on my neck now and I just lie there, trying not to move. Then he's in my ear, growling at me, "Stay still, bitch, stay fucking still," and I don't know what's going on. And he pushes me down, face in the sand, and I can barely breathe and he's sitting on my back or something. And something clicks in my head and I know I've got to try and stop him, so I start screaming and struggling and shouting, and it's hard cos he's trying to tie me up and my body's not doing what I want it to, but I manage to make some noise. That's when he punches me again. Oh my God, it hurt. Hurt so bad. Starts calling me things. Pushes my head into the sand so it's getting in my mouth, and I hate that, hate sand in my mouth. It's like a fear of mine, so I'm struggling and trying to shout and he's on top of me and that's when...'

She looks up at us, sees how we're looking at her.

'She just comes out of nowhere, launches herself at him. The woman he'd been fighting with earlier. And she gets him somehow and pushes him off me. So I roll over and I scramble to my feet, and there's the two of them just next to me and they're sort of struggling. She's sort of hitting him and screaming at him, and he's got his hands up to stop her and he's got this hood on. And then I see his hand and it's still got the knife in it and he pushes it sort of up and round.'

She stops talking as she tries to gulp in air, the horror of what she's recalling written starkly across her face. Her mum puts her hand to her shoulder and squeezes. Kayleigh catches her eye, gives her a slight nod, then continues.

'I can see her just lying there, blood everywhere, then something takes over and I run as fast as I can and pray my legs keep working. I go to the nearest buildings. I know he's right behind me. I run round this small wall, which isn't easy cos he's tied my hands with this plastic tie, and I go round the back and I find this tiny gap between some blocks. I don't even know what it is, but I just pull myself into there as quickly as I can and I lie there, just praying he doesn't find me. I keep as quiet and small as I can, just hoping, praying that he can't find me. Stay there for ages, not daring to move. After a while, I manage to get my hands loose from the plastic thing. And I just sit there and wait. Wait until you come along.'

She looks at me. There are no more arm movements now. She's just a ball of tears wrapped up in her mother's arms, shaking and sobbing.

I lean forward, lower my voice.

'This man,' I say, 'the one in the mask. You say he said things to the girl, said things to you.'

She nods in between the tears.

'Can you remember what he said?' I ask.

She nods, sniffs hard again, composes herself.

'He kept calling her dirty. Said she was a bitch. A dirty bitch. And he called her a slut. A dirty slut. Called me a bitch, told me to stay still, do what he said.'

Danuta looks at me, eyebrows raised. She makes another note.

I nod encouragingly.

'What did his voice sound like?' I ask. 'Did he have an accent at all?'

She looks at me for a second.

'An accent?' she asks.

I nod.

'Did he sound Spanish? Or foreign?'

She frowns, looking confused. Then shakes her head.

'He was, you know, English,' she says.

'English?' I say.

She nods.

'You're sure?'

She nods again. Big nods. Then buries her head in her mother's lap once more.

But my mind's racing, trying to compute everything I've heard. The man, the crude sacking hood, the two women, the rapes, attempted rapes, the violence and brutality, the credible witness to the attack. I come to the conclusion that the man she's talking about, the man with the English accent, can't possibly be Santiago.

I feel the cold ripple through me again, the sweat under my arms and on my forehead.

Danuta looks at me, her skin drained, concern on her face for the first time. I nod back and she swallows.

Then she turns to Kayleigh.

'Take a few minutes,' she says. She then gestures to me with her head, stands up and heads for the door. I reach over, put a hand on Kayleigh's back.

'You're brave, Kayleigh. So brave. You take your time,' I say, not sure if it's the right thing, and follow Danuta.

She's standing outside the apartment building, fag in her hand. I stand next to her and smoke wafts into my nostrils. I haven't smoked since my teens, but there's a part of me that wants to ask her for one right now.

She just stands there, staring out, wanting me to do the talking.

'So?' I say.

She turns to me. Shrugs her shoulders. Takes a drag on her fag.

'That's the murdered girl she's talking about, isn't it?' she says.

'We don't know for sure,' I say.

She looks at me, then looks away.

'We'll have to get the police here now,' I say. 'They need to know about this.'

She doesn't reply, just smokes away, thinking.

We both stare out at the sky, broken sporadically by small wispy clouds.

'You're going to get this picked up by one of the papers, aren't you?'

She looks at me and nods before throwing her cigarette onto the ground. She doesn't even crush it with her shoe, just watches it as it burns down to the filter, then extinguishes itself.

'I know it's a great exclusive,' I say. 'I know it's a great story for you guys, but the second you publish, the whole press pack will be down here and this guy will go to ground. We have to get the police onto this before something goes to print.'

She looks at me. It's hard to read her. No great emotion on her face, just stares at me like we speak different languages and she can't quite understand what I'm saying.

She moves away from the wall, starts to move towards the door of the apartment building. Then she stops and turns to me.

'I'm due to file something on this for tomorrow morning.'

She sniffs, then blows her nose into a tissue she has tucked into her sleeve.

'I'll put it off a day,' she says, then heads back inside.

Inspector Nabarro is here within the hour, accompanied by Miguel. Kayleigh runs through the same story she told us, with less emotion this time. The club, the walk, the beach, the assault, the struggle, the stabbing. They record it and I translate as she goes. They don't say much, just sit there like coppers, pretending not to show any emotion. I can tell they do care. The speed with which Nabarro makes his notes and that Miguel chews his gum makes it pretty clear.

At the end of it, they thank Kayleigh, tell her they'll be back with a written statement for her to sign, and head out. Nabarro is straight on the phone, barking instructions to his juniors, assembling a team of his Guardia Civil officers to meet in the next half hour.

Miguel says nothing, instead smoking two cigarettes and crushing the butts not far from where Danuta Barnes left hers.

I try to start a conversation, but he silences me. He offers me a lift back to the station and I accept.

On the journey, he's not in the mood for talking. I have a feeling he's thinking. Not his strongest area. We arrive a quarter of an hour later at Calvià Police Station and he takes me up to his office.

Just the two of us.

'Does she know about the other case with the hood?' Miguel asks, once I've settled into a chair. No offer of sherry this time around.

'Who?'

He closes his eyes, frustrated.

'The journalist woman.'

I shake my head.

'I don't think she'd have made the connection. Not many will. It was a long time ago, memories are short.'

He nods, relieved.

'What do you think?' he says.

I shrug.

'I think this is serious,' I say. 'A big deal. We thought we had the murderer – a twisted bouncer. Now it feels like more than that. It sounds like we might have at the very least a serial rapist here, and very likely a serial murderer.'

'We don't know that,' he says. 'They could be unconnected.'

'Could be. But the hood, you heard the description. Made of some sort of sacking. The two eyeholes. The same beach. Late at night. Preying on vulnerable girls. Someone British. Not Spanish, British. You know what that means?'

He nods.

'But we know Santiago had sex with the girl, on the beach. There can't be two rapists.'

'There can,' I say.

He looks at me, eyes narrowing.

'It's quite common,' I add. 'Happens a lot. Girl gets drugged and raped. Wakes up, not sure what's going on, in distress, vulnerable, and another guy comes along and takes advantage of her. Promises to walk her to safety, then assaults her in a dark alley.'

'You think that's what's happened here?' he asks.

I shrug.

'Possibly.'

'Which means we might have only one of the rapists,' Miguel says.

'And the most dangerous one's still out there,' I reply.

'So what we've got is someone who's committed a rape and attempted murder, and then a murder, four years apart. I can't quite believe it,' he says.

A short silence. Another shrug of my shoulders.

'You sure he hasn't been active between those incidents?' I ask.

He looks at me, narrows his eyes, then reaches over and picks up his office phone.

## 20

I don't remember much about the drive home, other than it was long, hot and dusty. By the time I park up, there's a message from Miguel. They've been back to search the sliver of space under the swimming pool, where I found Kayleigh. They've found a cable tie and they're hoping for a DNA match. He's hoping it might lead to a hit on the database.

When I enter the house, Nick's sitting on the sofa watching telly, looking unhappy. There's no sign of any booze, and he conspicuously has a glass of water on a side table. He's sweating and looking sour, his shirt showing big wet patches under the arms.

He turns off the telly when he sees me and stands up.

'How are you, love?' he says, coming over and giving me a kiss. For once, his breath doesn't stink of alcohol.

'Fine,' I say. 'How was your day?'

He shrugs and sits back down.

'So-so,' he says. 'I've not felt that well.'

I look at him, sprawled back on the sofa, just waiting to put the telly back on to nurse his splitting headache in peace. It used to be that I'd feel sympathetic when I looked at him in this state, aware of my part in his downfall. I'd try to do things to make him feel better, offer him a cup of tea or a bite to eat. But right now, as I stare at the man who's been sitting around the house all day doing nothing, all I feel is pity and a massive, overwhelming sadness. Sadness for the life we once had together. Sadness for the love that used to consume me every time I'd see his face. Sadness for the good times we had, and the bad times. Sadness for the tragedy that ruined us.

Just awful, fucking, tragic sadness.

I toss aside my bag and drop to my knees, tears rolling down my face, huge sobs gripping me. Dark thoughts in my head. I hear Nick shifting.

'Love, what's wrong?'

I just carry on sobbing uncontrollably.

The awful, fucking sadness.

I feel his arms around me. My body stiffens. He tries to grip me, to hug me, but I don't relax as I would have once.

He backs off. I can smell him a few inches away. Outdated cologne and cheap deodorant.

He lets me cry. Says nothing.

I sob, and sob, and sob.

After I don't know how many minutes, I stop crying and look up at him. He's sitting there, thinking, trying to calculate what's gone on.

I pull my handbag over and open it. It's an ageing Marks and Spencer model I bought on our last trip back to England. It's coming apart at the seams and the zip's long since gone, but I can't afford to buy another one, so it comes with me, a constant reminder of where we now are.

I pull out a tissue and wipe my face, doing the best I can with the streaks of mascara.

'It's me, isn't it?' he says, now looking out of one of the windows.

Does he really need me to say it? Really need me to spell it out?

He knows. He knows for sure what it is.

*The awful fucking sadness.*

I don't say anything, just carry on trying to make my face look respectable.

'Isn't it?' he says.

Now I stare at him, glaring, forcing him to look away after a few seconds.

I can see him, willing me to start discussing it, so he can 'there, there' me and promise he'll make everything better.

I sniff hard, stand up and make my way into the kitchen. I pour myself a glass of water from the bottle in the fridge.

Nick pads in, still wanting to talk.

'I'm sorry,' he says.

I look at him again, hands on my hips, head cocked to one side.

'What are we going to do then?' I ask, and his head snaps to attention.

'Do?'

I close my eyes hard to show my displeasure.

'I'll change,' he says. 'I'll sort myself out. I know I've let things go a bit recently. I've not been much of a husband, I know. It's just, you know... been difficult for me.'

'It's been pretty damn difficult for me too,' I say. 'One of us has been having to go to work to keep this household running, so you can keep buying the beer and wine you feel you need to get you through your day. One of us has been dealing with a murder and a missing girl and Christ knows what else besides. One of us has to get up every morning, go to work, put in a good eight hours, come back and keep this house together. One of us hasn't stopped trying. But that's the problem, isn't it? There's currently only one of us in this marriage, which means it's not much of a marriage at all. Is it?'

Am I being unfair? Am I taking things out on Nick that aren't his fault? Images of Santiago looming over me, then me slashing at his face with a knife pop into my mind.

Nick looks at me now, the puppy-dog eyes, the yearning and hope. The desperation for a crumb of comfort.

Not today, I'm afraid.

*The awful fucking sadness.*

Then it's his turn to break down. Right there in front of me, in the kitchen, he sinks to his knees on the worn flagstones. It's just tears and quiet sobs to begin with, then there's a primordial scream and he's wailing. Actually wailing.

I look away, try to ignore it to begin with. I'm not in the mood. But he's standing up now, walking towards me, face broken into creases and tears. He walks up to me and buries his head in my chest, his arms around me, grasping for comfort.

I manage one arm around him.

He hasn't earned two yet.

I give him a minute, then I gently push him away.

I run a hand through my hair, rubbing my head, then rubbing my jaw.

'I don't think I'm in a good place to do this tonight,' I say. 'Have a think. What are we going to do? Think about that. Stay off alcohol for a day or two, if you can. Then... I don't know. Maybe we'll talk. Do you understand?'

We share eye contact. The puppy dog again. The child inside.

'Do you, Nick?'

He nods, then looks away.

'Okay,' I say, and I walk out of the kitchen.

'I love you,' he says, and I turn around to look at him standing there, shirt half in, half out of his dirty old shorts.

It's my turn to nod before I face away and head up to the bedroom.

~

Double bed.

Our marriage bed.

Twenty-seven years in December.

It's a lonely place for one.

I lie there, staring up at the darkness of my bedroom ceiling. The shutters are drawn to keep the heat out, making the room pitch black even after my eyes have adjusted.

I'm assuming Nick's on the sofa. He usually prefers it to the spare room.

Spare room doesn't have a telly.

I can't sleep. Too much going round and round in my head. Nick, our marriage, my life out here in Majorca, Kayleigh and Michelle, rape and murder.

The Crude Hood.

My phone rings just after midnight.

Text message from Miguel.

They've had a DNA hit on the cable tie and it's not Kayleigh's. They've run it through their database and had two hits. I ring him straight away and he answers. He's still at Calvià Police Station. Just come out of a meeting with Nabarro and the Guardia Civil. Going to be a long night.

Two hits.

Two rapes.

Each almost exactly a year apart.

Last year and three years ago. Both were reported to the police. Both happened on or near the beach in Magaluf. Both victims had hazy recollections due to being under the influence of drink or drugs.

Both were British.

Which means we know for a fact that this man has raped three women and murdered one, Michelle Fraser. This year, last year and three years ago.

Probably four.

Four years ago. The Crude Hood. No DNA that time.

Four rapes, one murder and two more attempted murders in four years.

A serial rapist.

A serial killer.

And those are just the ones we know about.

What links them? Young women attacked in darkness on the beach. Under the influence. At their most vulnerable. In Magaluf for a good time. Victims of a sick, dangerous individual.

Miguel goes into more details. Says both of the victims reported their assaults to the police, and rape kits were used, samples kept. Both were in their early twenties. Both passed out on their way home from Kiss. One woke up in a side street, face down, a man on top of her, his hand forcing her head into the ground, his penis in her vagina. She tried to struggle but he was too strong. She was still coming down from a cocktail of drugs she'd taken. She passed out, then woke up an hour later and was helped to an ambulance by some passers-by.

DNA was found on a semen sample taken from her pubic hair.

Didn't see his face. No mention of any hood, but nothing to rule one out either.

The second woman was on the beach. Went down there after leaving the club. Planned to watch the sunrise but passed out instead. Woke up with bruising around her buttocks and vagina.

Went to a doctor. Referred to the police. The rapist had used a condom, but DNA was taken from a sweat patch on the inside of her thigh.

Didn't see his face. No idea if he used a hood.

Both were alone.

Of the four of them, three were alone. One was with someone. That guy who was stabbed nine times but survived.

Lots to link them. The DNA. The hood in two cases. The knife we know for certain in at least two cases. The MO, targeting vulnerable women on or around Magaluf beach. Three cases in the last week of August, one in the middle of June. The latest one.

It's not my job to investigate. Leave it to the police. Not something that requires consular assistance.

Four women. All British. All young. Raped, attacked, assaulted and, in at least one case, murdered.

This year, last year, three years ago and four years ago.

An annual attack?

What was he doing two years ago? A year off? A fallow year to let the ground recover? Or did he rape then as well, but no DNA was recovered? Or maybe nothing was reported to the police. Because that happens out here. Happens a lot. Sexual assaults of varying severity happen all the time. A non-consensual grope in the darkness of a nightclub. A hand up a skirt in the back of a bar. A drunk woman taken advantage of on a side street. A prostitute used, beaten-up and robbed.

It happens.

Happens a lot in Magaluf.

And it's often not reported.

I should know. I've met them the day after. Maybe two days after. They're in the consulate. They've lost their passport. A hazy recollection of a good night turned bad. Too much to drink. Snorted, popped or swallowed something they shouldn't have. Collapsed on the way home. Waking up in a stranger's bedroom, or worse. A vague memory of a man's hand where they didn't want it. Being held down. Trying to scream, trying to struggle. Can't remember what he looked like. Can't remember his name. Can't remember how they got there or exactly what happened. Think they might have been assaulted. The guilt, the shame, the embarrassment. Their own fault. Too drunk. Maybe they led him on. Maybe they said it was okay. It'll never stand up in court. Their word against his. Don't even know who he was or how to find him. Just too damn wasted to be a credible witness. They know they can report it. They sense they should report it. They'll think about it and maybe report it when they get back to the UK.

Maybe.

A rape or sexual assault not even documented.

Except by us.

The only record of it is on the consulate's files.

I sit up and take a moment to think.

Can't sleep anyway.

What's there to lose?

I step out of bed, flick on the bedside light and reach for my clothes. I get dressed: old jeans and the same blouse as yesterday. Grab my handbag, the ageing M&S one. Head downstairs.

Nick's asleep on the sofa, ITV2 blaring away on the telly.

I pick up my keys and head out to the SEAT.

Everything seems to work as it's intended at one in the morning.

The roads flow, traffic-free.

The traffic lights seem to be fixed green.

The streets are clear of rubbish where the night-time refuse teams have been. I can still smell the stench where the bin bags with their sweating contents have been removed.

I speed in.

I make it to the consulate in twenty minutes. I go up in the lift, through the main door, the reception door and the connecting door to the office.

I sit down and turn on my computer.

What was her name?

I have a hazy memory of her. She'd come in looking pale in a plain black T-shirt and neat knee-length shorts. She had frizzy brown hair pulled back in a bun, and a graze on her right temple.

It was Jane or Lauren or Sarah or something.

Said she'd lost her passport two nights earlier. Said she'd been attacked and that must have been when she lost it. Started crying, so I persuaded her to come through to one of the meeting rooms, and there she'd opened up.

I open the Aristotle drive on my computer – we log any casework that we do on it, particularly anything that might involve a crime.

I start searching, putting in the details I can remember. I look up two years ago, limiting the search to June, July, August and September. I put in assaults and then I change it to 'sexual assaults'. I add one further word: 'Magaluf'.

A string of hits come up – more than sixty for that summer alone – and those are just the ones that came our way (if the person doesn't want consular assistance, the police won't inform us).

I begin reading through them, eliminating as many as I can: any that name an attacker or where the attacker is known to the victim. Several of the sexual assaults are male on male. I eliminate those too.

I push on, looking for details that match my memory of the

incident: the girl with the frizzy brown hair, freckled skin and plain black T-shirt. She must have been about twenty-three or twenty-four. No more than twenty-five.

She was alone. I remember that. She was definitely alone.

My search narrows rapidly. Nothing left for June or July. Just a handful for August and September. A girl who ended up in an impromptu orgy in a hotel room complaining she hadn't consented to everything that went on. Eliminated. A girl who believed the man she had sex with might have filmed the incident. Eliminated. A man who woke up with a girl having sex with him against his wishes. Eliminated.

Then I get to Joanne Ainscomb and realise I've found her.

The facts jump off the page.

She'd been out with her friends to a nightclub. Doesn't say which, but I can guess. She'd drunk too much. No drugs this time, just drink. Cocktails, then beer, then more cocktails, then shots, then a bit more beer. She'd started feeling bad. No longer enjoying herself. Told her friends she needed some air. Planned to walk herself home.

She'd gone outside the club and headed, she thought, in the direction of her hotel. She walked for five, maybe ten minutes before she realised she was going the wrong way.

She turned around and headed back, but got lost.

Then she started to feel sick.

She'd paused by a wall in a street whose name she couldn't remember, had sat down and thrown her guts up. Then she had made a big error: she'd passed out.

She woke up to find a man with his arm around her waist, promising to help her. Said he would take her back to her hotel, back to her friends. She'd got antsy about him. Didn't like his arm around her. They'd argued. He'd gone off. She started walking, but still felt bad. She got to the beach and passed out again.

Then she made her second error: she woke up.

She was lying face down on the beach, a man on top of her, his weight forcing her into the sand. He was doing something to her. She wasn't sure what.

She'd started to struggle, tried to call out.

He'd forced her face harder into the sand.

Then she thinks he must have put a hand to her throat, that he throttled her. She couldn't quite be sure. All she remembered is waking up some hours later with the sun burning down on her face, and marks and bruising around her throat and genitals.

Her bag was missing. Didn't know if it had gone with the first man who tried to help her, or the attacker on the beach, but it was gone, and with it her passport. She was flying home the next night and desperately needed emergency travel documents, which was where we came in.

And one other thing jumps out at me that I hadn't noticed at the time. It hadn't seemed like a biggie, just another detail for the Aristotle database.

Her other memory of the man on the beach.

Him on top of her, him somewhere inside her, and the only thing he'd said during the whole thing.

'Slut, slut, slut. You dirty slut, slut, slut.'

I encouraged her to report it. Begged her to go to the police. Offered to go with her. Offered to translate for her. Emphasised the importance of making people aware of it. Tried to get across that whoever had done this to her needed to be stopped.

She had just cried and cried. Didn't want to go there. Didn't want any more stress or hassle. Thought it was her fault. She'd got drunk. She'd gone off without her friends. What did she expect, wasted and wandering around Magaluf in the early hours of the morning?

The most she would do was to agree to think about it. Said

she might report it when she got back to England and had 'come to terms with things'.

It was the last I heard from her.

*Slut, slut, slut. You dirty slut, slut, slut.*

It's now nearly four in the morning. Too late to ring Miguel. The exhaustion is beginning to kick in. I copy and paste my original notes into a Word document and save it to my desktop. Then I walk across the office, into the Family Room, where I spoke to Joanne Ainscomb.

The only one with sofas.

I slip off my shoes, drape my cardie loosely over my shoulders, close my eyes and hope that now some sleep might come.

I'm woken by the cleaners.

They get half an hour every day to give the office and reception area a pass. They have to finish before we open at 8am, so they're usually here by 7.30.

It's the younger of the two. A forty-something local with a face that tells of a hard life. She bursts into the Family Room, dragging an ageing-looking Henry hoover behind her.

They're here every day and I still don't know their names. Not sure I've ever said anything to them beyond good morning, please and thank you.

She gives a small shriek when she sees me, and I find myself apologising fast. I tell her I was working late and that I'm sorry for the mess.

She nods, gives me a look like I'm some kind of weirdo, then picks up her Henry by the handle and carries it out in a fanfare of crashes and cables.

My body desperately wants to lie back down, close my eyes for a few hours more, but my mind has things it wants to do. I sit up and rub the sleep from my face. I compose myself, stand up and head to the bathroom.

I lock the door, loosen my blouse and wash briefly under my arms and over my face. I dip into my handbag and apply what meagre make-up I have with me: a little mascara and a hint of foundation. I run a brush through my greasy hair, do my best to get it into some kind of order.

Then I walk out, grab my cardie and head through to reception. I'm nearly out of the door when I bump into Louise. She asks me where I'm off to and I tell her I've got to go to Calvià to see Miguel. It's about the missing girl. Missing *girls*. She looks at me, perplexed.

'I thought that was all sorted out,' she says.

I don't bother to reply.

I call Miguel from the car on the way. He doesn't answer. I leave a message. Tell him I've got information about the missing girl – girls. The Crude Hood. Tell him that I think I've found out what he did two years ago. Tell him we need to talk.

Then I drive all the way to Calvià Police Station. I park up, head into reception and ask to be put through to him.

Five minutes later, he comes down to meet me in person. His hair still looks neat and his demeanour is professional, but his skin looks drained, and I suspect he's not been home.

'You here about the story?' he asks.

What story?

He beckons for me to follow him and he takes me up to his

office. He opens the computer to the *Daily Star* website and brings up Danuta Barnes's piece. The headline is a shrill single banner: 'Dead girl saved me from Magaluf murderer'. It's a taut, personal piece about Kayleigh's experiences. Says cops are on the case, hunting down the killer. Warns young partygoers to be on the lookout. Tells women not to go home alone.

She hasn't made the connection. Hasn't realised about the hood.

No mention of a serial rapist.

'Could be worse,' I say, looking at Miguel. He makes a face, then sits behind his desk.

'Did you get my message?' I ask.

He shakes his head.

'You were struggling for a pattern. Over the last four years, there have been three documented rapes – four if we include the original case with the hood. But nothing two years ago.'

'Pretty much the long and short of it.'

'I think I might have found a link from two years ago. Which means, well, there is some kind of pattern.'

He asks me to explain, and I talk him through Joanne Ainscomb's case. I keep her name out of it, as she told me in confidence, in the Family Room. Then he takes me through to a large office on the far side of his floor. There's a wall with a map of Magaluf pinned to it, photos of each of the victims and writing next to them.

The incident room.

He brings in Nabarro and gets me to repeat everything I've just said to him.

I promise to try and contact the girl, to ask her permission to pass her number on to the police, to see if she'll give them a statement.

Four years.

Four rapes.

Two attempted murders.

One murder.

Nabarro is staring at the board, thinking hard. He picks up a board marker and draws a spot indicating our best approximation of the location of Joanne's attack. Alongside, he writes a date, time and place.

Looking for a pattern.

Joining the dots.

No one speaks.

Four years.

Four rapes.

We know the victims are similar. Young British girls under the influence, vulnerable, on or near the beach, attacked in the early hours, under cover of darkness.

Three were alone.

One wasn't.

A hood used in at least two cases, but no evidence of it in the others.

One other thing stands out.

'Four were attacked in the first week of August,' I say.

Nabarro and Miguel look at me, interested but vaguely suspicious.

'That's a pattern. An obvious pattern.'

Nabarro narrows his eyes.

Miguel says, 'Go on.'

'A British holidaymaker,' I say. 'Someone who comes out here on holiday the same week every year. Probably someone with a steady job, sticks to routine, doesn't like to change things.'

'And his holiday recreation is to attack and rape a girl every time?' Nabarro says.

I nod.

'He's a sick individual. He has violent sexual needs he perhaps can't fulfil easily back home in the UK. So he comes out here, where there are plenty of young, vulnerable, drunk girls and hardly anyone who knows him. Within a few days of each attack, he's probably safe and sound, back in England.'

Miguel's nodding slowly. He raises his eyebrows encouragingly at Nabarro.

'So a tourist, not a resident?' he says.

I nod.

'Does that make it easier?'

'Not really,' Nabarro says, clearing his throat.

'Couldn't you look at flight manifests for that week over the last few years? See which names come up each year?' I suggest.

'In high season, there's over 1,000 flights a day here, over a million people arriving each week. It would take us months to get all the names off the airlines. And that's if your hunch is right, that he's a tourist who has flown here and not come by boat,' Nabarro says. 'And then, of course, why does he move his week to June this year?'

I shrug.

'I know. Weird,' I say. 'Maybe he was ill. Who knows what goes on in his life?'

'Not much of a pattern,' Nabarro says, and goes back to staring at the board.

We sit there in silence for a minute or two, lost in our thoughts, trying to find a link, something to break the deadlock.

Miguel sits up.

'There is one other link, of course,' he says.

Nabarro and I look at him, searching his face for clues.

'The club – Kiss. They were all there. All the victims on the night of their attacks.'

I'm nodding. Nabarro is frowning.

'It's the main club in the resort,' he says. 'Everyone ends up there. I don't see how that helps us.'

'I'm just thinking,' Miguel says, shrugging, 'what if it's an inside job?'

A face pops into my head. Big and black, gold teeth and a smile that makes my skin crawl. I find myself gasping slightly and Miguel looks up.

'What is it?' he says.

I shake my head.

'No, nothing,' I say.

They're both looking at me now, foreheads creased with enquiry.

'Nothing?' Miguel asks.

I cock my head to one side.

'It's probably nothing.'

'Go on,' Miguel says.

'It's just, well, when you said Kiss, it's just, well, I'm not sure it's significant, but...'

They stand there, looking at me, eyes fixed, desperate for something, anything to seize upon. I feel guilty before I've even mentioned his name. It's so little to go on. Is it just me? Old, institutionally racist?

'Do you know Dante?' I ask.

They look at each other, a slight creasing at the corner of Miguel's mouth, Nabarro's eyebrows raised slightly.

'The DJ?' he says.

'Yes, well, it's just, he's been into the consulate, he and his entourage. He lost his passport, you see, on the night of the murder. Needed new documents to leave Spain.'

They're thinking now, concentration etched on Miguel's skin, trying to work through the permutations, running it through his brain to weigh up whether it's significant.

'I mean, it's probably nothing,' I say. 'Just a coincidence, and, well, it doesn't prove anything on its own really, does it? It's just, well, you mentioned Kiss as a link, and he is closely linked to it.'

Nabarro nods slowly, thoughtfully, then sniffs and wipes his nose and upper lip with the back of his hand.

'Interesting,' he says, before turning back to the timeline on his whiteboard.

We get no further so I leave the two of them sitting in their incident room, trying to pull the strands together into a workable whole.

Four years.

Five rapes.

One murder.

Two attempted murders.

No names. No suspects. No real leads.

They're going to talk it through. Brainstorm it. Bring in other officers. Work out a plan. Hit the ground hard. Do police work.

I get back in my car and start driving. I decide against going back to the office and, instead, head home.

My house has an unfamiliar smell when I arrive back.

Some sort of detergent.

Lemon and lime.

I find the source on his hands and knees in the living room, scrubbing the floor.

He jumps when I say hello.

'Christ, you scared the life out of me.'

He's dressed in his shorts and a clean polo top, an apron to protect his clothes, which makes him look odd.

'What's all this?' I ask.

He cocks his head to one side.

'Just cleaning up,' he says. 'Been too long since it was properly given the once-over.'

I nod slowly, trying to second-guess him. It might just be the effect of the detergent, but he smells clean for the first time in ages. He's shaved and there's a healthy colour to his cheeks.

Healthier.

He stands up, drops a wet cloth in the bucket behind him and looks at his feet, then up to me.

'I'm trying to make an effort,' he says.

I say nothing, just nod slowly again.

'I know I've been a state these last few weeks. I've let things go a bit. Lost control.'

I've wanted him to say it for so long, waited for this, hoped for this, and now, actually listening to it, it's excruciating. I can't look him in the eye. Instead, I stare out of the back window into the garden I've lovingly tended for seven years, at the hypericum that continues to thrive no matter how hostile the heat.

'I've been a mess. I *am* a mess. I'm just, well, I just wanted to sort of say, well, two things really. I wanted to say sorry.'

I have to look at him now. It would be rude not to. But I desperately want to turn around and just leave. Not a single part of me wants to see the man I love reduced to this.

'Sorry, and I know it has to stop.'

I take a few seconds, look across the room for something to distract me. Eye up our antique clock and the little model of a windmill we brought back from a trip to Holland many years ago.

'That's good,' I say.

He smiles, relief on his face. The sense he's got away with it. That the whole detergent and apron thing has worked.

'You know that it doesn't quite work like that though,' I add, and his whole face drops. 'You can't just say sorry and do a bit of housework.'

He's nodding now, keen to speak, but I don't let him.

'I've busted a gut in this house on my own for the last God knows how many months, going to work, coming back, buying the food, keeping things up, and you've done nothing but sit here drinking.'

He's looking at his shoes now, the hangdog lost puppy.

I go over to the sofa, a pale stain on the red cushion where one of his last drinking sessions has been washed off.

He just stands there, like an admonished schoolboy, waiting for his punishment.

I feel strangely powerful. It's not a position I'm used to.

'So what are you going to do about it?' I ask.

He looks up, trying to read me.

'It?' he says.

I get up and walk to the kitchen, grab the recycling bin, drag it into the front room, then push it over in a hail of clinks as bottles and cans come flying out. Trickles of residual beer and spirits drip onto his newly washed floor.

'This,' I say. 'What are you going to do about this?'

There are tears forming in his eyes now.

He takes a seat on the sofa, perching on the edge of the cushion.

'I'm off it,' he says.

'We both know that's easier said than done.'

The nodding again, using it like a defensive shield.

'You want me to go and see someone?' he says.

I look away, blow my cheeks out, getting hot and bothered.

'It's your problem,' I say. 'Your addiction. You know what urges you have. You tell me what you need to do about it.'

Defensive nods.

'I think I need to see someone,' he says. 'Go to a doctor or something, or maybe a group thing.'

'A group thing? You've really done your research, haven't you?'

'Elaine, please,' he says, the first stirrings of a backbone. 'I'm trying. I want to sort this. I'll do whatever it takes.'

'Good,' I say. 'Make sure you do. Then let me know the plan.'

I step over the bottles and cans and walk towards the door.

'It's not been easy for me either,' he says as I'm about to walk through it.

I turn back.

'What's that supposed to mean?'

I fix him with my stare now.

He holds my gaze and says, 'You don't have a monopoly on grief, you know.'

We lock eyes for a second or two more, before I turn away and head for the stairs, not wanting him to see my tears.

## 21

The stupid ringtone chime wakes me again.

It's just gone 6.30am and I've overslept.

For the first time I can remember, I don't put out an arm for Nick.

It's Miguel. Voice an octave deeper than usual: hard-edged and professional.

'We're going to hit Kiss,' he says.

I sit up, suddenly alert.

'Not because of Dante?' I say.

The line goes quiet. A terrible feeling of guilt ripples through me, making my muscles go stiff.

'It was the tiniest bit of information, Miguel, you can't honestly base a raid on what I told you. It's also off the record, entirely confidential. Please tell me it's not because of Dante.'

'Dante's just a part of this,' he says. 'All this GHB... we're pretty sure they're behind it. Everything that happens in Magaluf leads back to that place in one way or another. We need some answers.'

'When?' I ask.

'Tonight,' he says, '8pm. Before the doors open. Catch them napping. You want to come along?'

Images flash through my mind. A boot through a door leaving it hanging off its hinges, glass on the floor, handcuffs and cable ties, shouting and screaming, hard drives and box files being carried to a van.

'What would I want to do that for?'

'We're likely to need a fair amount of consular assistance afterwards,' he says. 'Plus, I could do with a good translator.'

I think through my day. Got the morning meeting, then off just after lunch to see how Riley's doing. Then it's the 100th birthday, handing over the card. Then Nick and I are meant to be having drinks with friends. Mike and Ines, our Anglo-Spanish neighbours.

'Eight p.m. you say?'

'That's when the doors go in,' he says. 'An hour before for the briefing.'

'I'll see how my day goes,' I say, already planning how to break it to Nick.

~

Eight a.m. at the consulate.

The morning meeting.

For once, everyone is there on time, even Rodrigo. Louise and Soraya look relaxed, Rodrigo self-satisfied as ever. I've barely slept and I must look a sight. I try to rub my eyes as inconspicuously as I can.

We run through that day's business: a group of six held overnight at Calvià for fighting in Magaluf (five are likely to be released, but one is being held for serious assault); a man's broken a tibia while paragliding and will need a transfer back to the UK; the mayor of Inca is trying to arrange a drinks party for British residents in an attempt to woo their votes; and a seventeen-year-old girl is in Son Espases, having had her stomach pumped after overdosing on ketamine.

Usual stuff.

I weigh up telling them about tonight's police operation. It's likely to generate a fair amount of work for us. Half the staff at Kiss are British, and the more arrests there are, the more visits we'll have to make. But it's a confidential police operation, and the last thing Miguel will want is gossip leaking out from our office.

I leave it.

We divvy up tasks: front desk for Louise and Soraya, emergency travel documents for Rodrigo (about all we can trust him with these days), hospital visits for me and Duncan.

I read out a supportive message from Vanessa, thanking us for our help on the Kayleigh Walsh and Michelle Fraser cases, and praising us for our efforts with a difficult and busy summer.

There's some nodding around as I read it out, then everyone's happy to break up and get started.

I've got the morning at my desk, looking through emails, gathering my thoughts. Once we shut to the public, I'll head to Son Espases to see Riley. I'm still trying to make up my mind about going with Miguel to Kiss later. While we occasionally go on police operations as a ride-along, PR exercise, we're not meant to get involved in police work in any operational sense. Miguel's never really come to terms with the fact that our staff are not here to act as interpreters.

Everything is telling me to avoid it like the plague.

And yet I can't stop thinking about it.

Then there's the guilt. Dante under suspicion, likely under arrest, because of my information, confidential information, circumstantial gossip. Am I naturally uncomfortable about a big black guy with a roll of euros in his pocket and a gold tooth in his mouth? But it's a murder inquiry. Gossip can be important. His passport lost the night she was murdered.

*Four years.*

*Five rapes.*

*One murder.*

Whoever's responsible for these attacks, whatever's gone on, there's something deeply concerning about Kiss and the hold it has over the island. It dominates life on the strip: it's where the revellers head, where the drugs get distributed and, inevitably, where the money gets spent.

Who knows what Miguel might flush out tonight?

I shouldn't go, I know it's a mistake, but at the same time I know I'm going to.

I go back to my desk and start on Riley's paperwork. If I don't do it now, it won't be ready for his Saturday flight.

I go through the usual checks. Put his details into Plato, Socrates and Aristotle. Name, address, date of birth.

The checks start coming back. Legitimate name, legitimate address. Impeccable passport history, until this moment. Three issued so far in his life, the last just four years ago. No one has yet reported it lost. I put in markers that this one has now been reported as missing, fill out the boxes explaining, as best as possible, where and when it disappeared, put in the details of the police report and a scan of it.

Then it's the DBS – Disclosure and Barring Service – check, just to ensure there are no warrants out on him that might prevent him from travelling.

The moment I put in his details, things are flashing up: red writing and asterisks next to his name. The sort of marks that didn't appear anywhere near Dante's.

Warning marks.

I click through to the next screen.

He has a criminal history.

I scan down the list: couple of common assaults, one actual bodily harm, a conviction for dangerous driving, and at the bottom, just six months old, one for domestic violence.

Nothing that would prevent him having a passport. Nothing that would prevent him travelling to the EU.

But a criminal history, nonetheless.

None of my business really, but my mind can't help joining a few theoretical dots.

A convicted criminal on the beach in Magaluf in the early hours of the morning on Monday the sixteenth.

A convicted criminal in a mystery accident after a night at Kiss, high as a kite on a cocktail of coke, ecstasy and crystal meth, the night Michelle Fraser is raped and murdered.

It's probably nothing.

Just the way my mind's working.

He doesn't look the type.

Poor guy's only just found out he'll be able to walk again.

But it gnaws away in the back of my mind – dots and asterisks and red warnings.

Riley and Dante.

Derek Williams.

Broken legs and mixing decks.

I take a deep breath so loud that even Rodrigo looks up at me.

It's 2pm by the time I get to Son Espases. I head up to the Atocha Ward, where Nurse Ariza is on duty again. She says Riley is down in the physio unit and gives me some basic directions.

I head down there. There's another bare, clinical waiting room covered in inspirational posters of people battling to walk and move again, with mottos strapped across them such as, 'Every journey begins with a step'.

There's another nurse on duty at the desk and she tells me Riley will be out of physio soon. There's a long glass partition behind her desk, which looks onto the small gymnasium where two groups of people are exercising.

Among them is Riley.

His wheelchair is pushed to the side and he's lying on a massage couch, flanked by two members of staff who are pulling and prodding him. Exactly what they're doing is shielded by one of their backs, but they seem to be concentrating on his hip.

Riley has his eyes closed, his mouth in a grimace, sweat on his brow.

I take a seat in the reception room and wait.

Ten minutes later, Riley is wheeled back into reception. When he sees me, his eyes briefly open in surprise before something clicks in his head and he manages a 'Watcha'.

I stand up.

'How are you?' I ask. 'How did the operation go?'

'Pretty good,' he says. 'Still can't feel my legs, but the physios have started working on the hip and the arm. I should be ready for home in a few days. Fancy a coffee?'

The Sol Café is in between blocks C and D of Son Espases.

I buy a latte for Riley, a strong and bitter espresso for me.

Riley orders himself a churro and dips it in his latte.

'Love these things,' he says. 'One of the things I'll miss most about Spain.'

'At least your time's not been completely wasted then,' I say, and he smiles.

We sip our drinks in silence, Riley making a mess of his churro as he stuffs it into his face.

'I've got something for you,' I say.

He looks up, a mixture of excitement and suspicion on his face.

I pull the buff A4 envelope out of my bag and pass it to him.

He opens it and pulls out the newly cut and pressed booklet with the royal coat of arms on the front.

The lion and the unicorn.

*Dieu et mon droit.*

'Emergency travel documents,' I say. 'Cinderella *will* go to the airport.'

He opens it, turns to the passport photo and grimaces.

'Jesus, looks like I've just lost a UFC bout.'

I smile, remembering what he looked like the first time I saw him, stretched out on that bed, yellow bruising all over his face, legs so bulky in the casts they were held in under that blanket, his voice working in rasps, the pain in his eyes.

'It's not too bad,' I say. 'I'm so pleased you're able to go back and that, you know, everything's healing well. I know there'll be ups and downs on the way, but it's really wonderful news.'

He looks a bit embarrassed, a slight red flush to his cheeks. He turns back to his latte.

'Have you got transport to the airport?' I ask.

'Going to be a taxi and a wheelchair. Mum's going to push me. It'll be fine, but slow.'

'What about at the other end?'

'Dad's hired a private ambulance to pick me up from Manchester Airport. From there, it's only about half an hour home. Going to jack myself up on codeine and just grin and bear it. Just bloody wish I'd got travel insurance, but there you go.'

I nod and he turns back to his coffee. Takes a slurp.

'A bit more's come back,' he says, not looking up.

'About the accident?' I ask, and he nods.

'Not a lot, but a bit more.'

'Go on,' I say.

'It might be nothing,' he says. 'I was out of my tree anyway and a lot of it's still all a blur and that, but I remember being on a street. I remember tarmac and palm trees and buildings and me looking to cross it, and then I remember a vehicle, a blur of grey or silver metal coming at me fast, and not enough time to get out of the way, and there's the grey metal again and then it's all a haze.'

'You're sure it was a car?' I ask.

'A vehicle of some sort. Probably a car. Something fast.'

'And that's it?'

'Pretty much,' he says, finishing his coffee. 'I don't remember any pain or any blood, or the actual moment of contact, or landing on the road, or anything like that. But I remember the vehicle, the speed, the flash of metal and one other thing.'

'Go on.'

'It might sound a bit funny.'

'It all matters, however small,' I say.

'Well, I remember this hat.'

'Hat?'

'On a sign outside a restaurant. Great big Mexican hat, the only thing really lit up there.'

'A sombrero?' I ask.

'That what it's called?'

'El Sombrero,' I say. 'It's a restaurant just outside Magaluf. Not far from the beach.'

'Right,' he says.

'In Torrenova.'

'Right,' he says again. 'Is that good?'

My mind's racing now, trying to think. That night, that beach, that sign, opposite that hotel: the hotel where Kayleigh spent the next few days hiding under a swimming pool.

The night Michelle Fraser was raped and murdered.

Mind racing, dots joining.

I look at him as he pulls his churro apart: acne, cropped hair, a glint in his eye, his whole life ahead of him.

Surely not.

'Depends what you mean by good,' I say.

I weigh up skipping the 100th birthday.

I want to get back to the office, get onto Aristotle and start checking dates.

It can't be. Surely not. Why would he be remembering things that might give him away?

But Torrenova, early hours of that morning, Monday the sixteenth, by the hotel, the mysterious accident.

I have to check it. And Aristotle will tell me what dates he's been in Spain in the last four years, the four years since he got his most recent passport.

Could they match?

The first two weeks in August – every year.

Except this year. This year it was in June.

He's going home this evening, so I need to check before he flies.

I weigh up getting out of the birthday. Calling McLellan and telling him that something's come up – the usual mass of apologies and best wishes.

But I can't.

I made a promise, and if I told him I couldn't go, I would just be lying.

That damn card from the Queen.

Instead, I drive the little SEAT onto the MA13 and make my way over to Santa Maria del Cami.

*Nice to do something pleasant for a change.*

The address he's given is a small block of sheltered apartments a few kilometres inland, but with windows facing towards the coast.

It's nice. Plain, red brick, squat and square, but practical for what it contains: a dozen or so European pensioners of mixed nationalities with a similar number of staff to keep them upright and functioning.

It's gone 4pm by the time McLellan meets me at the reception and takes me up to the communal lounge. He's delighted to see me, says he didn't think I'd come, and tells me I'll make his mother's day.

He passes me the envelope with the card in it and asks me to keep it a secret until the moment comes.

His mum is sitting in a wheelchair in front of a large television, a Spanish channel showing an old soap opera, the volume a little too loud for comfort.

She looks alert, taking everything in. Three other pensioners are sitting around her, all well over eighty, skin varying shades of walnut brown, nationalities hard to discern.

'What's amazing is, she's still got all her marbles,' McLellan says. 'She's none too steady on her pins anymore, but that's not so important. She still gets everything that's going on, still knows who we all are. Amazing really, when you think about it.'

'Does she speak Spanish?' I ask, watching as she gazes at the television set.

'Barely a word,' he says almost proudly. 'Been here nearly thirty years and still hasn't got past "hola" and "gracias". But she didn't come for the culture. It's that, isn't it?' he says, pointing out of the window at the cloudless blue sky.

I nod along and we stand there, shoulder to shoulder for a few moments, until I start to wonder what the plan is.

'When do you want to do it?' I ask, and he snaps to attention.

'Sorry, of course,' he says. 'They're just rounding up a few more of the old girls and then we'll have the cake and you can hand it over.'

I'm introduced to McLellan's wife, who forces a smile but generally looks a bit downtrodden. As she shakes my hand, I notice heavy make-up, poorly applied, but elaborately varnished nails.

There are two grandchildren – Evan, who looks about eight or nine, and Lyra, in her early teens.

'Parents let us take them for a couple of weeks a year while they go to Tenerife,' McLellan tells me.

The kids acknowledge my presence with brief nods before turning back to their tablets.

I'm just trying to think of a question to ask to keep the conversation going, when a nursing assistant asks me to move, and another lady, well into her eighties, is pushed past me in a wheelchair.

'The rest are sleeping,' the nurse says. 'That's all we'll have for the moment.'

'Righto,' McLellan says, and disappears to fetch something.

He returns five minutes later with a bundle of presents and a handful of cards.

Two other members of staff wheel a cake in on a small

trolley and start preparing glasses of fizz and beakers of orange squash.

McLellan nods to one of them and she goes over and turns the television off. There's an audible grunt of disappointment from one of the three ladies at the front. She says something in a language I'm pretty sure is Portuguese.

McLellan stands in front of the television and turns to face the old girls.

'I'm sorry to interrupt your day, but I just wanted to say a few words because, obviously, it's a bit of a special one today.'

Nods from his mother. Bemused looks from the women on either side of her.

'First of all, let me thank you all for coming.'

There are twelve of us in total in the room: four elderly residents, three members of staff, McLellan and his family and me. Only half of us appear to understand English.

'Now, it's very few of us that get to achieve what Blanche has achieved, and anyone that reaches the milestone of one hundred years can feel very proud of themselves. You all know Blanche, but you might not know everything about her. She worked as a clerk for the local council back in England for over thirty years, and did lots of good work for them. And, of course, she had me. Many of us, when our partners of however many years sadly pass away, we probably disappear from life a bit, but not Mum. She took it as a moment to embark on a new life, coming out here in search of some proper sunshine, and she's been here ever since. Mum, you've always been there for me. The one person who always has. The best woman I've ever met.'

Tears in his eyes now. Lip quivering slightly. About to lose it.

'A hundred years today. Absolutely incredible. I don't know what to say, but, happy birthday, Mum!'

And now there are tears, rolling down one side of his face. His mother, too, is breaking up. She tries to push herself out of her chair, but can't. A nurse rushes forward, grabs her under the arms and helps lift her so she can embrace her son. Then I can hear it. Everyone singing 'Happy Birthday', slowly in the background, the sound building.

I look around. Two nurses are pushing the trolley with the cake on it towards her. There are candles on it, but not 100. Nearer ten. One for each decade, I'm guessing. The singing continues in thick Spanish accents. I join in, lending my voice as microscopically as I can.

Blanche sees the cake. She claps her hands once in excitement, then turns to look at her son, gazes at him in wonder, then there's another embrace, her squeezing him as hard as she can.

*Sometimes there are the nice moments.*

'Well, blow them out,' McLellan says, gesturing to the candles. Blanche does her best to lean towards them. McLellan gets her under one arm, the nurse the other. She blows in the general direction of the candles but it's too feeble, so McLellan blows as well and eventually, between the three of them, the flames go out.

There's a small round of applause and then the nurse begins to cut the cake.

Blanche is still looking at her son, beaming. He looks up, catches my eye.

'Before you get your fingers messy with cake,' he says, 'there's one other thing.'

He nods at me and I step forward tentatively, moving my fingers on the envelope, leaving damp patches where they've been.

'There's another lady who wants to wish you a very happy birthday,' he says. 'She lives a long way away in a very big house, but she's sent you a message, and this kind lady,' he says, pointing his arm in my direction, 'has come here specially to give it to you. Elaine?'

I step towards her, open the dull brown envelope and pull out the high-class envelope inside.

I don't start speaking until I'm only a couple of feet away, so I'm sure she can hear.

'Blanche,' I say, 'my name's Elaine Martin and I'm the British Vice-Consul here on Majorca, and it's my absolute delight and privilege to give you this on behalf of Her Majesty, Queen Elizabeth the Second.'

As I hand her the envelope, something extraordinary happens to her face. Her eyes and mouth open like they can't get enough light or air. She looks up at me, not sure whether to smile or cry.

I press the envelope into her hand and encourage her to open the seal. She's struggling, so McLellan leans in to help. Between them, they get it open and pull out the card. Inside is an A5 photograph of the Queen in a powder-blue hat and jacket, smiling impassively.

Blanche looks up at McLellan in disbelief. He's grinning from ear to ear.

He opens the card.

'Would you mind reading the message,' he says, handing it to me.

'Not at all,' I say.

I start reading: 'I am so pleased to know that you are celebrating your 100th birthday,' I say in my Sunday best voice. 'I send my congratulations to you and best wishes on such a special occasion. Elizabeth R.'

Blanche is clutching one hand in the other, her cheeks bright red, her eyes glittering like a teenager's.

I hand her the card and give her a kiss on the cheek.

'Well done, Blanche,' I say, 'you're an inspiration to us all.'

*Sometimes there are the nice moments.*

She shakes her head in disbelief, then thanks me profusely. McLellan looks as proud as a new father.

'Will you stay for a glass of champagne?' he asks me.

I'm about to make my excuses when Blanche grabs my hand.

'Oh, yes do, please,' she says. 'Please.'

I look at her, then at the three other residents – all of whom look as if they have only a sketchy idea of what is actually happening – look at the nurses going about their work with nothing more than professional enthusiasm, look at McLellan whose eyes implore me to stay.

'Of course,' I say, and McLellan hands me a glass from the trolley brought in earlier.

I clink glasses with Blanche, then take a sip.

It's Asti Martini: warm and sickly sweet.

I take a couple of steps back and start talking to one of the nurses. She says Blanche is a pleasure to look after. They had thirteen residents until a fortnight ago, when one died. It's a mixture of British, Scandinavian and German retirees, with a couple of the wealthier locals thrown in for good measure.

I listen and nod politely, but my mind's already disappearing to Miguel, Kiss and tonight.

The raid.

I wonder what it will achieve. Santiago is long gone. Any contentious material that might have been there is probably long gone as well.

How will kicking down the front doors of a nightclub turn up a serial rapist or a killer?

McLellan comes over and the nurse creates space for him.

He clinks my glass and sips his Asti.

'Thank you,' he says, still looking delighted.

'Oh no, really, it was a pleasure,' I say. 'It's so rare we get nice things to do in this job. It really is lovely.'

'She's over the moon,' he says. 'She really is. I don't think she's had a day like this since she got married.'

I nod and listen politely. Five more minutes should do it, then into the SEAT and back on the road to Palma.

'I was so worried about her when she first moved over here, oh, must be thirty years ago now,' he says. 'It was such a big upheaval and she knew virtually no one. Except her friend, Eileen, who was living with her husband over near Inca. But she settled down so fast, it was amazing really.'

My mind starts to wander again, to kicking down doors, suspects trussed in cable ties, hard drives and documents.

'She absolutely loved it here from the off, was totally self-sufficient, until her walking got bad and her hearing declined. That's when I got her moved here.'

Miguel and Nabarro are right about one thing: GHB is all over this.

Where would you hide it in a nightclub?

Would you hide it?

'Amazing, really. Doesn't cost me a penny. Her pension covers most of it, and what it doesn't, the local council does. I mean, look at this place, it's beautiful.'

His voice is starting to grate, all gutteral vowel sounds and monotonous diction.

Would it not be brought in, in small amounts, by the dealers – the bouncers – who are happy to ply their trade inside? A few wraps of it in a sock? A few tiny phials of it in a pocket? How will bursting in and arresting people uncover that? How do you unravel the whole supply chain? The bigwigs. The people behind the dealers. The people who make the real money. The people who buy off the police and the officials, the local council and the mayor. How does raiding a nightclub get to them?

'Course, I don't get out to see her anywhere near as much as

I'd like. I'd be out all the time, but I've got stuff to do at home. I still work and I've got friends and family.'

'Of course,' I say.

That's where they really should be looking. The local council. Corruption in the town hall. Investigating the whole rotten edifice of the damn place. Drugs and drinks. Backhanders and bungs. Millions if not billions must be changing hands in Magaluf every year, yet the only sign of it is the odd Bentley or Maserati that gets driven around by the club owners.

Where's the real money going?

Who's really lining their pockets?

'But I make sure I get out at least once a year,' he says. 'Without fail. She'd miss me too much if I didn't. I'm her only child after all.'

My head spins round and I look at him and my whole body shivers.

'Every year, without fail, first two weeks of August.'

My stomach lurches like a medicine ball's been swung into it with force.

The same two weeks every year. Just like him. The Crude Hood. Five rapes in four years. One murder, one attempted murder.

'Except this year, of course. Had to bring it forward because of her birthday and that. Work weren't too pleased, but when I told them it was her hundredth, they understood why I needed to go in June.'

'Of course,' I say.

And now my heart's pounding like it's trying to get out of my ribs. My hands are shaking and I can sense my eyes darting around the room, throwing fidgety looks at anything and everything, just to prevent me having to look at him.

*The same two weeks every year. Five rapes, one murder, one attempted murder.*

The first two weeks in August. Every year.

Except this year. This year it was in June.

Brought forward. We don't know why.

Just like this man.

Just like Aiden McLellan.

I swallow hard and study his face, his eyes behind those thick glasses. I study the lines of his mouth and the contours of his jaw.

He's still beaming, still looking proud as punch, staring at his mother who's eating cake, looking at the Queen on her card, and sipping warm, disgusting Asti Martini.

The same two weeks every year. Except this year. This year it was June.

Just a coincidence.

Surely.

Aiden McLellan?

Sixty-seven-year-old Aiden McLellan.

He looks ordinary: clean-shaven and unexceptional in every way. A dull grey man at a dull grey event. No exciting international DJ. No globe-trotting dance music superstar. Just a dull grey man going about his day, bothering no one.

'Excuse me,' I say, not waiting for a reply, instead walking off to find a toilet.

There's one just past the living room. I go in, lock it, turn the ugly yellow light on and sit myself on the seat.

Surely not. This man? This unexceptional individual with his geriatric mother and two-week holiday every year?

There must be dozens of men who come out to Majorca the same two weeks every year. Dozens of men who moved their holiday this year to June.

Surely dozens.

There's a knock on the door and I look up.

'Just a minute,' I shout in English, then in Spanish. I reach up and flush the toilet. Stand up and turn the tap on. Run water over my hands, then splash some on my face. Look at myself in the mirror. Try to compose myself.

Then I unlock the door and walk out.

He's there, standing in front of me, and I nearly jump out of my skin. His eyes are narrowed, an inquisitive look on his face.

'Just checking you're all right,' he says, his brow furrowing. 'You went off so suddenly.'

I force a smile.

'Absolutely fine,' I say. 'Thank you again, you and your mother, both of you, for inviting me. It really is lovely. Nice to do nice things.'

I can sense myself gabbling but don't know how to stop. I bend my head, look at the floor, and push past him into the living room. I go up to Blanche, who's sitting with the card in her hand, studying its every curve and contour.

I kiss her gently on the cheek.

'Happy birthday, Blanche. I'm afraid I have to go.'

She looks up, disappointed.

'Won't you have more champagne?' she asks.

'I'm sorry, I can't,' I say. 'I've got to get back to work. But thank you so much for inviting me to your party.'

I hold her hand and squeeze it briefly. I wonder what she would think if she knew about her son, knew what he did when he came out to see her.

She mouths her thanks and I turn around to leave.

He's standing there in front of me, the same bemused look on his face.

'You're off then?' he says matter-of-factly.

I try to look him in the eye, but can't. I look at his chest.

'I must get back to work,' I say. 'Those travel documents won't issue themselves.'

Another glance up at him. Another brief, forced smile.

He puts his hand out for me to shake. I look at it, hesitate momentarily, then put my hand in his and he shakes it, a soft, clammy grip.

'Thank you,' he says, 'for everything. It wouldn't have been the same without you.'

'No problem,' I say, nodding once, then moving towards the exit.

My car's parked directly outside the home, under the skeletal shade of a nearby Aleppo tree. I get in and for once I'm not bothered by the heat. Instinctively, I push down the lock on my driver's door, and reach over to check the passenger side is locked too.

I turn the key in the ignition and the fan starts blowing the same old warm air around the car.

I throw it into gear and start driving away carefully, thoughtfully, thinking of distance and speed.

It's gone 7pm by the time I get to Palma. I park the car in an after-hours space outside the office, then head inside, using my pass and codes to get me into the main building.

The office is deserted, as you'd expect at this time on a Saturday night, but the air conditioning still buzzes away quietly and efficiently, and I'm grateful for the relief it brings.

I'm still rattled, my heart beating hard, a warm wetness under my armpits. I get a glass of water from the machine in the kitchen, then go to my desk and turn my computer on, counting the seconds as various icons wheel and count.

Could it really be him? Could an apparently unexceptional sixty-seven-year-old man do what he's supposed to have done?

But isn't it always the quiet ones?

I picture his eyes, the look on his face as I came out of the toilet, as I squeezed his mother's hand and wished her goodbye. It chills me now. I'm sure it's just psychosomatic, but they seemed different to me, as though some unexplained, unedifying thought process was going on behind them.

Finally, my computer's warmed up enough to let me access my databases. I open up Plato. Every time we run a check on it, it's traceable. It's a sackable offence to use it when you're not meant to. You're not allowed to check on friends and family, not meant to put in your nearest and dearest to see what comes up. It's strictly for professional use, and we all have to sign forms to say we understand the risks and responsibilities that access to it entails.

I'm not supposed to use it for things like this.

But I have to – I have to know.

I go through a couple of menus to get to the search function, wait for the little box to come up, and I put the name in.

Aiden McLellan.

Age: sixty-seven.

Put in his address from the information he gave us when he first requested the birthday card.

I click the box asking for a DBS check, hit search and wait.

It jumps back just a few seconds later.

A long list of entries.

Seven in all.

I scroll down them.

They date back over thirty years.

Indecent exposure in a park in 1988. Suspended sentence.

Another for indecent exposure in a car park in 1991. Suspended sentence.

Then, two years later, a conviction for assault against a girl. Nothing sexual about it, but he got eighteen months inside.

Then there's a break for fifteen years.

First up after that is sexual assault in 2008, six months inside. Time off for good behaviour. Another two years and another sexual assault: a nineteen-year-old girl in 2010. No further details. Two years inside. Three years later is a further six months behind bars for indecent exposure outside the toilets of a shopping centre.

And then, six years ago, 25 April, he's charged with rape. A seventeen-year-old girl in a side street in Harlow. Convicted and sentenced to six years inside. He serves two, which means he would have got out of prison almost exactly four years ago. Meaning he would have been out of prison for the first offence, the Crude Hood, four years ago.

A history of sexual violence against women, yet following the rapes that did yield his DNA, no one in Spain bothered checking it against UK records.

It ends there. No more charges, no more convictions. A clean record, in the UK at least, for the past four years.

Because, of course, he's switched tactics. Found a better place to ply his trade. Somewhere with a conveyor belt of young, drunk, vulnerable women to prey on. Somewhere he can pop in and out without looking suspicious. Somewhere with the right mix of vice and vanity for him to get away with it for years.

I need to speak to Miguel.

I pull my mobile out of my handbag and dial his number. It rings through to voicemail. I don't leave a message. I check the time. It's 8.15pm. He'll be either in or on his way to Kiss. In the middle of operations: kicking down doors, seizing box files and rounding up staff.

I switch off my computer, pick up my handbag and go out to my car.

I have to get there, get to Magaluf before Miguel makes a big mistake.

Because Dante didn't do it. Dante can't have done it. His dates don't fit.

Aiden McLellan's do.

I try Miguel again – voicemail. This time I do leave a message. I say I need to speak to him urgently. I say I think I know who it is. I say it isn't Dante. I say he needs to call me ASAP because this guy's on the loose.

Needs to call me because he's about to arrest the wrong man.

# 22

At least, for once, I know where Miguel's supposed to be.

I drive fast to Magaluf. I'm not bothered about speed limits. If the police pick me up, so much the better. The road is busy but clear. In twenty minutes, I'm parking in my usual side street, stepping out and making my way up to the strip.

I spot Kiss earlier than I normally would. There are half a dozen Guardia Civil vehicles and a couple of Policia Local ones parked outside it, sirens off but lights flashing. A handful of officers are standing around, chatting, comparing notes, smoking cigarettes and finding things to laugh about.

There's a big queue of clubgoers lined up outside the main entrance. The evening's events are proceeding as usual. I walk up to one of the officers and ask to speak to Miguel. He laughs. I explain it's urgent. He shrugs. I ask about Officer Nabarro. He says they're both inside and I should go and talk to the officers on the door.

I walk up the main staircase, avoid the queue and tell one of the officers on the door that I need to see Miguel. He says that's impossible. Says he's inside on important police business. I say I'm here on the same police business and that Miguel would want to know this. I explain I'm the British Vice-Consul on Majorca and I have important information regarding the murder of Michelle Fraser and the abduction of Kayleigh Walsh.

He tells me to wait where I am.

I spend a couple of minutes studying the queue: young men and women, brown-cheeked and bright-eyed, with their whole lives ahead of them, catching a few moments' pleasure before they return to whatever lives they live back in the UK. Do any of them ever truly know the risks they face out here? Do they ever realise just how close they all are to the forces of lawlessness and anarchy?

'Mrs Martin?'

I look round: it's the officer on the door.

'If you go round to the back, there's a staff entrance. Someone will meet you there and take you up to see Deputy Chief Fuentes.'

The back door.

The west door.

I thank the officer and walk back past the queue, ignoring the wolf whistles and catcalls, back down the stairs, past the officers in their vans, and take a right turn until I'm walking down the side alley called Carer Roser. I go past the amusement arcade and the estate agents. Past the spot where Karim received his beating. Past the spot where Michelle Fraser threw up. On and down until I reach the west door. There's no sign on it, no writing of any kind, no lock, no key code, no doorbell, nothing but a plain, black door – one meant to let you out rather than in.

I stand next to it and wait. I put my ear to it and hear nothing. I rap on it with my knuckles.

Still nothing.

I look behind me into the darkness, studying the gloom. Down the slope I can just make out the boardwalk and beach, dully lit by a single street lamp. Up the street I can see the bright lights and anarchy of early evening on the strip.

Still nothing.

I put my ear to the door again, but there's silence.

I form my hand into a fist to knock again, then something to the right catches my eye. Two things stand out: the glint of something metallic as it's brought towards me, and the horrible faceless form of the coarse sacking mask, as its two dark, bottomless eyeholes lunge towards me.

Instinctively, I jump back and put my fist up to protect me, as the bladed weapon, whatever it is, misses my face and instead catches against my knuckles. There's a searing pain and a noise I've never heard before as it scrapes off my knuckles and cuts through to the bones of the back of my hand.

I pull back and kick out at the hand as hard as I can, something primeval in me realising that knocking that hand off course is my best chance of survival.

There's a light groan as my foot makes contact with his hand and the sharp impact forces him to release his grip. There's a metallic sound as the blade hits the paving stone, and then he's on me, wrapping himself around me, a thick arm snaking round my back and pulling me into him.

I try to scream, try to kick out against his shins, wrestle with my shoulders and upper body, try to make my fist flail, but he's stronger than me and he pulls me in hard, until my face is pressed up against the cotton of his shirt and I can smell the sweat and odour of his chest.

Then his other hand has my neck in the crook of his elbow, and I can feel myself begin to suffocate.

He's pulling me now, a basic, non-consenting drag, as he wrestles me away from the club's side door and away into the darkness. I struggle, try to dig my heels in, look for my toes to catch something on the floor to stop us moving, but his strength is overwhelming. He's pulling, yanking, twisting and forcing me down. I feel my neck crick and a sharp pain races through it. My right hand is crushed against him and I can feel the wetness where the knife cut into it.

We're going downhill, towards the beach, where so much has happened for this man, and I realise that if I can't do something now, can't come up with a way of getting out of this, my fate is bleak.

'Stop struggling, bitch,' he grunt-whispers into my ear, the unmistakable accent of Aiden McLellan muffled by the sacking hood.

I force all my strength and weight into my feet and toes, do everything to dig them into the ground, until they're audibly dragging along. I can feel the leather being torn off them until it comes away completely on my left side, and I can feel the ground now scraping away the skin and nails of my toes.

But it's working.

I am slowing him.

'Stop it, bitch,' he says, and I feel a fist slam into my kidneys.

But it's working.

My right foot feels something, a gap in the pavement, something slightly raised, and it holds on for a millisecond. He wrestles violently left and right, using his strength to pull me away, and that's when I decide to stop struggling, to stop dragging my feet, to let my whole body go loose so there's no longer any resistance. I feel all my weight shift to him as he loses his footing and we both go sprawling onto the ground.

I land on top of him, a ten-stone middle-aged woman, my weight concentrated against his stomach and chest.

There's a stifled scream and a grunt as the wind's knocked out of him, and I do my best to hurt him, ramming my head into his defenceless face, feel it making contact, a crack of something hard, and then my fist and arms punching into his abdomen as I do my best to kick away.

He's forced to loosen his grip for a second as he concentrates on getting his breath back and reaches for his face, and in that second, I'm pushing off him and trying to get myself away.

I'm almost up, pushing myself off for my first step of freedom, when I feel his hand touching, then grabbing my heel. Half up, I turn around and launch a kick with my left leg against his wrist, and he's forced to let go.

Then I'm scrambling all the way up and pushing myself off into the nearest I can muster to a sprint.

I can feel the blood dripping from the gash in my right hand, and I wipe it on my skirt as I head up the slope, looking for an escape.

'Help!' I shout at the top of my voice, looking for reserves of energy in my lungs. 'Help. I'm being attack...'

But the force of his body impacting with mine blocks my last word. He's stronger and quicker than me. He must have got back to his feet sooner than I'd hoped, and a few paces have brought him level. Now I feel myself falling towards the ground, my hands out in front to break my fall.

Our fall.

I land hard, his weight fully on top of me now as I crash against the warm tarmac, my cheek scraping along the ground for a few inches before we reach a stop.

And now it's too late.

Now he's in his element.

Knows exactly what he's doing.

All those years of assault and rape and God knows what else coming to the fore.

He puts me into a headlock with one arm, then three rabbit punches in quick succession into my kidneys, like small steam hammers, taking the wind and the last of my resistance with them. As I struggle for breath, gasping and retching, he sends his free hand snaking under my stomach, then hauls and drags me along the tarmac, pulls me into a side alley, dark and unused, tarmac replaced by cold, rough concrete.

'Keep fucking still, bitch,' he says, and now I know it's over.

His grip around my neck is iron, the weight on top of me overwhelming. He squeezes and squeezes the arm around my neck until I'm still and compliant, wondering where my next air will come from. I can feel him wriggling and rearranging behind me. I try to move the muscles in my back, force my way off the ground, but can produce only a slight tremor through my body.

Then his mouth is in my ear, warm breath and spittle as he hisses out his words.

'Not a fucking sound, bitch.'

'Keep still, bitch.'

'This what you fucking want, bitch.'

'This how you like it, slut.'

Then the weight on my lower half is removed momentarily and I feel my skirt being pulled up and I realise, to my horror, that he's hard.

I feel new strength. I push and push with my back muscles, with my arms, with my legs, desperately looking for some sort of purchase.

Then I feel a hand working its way up the back of my thighs, working its way into my pants, pulling at them, trying to pull them down.

And that voice, hot and messy in my ear.

'This is what you like, isn't it, slut?'

'Isn't it, slut?'

'Slut, slut, slut.'

Then he moves to get the purchase he needs for what he wants to do, frees my right leg momentarily, and I kick it out hard, as hard as I ever thought I could, up between his legs, into his groin.

He screeches in pain, rolls his lower body off me while keeping his arm around my neck.

And I'm struggling now, struggling like a wild animal, kicking and pushing and wrestling and forcing myself this way and that, left and right, up and down, desperately trying to move him off me, move me away from him.

I feel his arm tighten on my neck, the air cut off again, my desperation for air overwhelming my desperation to get free.

'You fucking asked for it, bitch,' he says.

I feel him shuffle and wriggle on top of me, moving his right arm, rearranging something. But it's different from before. His zone of activity has moved away from my lower body, away from my legs and my backside, to something he's trying to do with his right arm, his right hand.

His breath in my ear again, hate and menace in his voice.

'This is for you, bitch,' he says, and I feel a sharp pain, like a sudden deep scratch, in the side of my body, then nothing. The pressure's still on my neck, the weight on my back, the breath in my ear, but his body is still, his activity concentrated on keeping me pushed down.

I feel a wetness in my side, a dull ache down in that direction, and a numbness starting to spread outwards.

I realise he must have picked up his knife at some point.

Realise I've been stabbed somewhere around the kidneys and that I'm slowly, surely bleeding to death.

'That what you wanted?' he whispers, his lips touching the inner curve of my ear.

'That how you like it? You and the others,' he says.

I want to reply, want to shout something back, tell him what I think of him, tell him how the police are going to get him, tell him how I left all his details on Miguel's voicemail, tell him how he's going to pay for the crimes he's committed against me and all those other women.

I can't because I don't have the strength to speak, let alone shout. I can't because my mouth is being slowly ground into the concrete and the air's being squeezed out of my lungs. Can't because the blood's slowly oozing out of my body.

'This how you...'

And then I feel the weight being lifted off me as his body is pushed, then hauled away.

Some shouting, some screaming, I can't really make it out, my lungs are too busy clawing for air.

Some scuffling, some dragging, some swearing, some violent movement as the two bodies, the two men, tear into each other.

'For all have sinned and come short of the glory of God,' Preacherman says as he lays into McLellan with all his might.

I want to get up, want to do what I can to help him, make sure he knows about the knife.

But I can't because the life's slowly but surely draining out of me.

## 23

Jonathan is smiling.

It's fleeting, breaking out on his face before being wiped away a second later, but while it's there, it lights up the room, it lights up my entire being.

It's his eleventh birthday and he's just opened his main present: a PlayStation. The one he wanted. The one we didn't think we could afford. The one his dad worked two weekends' overtime to have enough to buy him.

He rips open the paper, knows what it is the second he sees just a corner of the box, and he looks over at me and his dad and smiles.

And then he's off, concentration back on the box, ripping off the paper, looking how to get inside and at the contents within.

I look over at Nick and he's smiling, beaming even. We hold each other's gaze for a second. We don't need to nod or say anything. We both know what each other's thinking: that we did it and it was worth every second of that overtime.

Nick squeezes my hand and I look back at Jonathan trying to prise open the cardboard lip that will give him access to the box.

He squeezes my hand and says my name.

Squeezes it softly, gently and with love.

I open my eyes and can dully make him out.

Nick.

He's sitting beside me, talking gently, encouraging words, pressing my hand ever so softly, his face a little older and wiser than before.

As my eyes focus on him, he registers that mine are open.

'Elaine? Elaine? You're awake.'

I want to speak but can't seem to remember how it's done right now, the muscle memory groggy and tired.

'How do you feel?' he asks.

I turn my head to the left: another bed, a beige wardrobe and a table.

I turn my head to the right: a window with an institutional green curtain.

A hospital.

I look back at him. His eyes are wide and lively.

'What... what is this?' I say, my head finally working out how to form the sounds.

'It's okay, darling,' he says. 'I'm here. Been here all this time. You're safe now – absolutely safe.'

Safe?

Strange word to use.

Why wouldn't I be safe?

I think back, trying to search my recent memory. There was the alley and the feeling in my side, and the man on top of me and then he was pushed off and then... no, nothing.

The man on top of me.

The man who tried to rape me.

Tried to kill me.

Aiden McLellan.

The Crude Hood.

Safe now. Safe, thank God.

'What happened to him?'

'Him?' he says, looking blank, then registering who I mean. 'Ah, right, yes. He's gone,' he says.

'Gone?'

He nods, but doesn't say any more.

'How are you feeling?' he asks again.

'Okay,' I say, and try to sit up, but while I can just about move my hands and arms, they're weak, and the rest of my body's not responding. I put one hand on either side of my waist and try to push myself up, but I don't even manage a couple of millimetres.

'You're not to exert yourself,' he says, placing a hand just below my chest and rubbing my stomach.

'They've filled you with quite a lot of meds,' he continues. 'The doctor said it might be a few hours before they wear off.'

'Can you help me?' I ask, and try pushing with my hands again.

I can tell he's reluctant, but he leans forward, plumps up a couple of pillows behind my head, puts a hand under each arm, and pulls me gently until I'm sitting up.

'What happened to me?' I ask.

Nick sits back down into the armchair with its tartan cushioning.

'They had to operate more than once,' he said. 'You'd lost a lot of blood and they were worried about your lungs. Luckily, the stab didn't go through to the spinal column, so you should make a full recovery, but it was a close-run thing. He missed your heart by just a couple of centimetres.'

I hadn't been worried before, but now what happened creeps back into my mind. The knife and the stab wound, the assault and the memory of him, my body pinned underneath him as he scrabbled at me.

I swallow hard and ask for a glass of water. My throat is dry with a horrible, bitter taste in it.

Nick takes my hand in his again and squeezes it.

'How long have I...'

'Thirty-two hours,' he says, checking his watch.

'You look awful,' I say, seeing the bags under his eyes and the tiredness in his skin.

'Thanks,' he says. 'You don't look too great yourself.'

A smile plays at the edge of his mouth.

I smile back and his eyes soften.

'Where is he now?' I ask.

'You know what,' he says, 'it's probably best if Deputy Chief Fuentes fills you in on all that. You should carry on sleeping, but I suppose you'll want to know right away?'

I nod and he picks up his phone.

I look at my bedside table: a big jug of water, a paper cup, a single card with a picture of daffodils on it, and a laminated sheet of paper with instructions about using the payphone in my television console.

'Why did you choose daffodils?' I ask.

'I didn't,' Nick says, standing up and passing the card for me to read before wandering off a few metres to make the phone call to Miguel.

The inside of the card contains a few lines of elegant, sloped handwriting.

*Dear Elaine, I heard what happened. Get well soon, lady. You're a legend. I owe you big time.*

I feel a slight flutter in my tummy as I read the signature at the bottom.

*Karim.*

'Miguel's on his way,' Nick says, returning. He sits himself on the bed by my legs and picks up my hand again. He looks at me for a few seconds, studying my face, then I see his eyes beginning to water.

'I thought I might have lost you back there,' he says, the tears running now.

I shake my head and wait for him to look back at me.

'You'll never lose me,' I say, squeezing his hand with what strength I can muster.

Miguel arrives half an hour later, on his own but still in uniform. He and Nick shake hands, and Nick agrees to go and busy himself so we can talk.

He sits in the armchair recently vacated by Nick, puts his cap to one side and crosses his legs.

'So, how are you?' he asks.

I'm sitting up and beginning to get feeling back into my body. I'm on an antibiotic drip, so parts still feel fairly disconnected.

'Okay, considering,' I say. 'I can't feel much on my right side, but it could be worse.'

He gives me one of his smug grins and then winks.

'You could and should be dead,' he says. 'I'd say feeling a bit numb really isn't too much to worry about.'

We exchange smiles for a second, and then I remember why I'm in the hospital to begin with.

'Where is he?' I ask. 'What happened to him?'

The smile leaves Miguel's face and he sits back, takes a bit of a breath, works out what he wants to say, then speaks.

'We don't know right now,' he says. 'He disappeared and we tracked him as far as the beach, then the trail went cold.'

'Got away? He's loose on this tiny island and you still can't find him?'

He looks away, staring at my cupboard, then turns back.

'We will get him. It's just a matter of time,' he says.

'Time? You had four years. How could he have escaped?'

He shrugs, looking away, avoiding my gaze.

'We were too late. We went after him, but any trace disappeared once he hit the beach.'

I nod, trying to suppress an urge to scream.

A killer. A multiple rapist. A serial sexual abuser. The whole weight of Majorca's police forces and you just let him go. He disappeared into the ether on an island only 75 miles long and 100 miles wide.

'Preacherman interrupted him,' I say. 'While I was lying there, under him, Preacherman pushed him off me.'

It's Miguel's turn to nod now, eyes jittery, looking for something to distract him.

'Saved your life,' he says. 'Fought him off and raised the alarm.'

Something stirs inside me, something I haven't felt for a long time. A warmth, a brief flood of positive endorphins. Hope. Hope because there are still good people out there, people who will act on altruistic impulses – will risk their life for someone.

'I'd like to thank him,' I say. 'Pass on my gratitude.'

He swallows, looks down, then back up, uncrosses his legs and leans in. Reaches over for my hand and takes it in his clammy one.

Looks me in the eye.

'He was badly injured in doing what he did to help you. He's been put into a medically induced coma. It's touch and go if he'll survive.'

I feel the rigidity in my limbs again, feel the emotion welling up into my face, feel my body start to lose it again. More pain, more anguish, more useless, pointless death.

And then I'm crying again. Crying for another life shattered, more unnecessary grief and pain. A life hanging in the balance for mine. It doesn't seem right or fair.

I slump forward into Miguel's arms. I feel him embracing me, running his hand up and down my back, whispering into my ear like a baby, as I do my best to sob the past forty-eight hours out of my life.

Eventually, I stop and lean back into my pillows. Miguel hands me a tissue and I try to clean my face. He sits back in his seat.

'He was Matthew Houghton,' he says, his accent mangling the surname. 'Does that name mean anything to you?'

I try to think through the names and faces that have worked their way into my head over the last few days.

Nothing.

I shake my head.

'Me neither,' he says. 'Not at first. But then one of the guys in the team clicked. The first attack, four years ago. The woman raped on the beach and left for dead. The guy she was with stabbed nine times.'

He's looking at me and I nod as I think back to that first horrific attack. Laura Neil – the one I spoke to – still dealing with the horror of it all these years on.

'The guy she was with is him,' he says. 'Matthew Houghton.'

My stomach churns as I try to take it in.

'But that would mean he came back here and... oh God... was stabbed again?'

Miguel nods.

'By the same man?' I ask.

Miguel nods.

'We don't think it's a coincidence. We've spoken to his family. They say he's been coming out here every year since it happened. Comes out for at least a couple of months every year to look for him.'

I frown.

'Him?'

'For the man who stabbed him. The man who left him for dead. Comes out and combs the strip and the beaches and the bars and the clubs, looking and hoping to find him.'

I'm shaking my head, my mind turning. Hoping to find what? To see the hood? To hear a scream? He's come for the last four years to try and catch the Crude Hood in the act?

'Preacherman is Matthew Houghton,' Miguel says. 'He sat in plain sight pretending to be praying for people's souls when he was actually trying to save lives.'

It comes back slowly but in vivid pictures in my head. The man standing outside Kiss, screaming and shouting at us about our behaviour, about what we should be doing, about turning towards the Lord.

He's there every year, seen by everyone but barely noticed amongst the drunks and the pissants, the good, bad and ugly of that godawful half mile of hell.

The night my drink was spiked. Fumbling and bumbling my way down the strip, collapsing on the side, passed out and ignored. Preacherman was there. Preacherman helped me. Got me to hospital, made sure I was safe.

Preacherman saved my life.

It's touch and go if he'll survive – his reward for saving my life.

'You okay?' Miguel says.

I look up at him, his walnut eyes wide with sympathy for a change.

Preacherman doing the job that the police, Miguel and his men, should have done.

I shake my head. What else can I do? Shake it and shake it as if somehow it will get rid of all the awfulness, make it all make sense.

'What about Santiago?' I ask.

He shrugs his shoulders.

'The judge is still investigating him for the rapes. Could take a while, but he's not going to be out of prison in any hurry. Which is good, I suppose.'

He looks at me, hopeful of approval.

'I'd like to be alone now, please,' I say.

He frowns and sinks back into his seat.

'You sure?' he says.

I nod.

He hesitates a moment, then shrugs and pushes himself out of the seat. He picks up his cap, hesitates again, then walks slowly towards the door.

He stops, turns round.

'Call me when you feel up to it,' he says.

I frown.

'Call me once you've caught him,' I say. 'Don't bother getting in contact until then,' I add, before slumping into my pillows and waiting for the sound of the door closing so I can start to cry all over again.

# 24

It's some weeks later when I next hear from Miguel.

I've been back at work for a month or so. Had a week off. All I could afford – all I could justify.

Nick's making an effort, a real effort. He's not touched a drop since I've been home, just fusses around me, plumping up pillows, cleaning floors, cooking endless restorative meals. Says he wants to change things. Wants to make everything okay. Realises he's not been much of a husband or companion. Says he's going to turn things around.

He's got a job. Well, an interview for a job – in the kitchen of a café serving lunches in Palma. The pay's terrible, but the hours are okay.

The consulate's beginning to get its act together too. The season is winding down and it's returning to normal. Fewer lost passports, fewer injuries, fewer run-ins with the police, fewer tourists in general. Peak season is past and we're through the worst.

I'm composing an update for Vanessa on staffing over the winter – the latest in her attempts to surreptitiously work out who to sack – when my phone goes.

Miguel.

'What are you doing?' he asks.

'Admin,' I say, not bothering to elaborate.

'Come down to Cala Figuera beach. There's something you'll want to see.'

I look out over the office, see Louise and Soraya hard at work, a handful of people in the waiting area looking sunburnt and sullen, Rodrigo nowhere to be seen, paperwork spread across desks, everyone looking forward to lunchtime.

It'll wait.

It will all wait.

Cala Figuera beach is an hour's drive along winding coastal roads through the hills. On a day like today, with the sun at its late-summer best, catching the Med like a fisherman's net, it looks glorious.

In a patch of scrubland, which a single weather-beaten sign declares to be a designated parking zone, I see a clutch of police vehicles and unmarked vans.

I pull up just past them, find the nearest approximation to a patch of shade, leave my car and follow a dirty sandy track down to the beach.

The beach lies at the bottom of a high limestone cliff. Miguel is there, cap on, standing with his back to the sun, watching a team of boiler-suited forensics officers enter and exit a white tent that sits on the sand. A handful of short-sleeved colleagues stand talking to him, breaking into the occasional laugh.

I go up and say hello.

Miguel fixes me with a stare and a sly smile.

'How are you?' he asks.

'Never better,' I say, deadpan.

He nods, then speaks.

'We've got him,' he says, gesturing to the inside of the tent.

'You're sure?'

'Pretty sure,' he says. 'You're the only one here that's seen him alive. You might want to take a look.'

Now I nod. I do want to take a look. Want to look at him, whatever state he's in, to prove that I'm not afraid, that no one need be afraid of him ever again.

'Go on then,' I say.

'You're sure?'

I don't reply, just stare him down until he makes a face and disappears inside the tent. He comes out a minute or two later with some white overalls and masks in his hand, one set for him, one for me.

We garb up silently: suit, mask, shoe covers, gloves. When I'm ready, I look over at Miguel and nod. He lifts the flap at the back of the tent and gestures for me to go inside.

Inside, a woman and a man in white boiler suits are attending to the body with various kits and chemicals that I don't understand. Miguel asks them if they'll give us a minute, and neither argues.

As they leave, I can make out the body. It's lying face down, clothes dirty and torn, bloodstains on the surrounding sand.

Miguel walks to where the head is and pulls it up.

The face staring at me has the top lip pulled away from the teeth in a snarl, the eyes rolled back in their sockets, the skin stubbled, bloodied and pale, a weak chin and sunburnt cheeks.

'That's him,' I say.

Miguel looks at me, checking.

'Definitely,' I add. 'No doubt at all.'

He lets the head drop back into the dent it's made in the sand.

'Good,' he says, and shows me out.

We walk back towards the car park, side by side on the sandy path.

'How did you find him?' I ask.

'We got a call early this morning. Local was complaining about a homeless guy who'd been stealing from his garden. Reckoned he was living rough somewhere round here. My guys tracked him to a disused hut on a bit of scrubland just the other side of the cliff. Soon as they heard him shouting and swearing at them in English, they had a pretty good idea it was him – we've all been scouring the island for weeks.'

'So how'd he end up down here?'

He turns to me, gives me a cocky smile.

'There was a bit of a chase, ended up on the edge of the cliff. Bit of a struggle kind of a thing and, you know how these things go.'

'Do I?' I say, stopping and staring at him, making him hold my gaze. 'Did he fall, or was he pushed?'

He manages a weak laugh.

'Do you care?'

'As a matter of fact, I do.'

He shrugs, puts his shades back on.

'Officially, he fell,' he says, and starts to walk on.

I stand for a moment, trying to take it in, then I walk quickly to catch him up.

'And unofficially?'

The shrug again.

'Unofficially, he got what he deserved.'

'He deserved a trial,' I say. 'The victims deserved to see him hauled into court, to listen to his crimes and have to answer for them, to get the justice that was coming to him.'

'And have the whole of the British press decamp here for weeks at a time, dredging up every bad thing they can think of about Magaluf, about the island, about Spain? Six months to a year of more tabloid hysteria? I don't think so. It's better this way.'

We've reached the car park and Miguel heads to his squad car. I stop and look back to where we've come from, a view across the Med, the sea glistening and pristine.

More violence, more death, another body washed up on a beach. Another corruption of justice, more men deciding they know what's best for the world. Closure for Miguel and his men, maybe, but for who else? For the victims? Maybe. Who am I to judge? But not for me. My life is spent trying to make people realise there are rules, regulations and acceptable ways to behave and, even out here, even when it's a scumbag like McLellan we're talking about, that matters.

I walk up to Miguel's car. He's sat in the driver's seat with the door open, studying his phone.

'Next of kin?' I ask.

'His wife's been informed,' Miguel says. 'Nabarro's on his way to the old lady in the home now.'

'I hope he puts it gently. At her age, she doesn't need to know the full details.'

'Of course,' he says. 'The Guardia Civil are a case study in sensitivity.'

'Any more idea why?' I ask.

He looks at me, his forehead crumpled quizzically.

'Why what?'

'Why he might have done it? What compelled a man with a wife and children to rape and murder young girls?'

'Even speaking to the UK police and people who knew him, it's hard to tell. He'd only been married a few years. The grandchildren are his wife's. She's a lot younger and had no idea about his past. Never showed any dubious signs towards her. Had a fairly normal upbringing; parents were poor but hard-working by all accounts. Somewhere along the line, he just developed a deep and violent hatred of women, particularly young, sexually active ones. Can't say for certain, but a friend of his has said he thinks it comes from when he got rejected by a couple of girls when he was a younger man. Never dealt with the anger well. It's around the time his first offences started, but no one ever thought it would end up like this.'

I stop, stand bolt upright, as I feel it coming on. Miguel stands up and I put my hand out, grab his arm for support, as the waves and waves of emotion sweep over me in great big heaves of upset and tears.

It's all so damn awful. So pointless, so horrible, so much needless hurt and loss and grief.

I don't know how long I'm crying for, probably just a minute or two, but it feels like a lot longer before I feel composed enough to blow my nose and apologise to Miguel.

'What happens now?' I ask.

'The usual,' he says. 'Forensics and investigation. Cause of death and then we'll see what we can find out. My guess is not a lot.'

'Why do you say that?'

'I don't know,' he says, looking around, eyes moving between a couple of officers smoking by the sand dunes.

'Majorca's a funny place,' he says. 'There's a lot of different people here, different views, different politics, wanting different things out of life. Some are important, some have influence, some have money. I spend a lot of my time trying to work out the good ones from the bad, trying to make sure the right people have the right things happen to them. A lot of people don't like me because of it. They have their own way of doing things. But it seems we can all agree on one thing... that this guy,' he nods back towards the beach where we came from, 'is better off like that, and I can't see many people disagreeing. I reckon they'll think it's some kind of justice.'

I look at him, study his face, the Mediterranean skin, overnight stubble, the opaque eyes and the mind that lies behind.

I don't agree with him.

Everyone deserves justice, whatever they might have done.

And I'm pretty sure a lot of the right people on this island have had the wrong things happen to them.

But right this minute, by this beach, under this heat, on this island, I don't have the energy to argue.

For the first time in a long time, my thoughts turn to Nick. The old Nick, stood in the kitchen, in his apron, cooking up some stew or other, the radio on, a glass of wine poured for each of us. It's a good feeling, one full of warmth and reassurance. Can it be us again? I don't, in all honesty know, but I'm not ready to give up on it quite yet.

Miguel and I shake hands and kiss on both cheeks, then I'm in my car, pulling out of the car park and heading back to the main road.

THE END

## A NOTE FROM THE PUBLISHER

**Thank you for reading this book.** If you enjoyed it please do consider leaving a review on Amazon to help others find it too.

**We hate typos.** All of our books have been rigorously edited and proofread, but sometimes mistakes do slip through. If you have spotted a typo, please do let us know and we can get it amended within hours.

**info@bloodhoundbooks.com**

Printed in Great Britain
by Amazon

24869279R00179